KU-387-179

The Boy from Berlin

By the same author

NORTH SLOPE

SHADOW OF THE WOLF

HELL'S GATE

THE EAGLE'S COVENANT

THE DEVIL'S TRINITY

THE THIRD SECRET

A COVERT WAR

The Boy from Berlin

Michael Parker

ROBERT HALE · LONDON

First published in Great Britain 2011

ISBN 978-0-7090-9353-4

Robert Hale Limited
Clerkenwell House
Clerkenwell Green
London EC1R 0HT

www.halebooks.com

2 4 6 8 10 9 7 5 3 1

Typeset in 10.5/14pt Sabon
Printed in the UK by MPG Books Group

PROLOGUE

Edna Mahan Correctional Facility, Newark, New Jersey. 2010.

BABS MASON KEPT *picking at the loose thread in her prison skirt. It was almost like an unconscious gesture, twisting it in her fingers as she looked around her cell, and up at the bulkhead light recessed into the ceiling. When the young writer sitting opposite got no response to her question, she put it to Babs again. She had a small voice recorder beside her and a notepad resting on her lap.*

'What year was it?' Babs repeated the question finally, turning to look at the young woman.

'Yes, the year you met your husband.'

Babs couldn't think for a moment. Her mind refused to batten down and concentrate, set as it was on other things. The young woman's presence didn't help either. Babs envied her youth, her freshness and most of all, her freedom. It distracted her and became a point of focus, almost. The irony was that she had specifically asked for the woman to visit her and record the events leading up to her imprisonment, so she had no reason to wish the young woman wasn't there. The prison administrator had taken some persuading, but Babs still had powerful connections outside, and that had helped.

'The year I met my husband,' she muttered and lowered her head in thought, trying to take her mind back several years. 'It was when I was having an affair with his father, William. He liked to be called Bill. It was in the late sixties. I was about eighteen or nineteen. I was studying for my degree in Chemical Engineering. I met Bill at a University Ball. He was a handsome, strong, forceful man. I was fascinated by him.' She sighed, recalling the memory. 'The affair

burned itself out. That's when I got to know Gus. He was about fifteen years older than me, give or take.'

Babs thought of her youth, her beauty, now faded. The silky blonde hair had become dry and grey, like thin cords. It was no wonder; she was over sixty and her years in prison hadn't helped. She studied the backs of her hands where the truth always rested. Whatever face a woman tried to present to the world, whatever falsehood about her age, the truth was in the hands.

'William Mason, Bill, you said,' the young woman reminded her. 'How old would he have been then?'

'About forty-five or so.'

The writer scribbled on for a short while. Babs watched her intently. The young woman looked up and brushed a small, wisp of hair from her face.

'Would you say that that was when it all began?'

Babs smiled. 'The truth is that it began a long, long time before that, but none of us were to know. Not then anyway.'

'Could you elaborate on that?'

Babs thought about the statement she had just made, about it all beginning a long, long time ago, and the names of people she had never heard of; names that meant nothing to her, some who had died before she had been born. Now she knew them all; each and every one of them. Their destinies were as much hers as they were theirs. Their paths began in different places, in different times, but each path had moved inexorably closer until they were linked as one. And that single path finished in the walls of this cell and would be consigned to the pages of the young writer's notebook. In there would be the names of the strangers, of the loved ones, of the deceit, the cunning and the violence, of the life and death of Babs Mason.

'Well perhaps I should start at the moment I knew my husband was going to become President of the United States of America.'

PART ONE

ONE

Newark 1994

BABS MASON WAS waiting for her husband, Gus outside the New Jersey Supreme Court house. It was a warm evening, pleasant with a little breeze. There wasn't a great deal of traffic about, but plenty of pedestrians and some joggers making their way across to the park. Kids walked by with their earpieces in listening to their MP3 players, and youngsters carrying backpacks hurried along, fresh out of school. Babs had positioned herself so that she could see right through the doors of the court house, knowing she would spot her man as soon as he walked into the huge lobby.

Babs Mason was forty-seven and still a very attractive woman. Her figure was trim from the jogging she enjoyed down by the lake, and the fact that she paid attention to her fitness regime and diet. She and Gus Mason made a fine couple and were enormously popular among business acquaintances and the various clubs of which they were members. Babs felt privileged to be part of Gus's life. They had no family other than Gus's father, William. He liked to be called Bill, and could be a strange fellow at times. Babs had known him intimately once and still had a sweet spot for him, which she would often deny to herself. Her relationship with Gus's father was how she came to meet Gus. At first, many of their peer group thought Babs and Gus were seeing each other, but the truth was that Babs and Bill Mason were indulging themselves in a passionate affair. It burned itself out eventually, and Babs found herself attracted to Gus, although she sometimes wondered if it was an attraction borne out of a suppressed desire to remain close to his father.

She caught sight her husband as a group of people came through the open doors and raised her hand. Mason lifted his and waved when he saw her. Babs could tell by the look on his face it was good news. He was such a handsome man, she thought; it was no wonder other women showed an overt interest in him.

Mason slung his arm round her and kissed her briefly on the lips. Babs responded and then pulled away, hooking her arm into his. She fell into step beside him and they walked to her black Lincoln convertible, which she had parked in the Memorial Field parking lot across the road from the court house.

'Well, how did it go?' she asked. There was a marked anticipation in her voice which she found hard to disguise; part of the game really.

Gus Mason looked down at her lovely face as they stepped on to the sidewalk on Washington Avenue. He couldn't keep her waiting any longer.

'He's going to back me,' he said, and squeezed her hand.

Babs stopped and turned towards him, looking straight into his lovely, blue eyes. 'That's wonderful news, Gus.' The noise from the passing traffic was lost to her as she pulled him close and kissed him again. 'Really wonderful news.'

Gus Mason was the archetypal modern American. He had graduated *cum laude* from Harvard Law School and joined the United States Attorney's Office in Newark. He ran the criminal division until being named chief counsel, and would have almost certainly been appointed attorney general. But Mason had no intention of becoming a permanent trial court lawyer; he had his eye on the bigger prize in Congress. His first step along that most insecure road was to become elected as a representative to the Newark State Senate. Between them, Gus and Babs had deliberately cultivated friendships among the big hitters in the local community. But to seek representation meant winning the support of those men and women who were at the heart of local politics and could help give Mason the step up he needed.

Gus had never had any problem mixing with other people, although in some cases he had to work on a relationship and ensure it didn't look contrived. But in the main it was as though everything was preordained in his life; a privilege accorded to few people. He had achieved a high standing among his colleagues, both as a lawyer and as a friend. But to seek the advancement he wanted, he needed the backing of one of the men most likely to help his cause, and that was Henry Lawrence, an associate Supreme Court justice.

Lawrence had worked at the Newark court for almost twenty years and had risen through several offices, holding senior positions until he was nominated by President Reagan as associate justice of the United States Supreme Court. He still maintained an office in the Newark court and had many influential friends in high places around the political system in America. His standing among the community was exemplary, and it was Lawrence's support that Gus Mason had been promised. With Lawrence's influence, Mason stood an excellent chance of being elected to the State senate, providing they could swing the governor's approval and secure Mason's nomination.

'Gus, honey,' Babs said as they settled themselves into the soft leather seats of the Lincoln. 'I've arranged a little dinner party this weekend; kind of a celebration.'

Mason clipped his seat belt into place. 'What's it in aid of?' he asked glibly.

Babs tossed her head and allowed her blonde hair to fall back over her shoulders as she gunned the motor into life. 'As if you didn't know,' she said, her eyes twinkling.

She swung the Lincoln away from the parking lot and into the traffic flow with barely a glance at the road in front of her. The car bounced a little as it rolled on to the tarmac. 'We're meeting Ann Robbins,' she said, looking at him quickly. Her eyes sparkled, but there was a question there.

Ann Robbins was a state senator. She was divorced and something of a man-eater. She could also make or break people, and was another one that Mason needed on his side.

Gus frowned. 'She doesn't like me, Babs, you know that.'

Babs pulled the car out of the nearside lane and passed a truck. The diesel engine roared at them as she slid by.

'Well you're going to have to change that, honey.' She pushed the throttle down and powered her way up Washington Avenue. 'Otherwise you won't make state senate.'

Ann Robbins was the kind of woman who wanted men on her terms. And to play Babs's Mason's game with Robbins could spell disaster for Mason. He knew exactly why his wife believed they should curry favour with the senator, and how they should go about it. Robbins had already voiced the opinion, albeit discreetly, that Gus Mason would not be an asset to the state legislature. The one thing that concerned Babs and her husband was the quaint but deadly tradition of senatorial courtesy. With this odd concession to incumbent senators, any one of them could block the governor's nomination of a candidate without having to justify their reason for doing so. And unless Gus Mason could get into Senator Ann Robbins' good books, Babs was convinced she would block his nomination.

Hence the dinner party.

The young woman stopped writing and looked up from her notepad.

'So Ann Robbins was a hurdle you had to overcome?'

Babs nodded, wishing she'd never met the senator. 'You could say that. Ann Robbins liked men, but she also liked power, control. She wanted to get my husband into the sack, no doubt about that.' Babs clenched her teeth and squeezed her lips into a compressed grimace. 'Pure bitch, that one,' she added, shaking her head slowly, missing the irony. 'She probably would have enjoyed my husband's rough sex.'

The young writer looked at Babs, a shocked expression on her face. 'Your husband...?'

Babs nodded and smiled grimly. 'He might have looked sugar and spice on the outside, honey, but he was a different animal on the inside.'

'And yet you deliberately arranged the dinner party,' the young writer pointed out. 'Surely you were taking a risk?'

Babs agreed. 'Yes, but I believed it was a risk worth taking.' She shrugged philosophically. 'But it didn't end the way I planned it.'

'So what happened?'

'Nothing, actually,' Babs answered. 'Not at first, anyway, but I do remember the evening as if it were yesterday.'

She lowered her head and peered over the top of her half-moon glasses at the young writer. 'If only it were yesterday,' she admitted.

*

Ann Robbins arrived punctually at the Masons' home overlooking the Deerfield Golf and Tennis Club. She had used her own car; it meant she would have to avoid alcohol. That way she would remain in control during the evening and not run the risk of being breathalyzed by over zealous police on the drive home. It was small things like this, the attention to detail and the preparedness that made Senator Robbins such a formidable opponent in the legislature.

Babs welcomed her at the door with a fixed smile, and led her through into the lounge where Gus Mason was scanning an old *Newsweek* magazine. He was dressed casually in an open-neck, short-sleeved shirt and tan slacks. He stood up and put the magazine down, then greeted Robbins with a kiss on both cheeks.

'Good to see you, Senator.' He could smell her perfume. It was fragrant, but not excessive.

Robbins laughed. 'Ann, please.'

Mason's eyes widened. 'You look good.' He pointed to the drinks cabinet. 'Can I get you something?'

'Sparkling water, please,' she told him, 'with a little ice and lemon.'

'I'll get that,' Babs offered. 'You two chat.' She turned on her heel and left them to talk.

When the senator had her drink, Mason gestured towards an armchair beside the fireplace. Robbins smiled and lowered herself carefully into the chair, smoothing her skirt beneath her as she sat down. When they were both settled, Mason began the small talk that usually precedes the more relaxed conversation. They generalized about the weather and each other's well-being. While they were talking, Mason took the opportunity to study her.

Ann Robbins was about forty years of age and very striking. It wasn't difficult to see how men could be attracted to her. Her hair was cut in a short style, blonde with just the hint of dark roots showing. She still had a very good figure and showed no signs of weight problems. She had a lively personality which was the key to her attractiveness, but Mason knew that she was quite adept at hiding the spiteful side of her character, so her personality surfaced easily above her dark side. And all the while he was studying her; he knew he was being studied too.

Babs came through to the lounge. 'Ann, Gus, dinner is ready.' She didn't wait for a response. 'Would you like wine with your meal?'

The senator stood up. 'No thank you, Babs; I'm staying sober tonight.' She followed her into the dining room with Mason taking up the rear. The table had been laid with simplicity, but with a touch of elegance. Around the room Babs had placed candles which were now fluttering and throwing distinct shadows over the walls, which enhanced the subdued lighting.

While the three of them ate there was an edge to the atmosphere around the table. It was nothing to do with the food, nor the furniture, but the fact that all three of them knew why Babs had invited Ann Robbins to dinner. There was an affectation in Babs's manner that her husband noticed. It made him feel self-conscious, and he wondered if it wasn't having the opposite affect that his wife had intended. It wasn't easy to detect a similar attitude in Ann Robbins though, such was the clever way in which she was able to hide her true feelings, but Mason knew he and Babs would have to be on their guard.

'I understand you have Henry Lawrence's backing for the Senate?' she said to Mason, referring to the decision the judge had made.

'I certainly have. It took a great deal of persuasion,' he told her. 'I think he was a bit reluctant at first.'

Babs winced. She thought her husband was being a little too honest.

'Why do you say that?' Robbins asked him.

He shrugged. 'It was like walking on eggshells, you know. I couldn't just go up to him and ask for his backing; I needed to do it with a certain amount of care.'

'Has he spoken to the governor?'

Mason arched his eyebrows. 'Jack Berry?' He shook his head. 'I don't know, but I don't think he would be prepared to endorse me if he hadn't spoken to Governor Berry beforehand.'

'Quite. I'm sure he would have done. Have you met him socially?'

Mason nodded. 'Often, but most of the time I see him, it's like two ships passing. Always busy,' he added.

Robbins frowned. 'Pity. It would have helped had you known him a little better.' She glanced quickly around the table. 'A little dinner party like this to gain favour with him, perhaps?'

Babs winced again at the obvious innuendo.

Mason caught the barb and ran with it. 'How else can we get to know our peers outside of court rooms and golf courses?' He looked directly at her.

'By making friends on the way up?' she suggested. 'You know what they say about meeting them on the way down.'

'And what about you, Ann,' Babs asked. 'Have you made any friends on the way up?'

She shook her head. 'No more than I need to. I cultivate the friendships I need.'

'How?' she asked. 'With dinner parties?'

Robbins shook her head again and looked directly at Gus. 'No, I use other methods.' There was a slight inflexion in her voice.

'In what way?'

'Personal and intimate.' She didn't elaborate.

Babs thought the senator's voice had lowered a notch as she said that.

The conversation continued without the animation one associates with informal dinner parties. It was more affected than spontaneous. Both Babs and her husband sensed it. The senator, though, seemed to be leading the table talk, which was beginning to get under Babs's skin. There was very little sign of any real intimacy developing between the three of them. Babs wasn't sure she wanted her husband to get that close, but something of a softening of the table talk and more humour would have helped.

Mason was not making any progress with the senator, and Babs could see that her husband was holding back. He was a notorious flirt, and most of their lady friends enjoyed the usual banter between them. But this was different; the senator was being aggressive, almost. Babs wondered if this was more of a job interview than a friendly dinner party. She was certainly leading the conversation.

She cleared her throat discreetly and stood up. 'I'll just clear these things away and bring the coffee through. Perhaps you two would like to retire to the lounge. We'll take coffee in there.'

As Ann and Gus got up from the table, Babs controlled her frustration and growing anger by getting on with the task of clearing the plates and making coffee. But she made sure she was quiet enough to follow the conversation in the other room.

'Have you ever blocked anybody from the Senate?' Mason asked her.

She nodded. 'When it has suited me.'

'Do you base that on politics, personalities or what?'

'Rarely politics, Gus. If I don't like the bastard, he doesn't get in. It's as simple as that.' She laughed. 'But I'll deny ever having said that.'

He understood how mendacious politicians could be when it suited them. Ann Robbins was no different. 'You'd have the newspapers snapping at your heels like a pack of wolves if they thought that of you,' he said, smiling.

'They'd have to catch me first.'

'You keep yourself fit then, Ann?' he asked. 'Do you use the gym?'

She shook her head. 'I prefer jogging. I like to run down by the lake.'

He arched his eyebrows in a show of surprise. 'Aren't you bothered by people coming up to you at all?'

She shrugged. 'If they can run and ask me questions at the same time, it will help to get them fit.'

They both laughed as Babs walked in with the coffee. At last, Babs thought to herself, things were warming up.

'Ann tells me that she likes to go jogging down by the lake,' Mason said to his wife.

Babs's expression changed. 'I do as well. I've never seen you though, Ann.'

Robbins shook her head in a short, sharp movement. 'I'm always there at six in the morning. I like to get out in the early morning air. Not so many people about either.'

Babs chuckled softly. 'Too early for me, I'm afraid. I usually get there about 9.30.'

She was still holding the tray of coffee cups. She put it down on the coffee table and poured a cup for the senator.

'Perhaps we should run together one day,' she suggested.

Robbins ignored the offer, but smiled thinly and turned her attention back to Gus Mason.

'As I was saying, Gus, getting into the Senate is not as easy as you might imagine. It isn't just powerful backers that you need, but powerful friends too.' She let the last statement sink in like a heavy stone settling on soft mud until it slowly disappeared from view. 'And those friendships are not easily come by; you have to work at them.'

Mason believed her advice was filled with innuendo, and it irked him to think she might be suggesting a liaison. He glanced at Babs who had a fixed expression on her face, holding back on what could be a fairly explosive temper. He decided to change the subject. Or at least steer the senator away from the idea of working his way into the State Senate by way of Ann Robbins's bed.

In the end the evening turned out to be something of a disaster for Babs and her husband. Once Senator Robbins had left in her car, they turned and faced each other in the drive as it disappeared into the night and shook their heads.

'It didn't work, did it Gus?'

'No.'

They stepped up on to the porch and stood there for a while listening to the sounds of the night. The moon was up and throwing its soft light everywhere. It could have been romantic.

'She's going to block you, isn't she?'

He didn't say anything at first but continued to stare into the night.

'Yes,' he said at last. 'She's going to block me.'

Babs's features hardened in the shadows. 'There must be some way to stop her,' she muttered.

'Some way,' he replied grimly, 'even if it means getting up early and taking up jogging.' And with that he spun on his heel and went back into the house.

TWO

THE YOUNG WOMAN *paused and put her pen down. The small voice recorder was still recording quietly on the table between her. She noticed that Babs would keep picking at the folds of the rough skirt she was wearing. Probably a thing about being confined, she decided. It was no wonder; the prison cell felt pretty bleak and restraining. How different, the young writer thought, to Mason's previous life where glamour and power went hand in hand.*

'What about the German guy?' she asked, referring to a large pad that she had placed beside her.

Babs tossed her head back. 'Oh, the German guy,' she repeated. 'Gunter Haman. I never knew he existed.' She stopped and looked across the cell at the young writer. 'Never heard of him. Never met him.'

'But he was the one who started it all really, wasn't he?'

Babs shook her head. 'No, there were others. What Haman did was an act of penitence. He had no way of knowing how it would end.' She closed her eyes briefly and remembered how utterly appalled she had been at the disclosure of Haman's innocent involvement. He would have had no idea what he was about to start.

Gunter Haman opened his eyes in the darkness of his bedroom and thought once more about the dream. It had come again, but this time with remarkable clarity. Before this the images had been a little vague and confused, melding with pictures of the present. Although it was clearer, it still troubled him.

He could hear his wife breathing softly beside him, and turned his head to one side so that he could just make out the shape of her head on the pillow. Beyond her, on her bedside table the digital clock display showed that it was 4.30 in the morning.

He yawned and blinked his eyes to clear the dryness from them, and as his eyelids closed, so the images came flooding back. He could see the young woman's arm beginning to scorch as the flames took hold and blistered the skin. The number tattooed crudely on her arm blurred and charred, vanishing in a moment. But although the number had disappeared quickly, Haman would never forget it; 180328. It was his date of birth: 18th March 1928. Sixty-seven years ago.

When Haman had first seen that number, it meant nothing to him other than it was the date of his birth, but over the years he had come to understand. Now it poured over him like a flood, and swamped him with a pervasive and damaging feeling of guilt.

He sat up, threw the covers back and swung his thin legs over the edge of the bed. With his arms supporting him, he sat there staring down at the floor, seeing nothing except the woman's burning arm.

'What's up, Gunter?' Her voice was thick with sleep.

He turned his head a little to one side and answered his wife's mumbled question.

'Nothing, a bit of indigestion, that's all.'

He felt his wife move as she propped herself up on her elbow.

'You having that dream again?' she asked, reaching out a hand and touching him gently on the shoulder.

Haman turned and looked at her in the darkness. 'Go back to sleep, sweetheart; I'll be OK.'

His wife moved away from him and switched her bedside lamp on. The room was immediately flooded with light.

'I'll go and make us some coffee,' she told him and clambered out of bed. As she fastened her dressing gown around her generous proportions, she looked at him with genuine concern. 'It's happening too often, Gunter. You need to talk about it.'

Haman reached for his dressing gown which was hanging from a hook behind the door, and put it on. His wife shuffled out of the bedroom, turning the main light on as she went through the open door. Her grey hair, usually well groomed, was now a little unkempt. Haman smiled at the untidiness, but at least his wife had a great deal more hair than him.

They sat on opposite sides of the table in their well-appointed kitchen, sipping their coffee. Haman's wife put her cup down.

'How many times have you had this dream?'

Haman shrugged. 'I don't know, Angela; ten times, twenty maybe.' He shook his head and spilled his coffee. 'Damn!'

Angela reached over the table and put her hand on his arm. 'I'll do it.'

He watched as she got some kitchen roll and mopped the spilled coffee. She took his cup from him, wiped it and put it down on the table.

'Sorry, Angela.'

'Never mind about that,' she told him as she sat down again. 'Now, about this dream.'

He put his hands to his forehead for a moment as if he was about to burst into tears. Then he lowered them and straightened up.

'You know I served in the Hitler Youth.' Angela nodded; she knew his history. 'My last few weeks were spent in the Reich Chancellery.' He shook his head slowly. 'I was just a kid.' He sighed and drew in a deep breath. 'They told me I had one last job to do; one last task that would serve the Fatherland.'

'Yes,' she interrupted, 'you've told me about that many times.'

He fixed his eyes on her, the woman he loved and had loved for over forty years. Would she be able to cope with the truth, he wondered? Or would she look on him as some kind of Nazi butcher?

'But not the last time,' he responded, making up his mind to tell her and hopefully to ease the burden. 'Not the last time,' he said again.

She picked up her cup. 'What last time?'

He cast his eyes down and looked forlornly at the table top. He knew he had to open up, to share his own, perceived guilt with her.

'Angela,' he began, 'the world believes that Hitler and Eva Braun died together in the Chancellery.' He looked up at her, shaking his head. 'But that isn't true. Eva Braun did not die. She wasn't even there.'

Angela's eyes widened and her mouth fell open. Haman put his hand up.

'Well, she was there, but not when Hitler was shot. She was taken out of the room.'

Angela peered at him, her eyes half closing. 'By you?'

He shook his head. 'No, somebody else.'

'But what about...?'

He nodded briskly. 'I know; what about the two bodies?' He could feel himself trembling slightly as he began to recall those last moments. 'They brought a young woman in. She was about the same height and build as Fraulein Braun. She was forced to kneel beside the body of Hitler.' He stopped for a moment to gather his thoughts and to compose himself. 'She couldn't have known what was about to happen because she was blindfolded. They shot her in the back of the head and arranged her body next to the Führer's.'

'You saw all this?' Her voice was a whisper.

He nodded. 'I was then told to burn the bodies and to make sure they couldn't be identified. It was for the sake of the Fatherland, they said. I was on my own.' He looked into his wife's eyes, searching deep into her soul. 'I was barely seventeen years old, Angela. Seventeen.' Tears began to roll down his face. 'I poured gasoline over them. It had been left there for me. When it was done I lit a piece of paper with a cigarette lighter they had given me. I tossed the paper on to the bodies and ...' He stopped and shook his head. 'The flames just erupted.' He was silent for a few moments. 'And then I saw the number on her arm.'

'Number?'

'A tattoo. A number on her arm. I didn't know what it meant, not then. But it was the date of my birth – 180328. I couldn't take my eyes away, even when her flesh burned and the number disappeared.' He reached across the table and took Angela's hand. 'The dream has scared me, Angela; scared me to death. It's as though the dead woman is pointing the finger at me; as though she is saying "this is your fault; your responsibility". Then I see the flames burn her flesh away and the tattoo with it.'

Angela put her hand over his and kept squeezing it as though she was gently kneading bread dough. He could feel her trembling and the pressure from her fingers was growing stronger. He drew his hand away and studied the look of astonishment on her face.

'I've lived with that all those years, Angela, but could never bring myself to tell anyone.'

'But you were a mere child, Gunter,' she said softly, shaking her head. 'Nobody would have blamed you.'

'It wasn't the blame or the guilt that stopped me from telling the truth. I was simply carrying out orders as any soldier would.'

'Tosh!' she said suddenly, straightening up. 'You were no more than a boy scout; soldier indeed!'

He smiled. 'I thought I was a soldier.' He said nothing for a while; just looked at his wife.

'I'd almost forgotten about it,' he went on, 'you know; managing to keep it at the back of my mind. Until the dreams started.' He lifted his eyes until he was looking over the top of her head, looking at something far off, something dredged from the deep recesses of his mind. 'Until the dreams started,' he said again.

'Do you think you should talk to someone about them?' she asked.

He smiled again and shook his head gently. 'I'm talking to you, Angela. I don't need anyone else.'

'But the dreams are bothering you,' she pressed. 'That can't be good for you.'

He shrugged and took a mouthful of coffee. 'I need to find out who she was,' he said as he put his cup down. 'I think that's why I'm having the dreams.'

Angela's mouth fell open. 'Don't be silly, Gunter. Why on earth do you want to know who she was? And how would that help anybody? It certainly wouldn't help that poor woman.'

'For some reason Angela ...' he paused, trying to pick his words carefully, 'I feel that someone should know what happened to her; someone who was part of her family.'

'If she was a Jew, Gunter, she wouldn't have a family; they killed them all.'

He arched his eyebrows and gave her a rather condescending look. 'Sweet Angela, you're right of course, but there are always miracles and somebody could have survived. It has happened.'

'And you think this would stop the dreams?'

'It might help.' He got up from the table and took their cups across to the coffee pot. He filled both cups and returned to the table, setting them down. 'It's as though the woman is reaching out to me in the dream.' He sat down. 'I'm sixty-seven years old now, Angela. Only God knows how long I have left. But if I could find out who she was, I believe I would go to my grave a happy man.'

'A kind of redemption?' she offered. 'Rather silly, isn't it?'

He chuckled. 'Some redemption; I was never brave enough before, and now most of the guilty ones are dead I decide to set out on some kind of crusade.' He chewed his bottom lip. 'Do I sound like a coward?' he asked.

Angela reached over the table and took his hand. 'No, never a coward.' She leaned back in her chair, pulling her hand away. 'So how will you go about this crusade at your age, and what will you do when, and if, you find out who the poor woman was?'

He nodded towards the small room he used as a study, his 'indoor shed' as his wife called it. 'I'll go down to the public library, see who I need to contact, what I have to do.'

'What about the people who were in the Chancellery with you? Won't they be able to help?'

He laughed. 'If they're still alive, they'll all be over a hundred years old.' Then he shook his head and lapsed into deep thought for a moment. Eventually he looked up. 'I'll make a start in the morning.' He glanced at the clock on the wall. 'Well, later, anyway.'

Angela knew then that Gunter would begin his quest as soon as he had had his breakfast and showered. Once he had his teeth into something, he was something of a Rottweiler and wouldn't let go. She just hoped he would meet a dead end on this one and let the whole thing drop. But more importantly she hoped that it would get the dream out of his mind and there would be no harmful consequences.

She hoped.

It was some time before Gunter Haman learned about the International Tracing Service in the town of Bad Arolsen. He had had many false starts, but soon discovered the facility by doing a search in his local library at Aachen. He used the new service known as the 'Internet'. It was in its infancy but the librarian was very helpful and Haman's search was reasonably short. The International Tracing Service, known as the ITS, was just a couple of hours' drive from Buchenwald, which was just a few miles from the town of Weimar after which the early German Republic had been named, later to become the Third Reich. He made an application to the ITS to search through the records of those people who had perished in the concentration camps.

When Haman had submitted the application, it had taken a great deal of time for a reply because of the nature of the bureaucracy that controlled the centre. It was headed up by eleven different nations, and each one had to agree to a search application before it could be issued. It meant several weeks of waiting for Haman, but he had learned to become patient.

While he waited for a reply, Haman began other, local searches. It meant he had been away from his wife now on many occasions over the ensuing weeks, and it was beginning to tell on him. He had visited many places in his quest while he waited on the ITS. He realized that it was one of the best kept secrets of the post-Holocaust era, and was under intense pressure to open its doors to the general public. He phoned his wife whenever he was too far from home to return in the evening, and every day she insisted he give up his search and return home. But Haman always refused because he felt his hardship could never match the hardship endured by those unfortunate people who had been incarcerated behind the wire at all the notorious concentration camps in Europe. And incarcerated by his own people too.

When he finally received the reply he had been waiting for, Haman hurried to the tracing service centre. At the reception desk, he found a smart young woman. She seemed the opposite of what he expected to find. She looked up at him and smiled as he showed her his written permit. He asked what he had to do and where he should begin.

'Do you know who you are looking for?' the young woman asked.

He shook his head. 'No, I only have a number.'

'What is it?' He told her and she tapped the number into a computer. A few moments passed and she wrote the name

Buchenwald on a notepad, tore the page off and handed it to Haman.

'You'll find details in the file marked *Buchenwald*,' she said, handing him the paper. Then she pushed her swivel chair away from the desk and stood up. 'I'll take you.'

He was shown into a room that contained row upon row of steel filing cabinets. The young woman pointed down the aisle and left him to it, promising him help if he needed it. Haman began walking slowly down the aisle, crowded in by shelves and shelves of heart rending misery.

On each cabinet was a plate containing the letter, in alphabetical order, of each file held within that cabinet. On other cabinets were the names of the camps: Auschwitz, Bergen-Belsen, Breendonk and Buchenwald. The list of names and letters seemed endless.

Haman opened the draw marked Buchenwald. Inside were ledgers. He withdrew one and went to the end of the row to find a table, one of many that had been conveniently placed. He laid the ledger on the table and opened it. There were columns of names and numbers. Alongside each name had been written something about that person. It included such mundane information as to whether that person had lice, how many teeth, false or otherwise, gold or silver.

As Haman ran his finger down the archaic, brown stained pages, he began to feel a sense of bitterness towards his own country. Each line had stripped bare a human being, taking the poor soul down to the basest of dignity. There was nothing there about the character of the man or the woman, simply what they possessed that could be quantified and valued. The fragments of their living were more valuable than their lives.

After two hours, Haman had worked his way through a dozen ledgers. His eyes were beginning to react to the constant scanning of aged writing. There were times when he was distracted. Not by other sounds or the occasional visitor, but by the sheer, overwhelming sadness of each entry. He knew that someone would have carefully penned the entry; probably blotting it like a clerk would after making an entry in a warehouse ledger or financial account. He wondered how that nameless person must have felt. But then he real-

ized that that person would have been like the young, 17-year-old Hitler Youth who had been ordered to burn the bodies of the Fuhrer and Eva Braun; he would have been doing his duty.

Haman took a break and went across the road to a bar where he had a coffee and collected his thoughts. He could have used the small reception area where there were some automatic dispensing machines, but he felt the need to escape from the place for a while.

He didn't know what he would do when he found what he was looking for. Once he had the name of the woman who was murdered in the Chancellery, he would need to trace her and learn whether she had a family or not. The chances were that if indeed she did have a family, they would all have followed her to their deaths in the revolting gas chambers. He finished his coffee and went back to the building that he had come to regard as a house of death.

He began his search again wondering how long it would take him to work his way through the endless rows of cabinets before, or if he found what he was looking for. But suddenly the number was there, neatly inscribed and showing deft penmanship: 180328. But there was no record of her fate; all that had been written in a firm, steady hand was the woman's name, Rosmaleen Demski, followed by the word '*Zugeordnet*': assigned.

Haman knew that Buchenwald had been a sink hole where the unfortunate Jews and people who were anathema to the Nazis met their fate. And he knew from the records through which he had been reading that each entry contained the fate of practically all those who had been listed. He hadn't come across the word *assigned* before, so now he was baffled; he didn't know what to do. He closed the ledger and took it back to the filing cabinet, replaced it and slid the long drawer home. It was almost as if he was closing a drawer in a mortuary.

The young woman at the desk looked up at Haman as he walked into the reception area. She smiled. It was a pleasant smile; so out of place in the house of horrors.

'Did you find what you were looking for?' she asked.

Haman shrugged and shook his head. 'All I could find was that my friend had been assigned.' He shrugged again. 'I don't know what that means. You know; what happened to her.'

Her head bobbed up and down. 'Yes, I think you'll have to look through the records at the camp your friend was at.'

'Buchenwald,' he reminded her.

'Of course,' she remembered. 'If you'll just wait for a moment.' She typed in Haman's details on the computer and asked for the number for which he was searching. He told her. She finished typing then punched the print button. Once the printer had finished, she pulled out the result and handed it to him. 'Hand this in at the Buchenwald desk with your application. Should be all you'll need,' she reassured him.

He thanked her and left the centre. Tomorrow he would begin the next part of his quest.

Buchenwald was a statement about man's inhumanity to man. Despite the efforts to make the camp look pristine, there was nothing anyone could do to shake off the invisible cloak of terror that stalked each blade of grass and each wall of that forbidding monument to the Nazi horror. Haman felt his skin crawl as he sat in front of the computer screen, checking column after column of names and their fates.

As much as Haman wanted to find out what happened to Rosmaleen Demski, he was drawn by some powerful emotion to the names that scrolled past. It was as though he felt compelled to suffer the fates of those inmates by some kind of metamorphosis, as page after page of horror written with a casual hand that could not even begin to understand or empathize with the victims, were now making his flesh crawl. He felt guilt, and it was not guilt by association, but guilt by birth. He was born a German and felt the weight of the nation's guilt on his shoulders.

He blinked the tears from his eyes and continued his weary toil until he came to Rosmaleen Demski. It was not the first, but about the fiftieth woman with that name. But this was the woman he had been searching for. Rosmaleen Demski, number 180328; assigned to Reich chancellery. Haman nodded; he knew that. Well, he realized what the assignment was but the date was March, 1945. The woman who had been murdered in place of Eva Braun died in April. So why was Rosmaleen Demski taken away earlier if all they had

planned to do was to shoot her? Probably to fatten the poor woman up, he decided.

But it was the following entry that caught Haman's eye. She had a son. His name was Isaac. Ten years old. And his number was written alongside his mother's entry, just to keep the records straight. So correct in everything they did, so fatal to everything they touched. He shook his head and read on. Isaac, number 180329, was taken away from his mother and returned to Auschwitz. Haman looked up at the ceiling. He knew that thousands of the Jews had been processed at Auschwitz before being sent on to places like Buchenwald. It looked as though young Isaac Demski had been returned there to be reprocessed perhaps.

He looked back at the screen. There was nothing else there that could help him. It meant he now had to return to the ITS at Bad Arolsen and begin his search for Isaac Demski.

Babs let the memory fade away. She had never met Haman. And if it hadn't been for the German's dedication, she would never have met Jacob Demski. Smart bastard he was, she recalled, but so dangerous.

She looked at the young woman who was still writing and waited until she had put her pen down.

'You never know who you are connected to, you know, until it's too late.'

'Too late?'

She peered over her glasses at the young writer. 'It's like having a relation turn up at a family wedding. Someone you wouldn't be seen dead with. Or the black sheep of the family.' She sighed deeply. 'The one who shatters that carefully contrived appearance that you reserve for the outside world.'

'Reveals the truth about you, is that what you mean?'

Babs leaned forward assertively. 'Yes, but it isn't always a truth that you are aware of.'

'A skeleton in the closet?'

Babs grimaced. 'You could put it that way.' She stopped and thought of something. 'But in this case, more than just a skeleton in the closet.'

The young writer wondered if that was a reference to the concentration camp, but let it pass.

'Let us go back to the dinner party for a moment,' she said after a

while. 'You said you used to jog in the middle of the morning. But what about your husband, did he take up jogging?'

Babs stopped fiddling with the loose thread in her skirt and looked across the cell at the young woman. 'Yes, but I didn't know it at the time. I would go for a run about nine, 9.30.' She shrugged. 'Sometimes it would be late evening. Mostly it depended on what Gus was doing at the time.'

'It did rather point the finger at you,' the young writer told her. 'Pre-planned?'

'It looked that way,' she admitted. 'But I wanted to bump into Senator Robbins in a more subtle way so that it looked like chance. I needed to get into her good books.'

The young writer scribbled something down on her pad. 'She wasn't keen on you though, was she?'

Babs shook her head. 'No, and that's the damming thing about it. If it hadn't been for my presence in Gus's life, I'm sure she would have been all over him like a rash.'

The young woman laughed. When she quietened down she said: 'So Ann Robbins' intention to block your husband's admission to the State Senate was simply because he was married to you, right?'

Babs eyed her rather sternly. 'Ann Robbins wanted my husband like there was no tomorrow, but he wanted no part of it, and that stuck in her craw.'

'It gave your accusers a motive, didn't it? The irony is that, well, there really was no tomorrow for Senator Robbins, was there?'

Babs was a little surprised at that. 'Why, because she fancied my husband? She fancied most things in pants.' She looked away. 'The prosecutor claimed I had a motive because Senator Robbins was going to block Gus's election to the State Senate, not because she was showing signs of wanting to get him in the sack.'

The young writer turned her attention to the notepad and wrote for a little while. Then she looked up and tossed her head back, and ran her hand over her head.

'Was it common knowledge?'

'Was what common knowledge?'

'Senator Robbins' intention to block your husband?'

'Judge Lawrence knew.'

*

Gus Mason sat across the table from Judge Henry Lawrence in the diner. It wasn't an unusual place to find members of the court. Although there were more elegant places for people like Judge Lawrence to eat, there were fewer prying eyes and open ears in the diner. The other customers in there were more interested in their own lunch breaks, tucked into the booths, than they were in whatever was being said, or plotted at other tables.

The waitress poured them both fresh coffee and took their orders, then left them to themselves. The diner was busy, and that suited the two men. They could talk freely and know that they wouldn't be overheard. Outside the diner, the traffic on Washington Avenue rumbled by. The noise was only intrusive when the main door of the diner was opened, but not for long; inside it was just the general hubbub of conversation and the sounds of knives and forks on plates.

Lawrence lifted his cup and took a mouthful of coffee. The cup was almost lost in his huge fist. Lawrence was a big, imposing giant of a man. He was about six feet three inches in height and weighed about two hundred pounds. In court his presence was so intimidating at times that it was said that he literally frightened the defendants into pleading guilty, whether they were or not.

His dark hair was swept straight back over his head and reached to his shirt collar. His dark suit and massive shoulders made him a fearsome sight. Gus Mason knew the judge had tremendous strength and had been a legend in his college football team. He once signed for the Dallas Cowboys, but a foot injury put paid to what would have been a promising professional career.

Lawrence was also well known for his right wing views. Some members of the left wing newspapers argued that a man with extreme views like Lawrence's should not be a judge, but it was expected that he would be appointed to the Supreme Court once a Republican president had been elected.

'She's going to block you, Gus.'

Mason nodded over the top of his coffee cup. He put it down. 'I know,' he replied levelly. 'I've got to figure something out; something that will either change her mind or ...' He shrugged and left the rest of the sentence die on his lips.

'Have you tried the direct approach?'

Mason smiled and raised his eyebrows. 'You mean like sleeping with her?'

Lawrence nodded. 'She'd be eating out of your hand. It's worth thinking about.'

Mason nodded back. 'And Babs would be delighted, eh?'

They both laughed. Then Lawrence got serious. 'We've got three weeks until the nominations are accepted, Gus. That should give you some time. It wouldn't be the end of the world if she blocked you, but it might sow some doubt on your credibility.'

He shook his head. 'We had her over for dinner. Waste of time.'

'Too open. You need a little more subtlety.'

'Like blackmail?'

Lawrence's eyebrows lifted. 'You have something on her?'

'Of course not. She's untouchable.'

The waitress turned up with their orders. Ham on rye bread for Mason, and a beef burger with fries for Lawrence. She refilled their cups and left them to their meal.

'I'll speak to her, Gus,' Lawrence told him, his jaw rotating as he munched on the burger.

'Really?' Mason was surprised at the judge's offer. It wasn't expected of senior judges to interfere in what could only be seen as a political decision. Not that it was very democratic, such that a senator could block an aspirant simply because of a personal prejudice. But Mason welcomed the judge's offer.

'That's very good of you, Judge,' he admitted, 'but isn't it a little risky?'

Lawrence shook his head. 'Counsellor, we need you in that Senate, and one way or the other, we're going to get you there.'

Mason was surprised at Lawrence's openness, but he let it pass, grateful that he was being given such powerful backing. But he did wonder exactly how Lawrence was going to swing it.

THREE

Lieutenant Amos of the New Jersey State Police stared down at the body of Senator Ann Robbins. She had been pulled from the water and looked quite peaceful. Her hair lay in wisps across her face which had turned white because the blood had drained away, seeking the lowest point in her prone body. She was wearing an expensive jogging suit with the distinctive 'whoosh' logo emblazoned across the front. There was no sign of any make-up on the woman, and there was no obvious sign of violence.

Amos pulled the zip up along the body bag until it closed over the senator's face and stood up. He looked around at the crime scene which was now cordoned off with police tape. It fluttered in the breeze like a warning to anyone who might come along in a hurry, as some joggers tend to do.

The lake was on his left as he faced back along a blacktop path, wide enough for most traffic. The trees on his right were on the edge of a small copse. A well-worn path, not tarmac, sloped down from the high ground. The path could not be seen from his vantage point other than the few yards that came out of the trees and joined the track that ran around the edge of the lake.

'Has she been in the water long?' he asked, still looking at the path.

The police doctor pushed his bottom lip out as he considered the question.

'Difficult to tell at this stage, Amos. Should get a better idea from the pathologist's report, but I would say no more than thirty minutes.'

He turned to the police officer who was standing close by.

'Who found her?'

The patrolman looked beyond him and tipped his head towards a Crown Vic patrol car that was parked on the narrow road.

'Young jogger, a woman no more than about eighteen. She's over there.' Amos turned as the officer was talking. 'But she's pretty shaken up.'

He nodded. 'I'll go careful,' he said and walked over to the police car.

The young woman was sitting in the back of the Crown Vic. She was wearing a good quality jogging outfit and what look liked decent trainers on her feet. She had her hands in her lap and Amos could see she was trembling. He eased open the door and slid in beside her. He could see her blanched features quite clearly and realized it must have been a terrible shock to the poor woman.

'Morning ma'am. I'm Lieutenant Amos. Everybody calls me Amos. Thank you for agreeing to wait. I won't keep you long. When we're finished up here one of my men will take you home. You can call in at the precinct office and make a statement later, or we'll send somebody round to your home if you wish.'

She moved her eyes towards him and shivered, but it was not from the cold.

'Thank you,' she said quietly. 'I would sooner you send somebody round.'

'What time did you find the body?'

She looked away from him and stared through the windscreen. 'About seven o'clock this morning.'

He glanced at his watch. 'Was there anybody else around at that time?'

'Couple of joggers.'

'Do you know them? Would you recognize them if you saw them again?'

She shook her head. 'I didn't know them, not personally. I only see them occasionally.'

'Any strangers?'

'No.'

'When you found the body, what did you do?'

She looked at him. 'Phoned 911.'

'Of course. Thank you.'

She smiled thinly at him as he moved away and climbed out of the car. Then he turned and leaned on the coachwork, holding the door open with his bulk.

'I'm going to ask one of my men to take you home now. I'll have a policewoman come round tomorrow; take a statement. You sure you wouldn't prefer to come to the office?' She shook her head. 'Thank you for your cooperation,' he told her and closed the door gently before going back to the scene of the crime.

'Well?' he asked the doctor when he got back.

The doctor knew what Amos wanted because they always wanted answers that couldn't be given immediately.

'It's too early to tell. She could have drowned. There are no obvious signs of violence, no tell-tale signs of a struggle, nothing; could have been a heart attack, anything.'

Amos thanked him, knowing that the lab report would almost certainly reveal how she died. He would just have to wait. He hoped for the sake of public relations between the department and the public that Senator Ann Robbins had died of natural causes.

But somehow he doubted it.

Gunter Haman stared at the computer screen unaware that his wife was standing beside him with a cup of coffee in her hand.

'Gunter?'

He was in such a concentrated state of mind that his wife's voice startled him. He shook his head quickly and looked up at her as she leaned over his desk and placed the mug by his elbow.

'Sorry, Angela, I was miles away.'

'I think you're spending too much time on that thing,' she told him as she straightened. 'You need a break.'

Haman could understand his wife's concern. Since his return from Bad Arolsen he had made it a daily commitment to find Isaac Demski. It meant hours of trawling through websites devoted to survivors of the Holocaust, and, in particular, children who had survived.

He had tried an Israeli site called Yad Veshem. It was an online site where there were pages of testimonies from survivors of the camps, but his searches achieved nothing useful. He had tried other sites in Europe and Russia, but always found himself wandering up blind alleys, through false dawns and giving up each day in frustration. But one day he logged on to the German Red Cross and discovered that they had a tracing service for families of the Holocaust. He chastised himself for not going there in the first place, but it meant that he had at last opened up a door through which his inquiry could go.

What transpired then was a delay of several weeks. He was only able to request a trace for Isaac Demski, having supplied the necessary information, which included the fact that he wasn't a relative. This meant that the Red Cross would try to make contact with Demski and ask if he was prepared to accept a message from Haman.

'Well?' his wife demanded.

He smiled and leaned back in his chair. He had a huge grin that seemed to spread across his face. 'I've found him,' he declared triumphantly, picking up his coffee.

'Demski?'

'His son.' He pointed at the screen. 'He lives in America. He sent me an e-mail. Says his father can't respond but has asked him to. Look.' He pointed at the screen.

Angela came round to his side of the desk and read the message. Then she looked at Haman and put her arms around his shoulders, squeezing him gently.

'After all this time,' she said. 'I'm pleased for you, Gunter.' She let him go. 'What now?'

He shrugged. 'I suppose I'll have to pay him a visit; can't expect him to travel over here.'

She agreed and put her hand on his shoulder. 'Then I want you to put an end to this,' she told him. 'You've done what you set out to do. All you have to do now is tell this man what happened.' She straightened up beside him, leaving her hand on him.

Gunter glanced up at her, closed his hand over hers and smiled. 'You're right.'

Then he turned back towards the computer screen and began typing. His wife walked out of the room and once again found herself hoping that that would be the end of it.

*

'You referred to "many skeletons",' the writer asked, looking down at her notes. 'Was that a reference to Buchenwald concentration camp?'

'I suppose it was,' Babs admitted. 'It all began there.'

'But you had no knowledge at all of Isaac Demski's past?'

Babs shook her head quickly. 'No, of course not. I wasn't born then. What happened then was, well ...' she stopped and wondered how she could explain it to the young writer. 'This was something Gunter Haman was doing that had absolutely no connection to the business of getting my husband elected into the state Senate. He had no idea we existed.' She paused. 'There was no way we were ever likely to meet Demski either. He was not one of us.'

'Can you explain that?'

Babs smiled. 'He was head of the Jewish Mafia.'

Jack Demski stood some distance away from the arrivals door at Kennedy Airport. It was a habit; he tried to avoid standing in a crowd. The people in front of him had no such concerns, they were there to meet loved ones, friends, guests and quite possibly, business associates. But Demski was there to meet someone from his father's past; a complete stranger. He watched as the passengers filed out, their faces lighting up in recognition as they spotted the person who was there to meet them. Some waved; some just lifted their eyebrows in recognition. Some dallied in the open door as children ran to them, flinging their arms out in joy. Other travellers piled up behind those innocently sharing the beautiful moments with sons and daughters, grandsons and granddaughters. Demski smiled; he'd done it himself.

Then Gunter Haman appeared. His face showed that mixture of expectation and concern: the expectation that someone would be there to meet him and the concern that perhaps there might be no one there. But Demski's obvious Jewish heritage was a dead giveaway, and Haman's face brightened as he spotted the dark curls and the unmistakeable curved nose. Standing beside Demski was a giant of a man. He was dressed in black and his head was freshly shaven. Haman wondered idly if the giant had ever seen photographs of the unfortunate prisoners in places like Buchenwald who had never been given the option of whether they wanted their heads shaved or not.

The big man beside Demski leaned forward slightly, bending down to say something. 'This him?'

Demski nodded. 'Just like his picture.'

He stepped forward as Haman cleared the throng and held out his hand.

'Welcome to America, Herr Haman. Did you have a good trip?'

Haman dropped his suitcase on to the floor and shook the offered hand. 'Yes, thank you. Jack? Do I call you Jack?'

'Jack's fine,' Demski nodded and turned to the big guy. 'Take Mr Haman's suitcase.' Then he pointed to the exit doors. 'This way. We have a car waiting.'

'Please, call me Gunter.'

Demski looked at him. 'Sure thing, Gunter.'

And so they walked out of the airport; the German, the Jew and the big, shaven-head American.

Babs had just showered and changed after her morning run down by the lake. She had carefully avoided the route where Ann Robbins had been found. The police were still there although the forensic team had departed, and Babs preferred to keep her distance. She walked through to the front door in response to the chimes from the doorbell. As she passed by the open door of her lounge, she could see the police car at the end of her drive. She frowned as she pulled the door open and found it difficult to suppress a gasp at the sight of the black guy standing there.

'Morning ma'am,' he said pleasantly, showing her his police badge. 'Lieutenant Amos, New Jersey Homicide Division. Mind if we talk?'

Babs stepped out of the house and closed the door behind her. She glanced up and down. 'What do you want to talk about?'

Amos noticed the door had been shut in a very deliberate way. He preferred to interview people at first in their own homes. He always felt it gave him an opportunity to study the person in their own surroundings. It gave him a clearer perspective. But the act of closing the door was almost like a statement from Babs Mason. He shrugged mentally and began the interview where he stood.

'I'm investigating the death of Senator Ann Robbins. I presume you have heard that she died.'

Babs nodded. 'Yes, very tragic. Quite young too.'

'You knew her, I believe?'

'Not really. She wasn't a friend of mine.'

'But she was an acquaintance?'

Babs nodded, her face almost expressionless. 'Yes.'

'She came to your house for dinner one evening?' he asked. 'Couple of weeks ago?'

Babs frowned. 'Yes, about three weeks ago. How did you know that?'

'Were Senator Robbins and your husband good friends?' he asked, ignoring Babs's question.

Babs shifted the weight, moving from one foot to the other. 'Their paths crossed at times, but I wouldn't have called them good friends.'

'But they did know each other?'

'Yes.'

'When did you last see Ann Robbins?'

Babs considered the question for a while. 'Must have been the night we had dinner together. Yes,' she decided, 'it would have been then.'

'I believe you go jogging down by the lake?'

'Yes.' Her reply was drawn out slowly.

'Did you ever see Miss Robbins while you were out jogging?'

'I might have done,' she conceded.

Amos pulled a small notebook from his jacket pocket and flipped it open. He thumbed the pages.

'Miss Robbins was seen in conversation with a woman that morning. Could that have been you? Could you comment on that?'

Babs shook her head. 'I couldn't possibly. I meet so many like-minded people down by that lake. I may have seen Miss Robbins, but I don't remember having a conversation with her. I might have said "good morning", but that hardly constitutes a conversation, does it?'

Amos agreed. 'No, of course not.' It wouldn't have been the first time a so-called witness had embellished a story. It was quite possible that a simple 'good morning' had been turned into an entire conversation.

'I understand that your husband has put himself up for election to the state legislature, and that Senator Robbins was opposed to his admission. Were you aware of that?'

Babs felt little prickling sensations round her neck and her cheekbones. She swallowed hard and continued to stare at the lieutenant.

'Are you implying something?' she asked him.

He shook his head. 'Just asking questions, ma'am, that's all. Were you aware of it?'

Babs tried to relax. 'That was politics, Lieutenant; something we prefer to keep "in house". Whatever Senator Robbins' opinion of my husband was, he never mentioned it.'

'I understand your husband is highly regarded in legal circles,' Amos told her. 'If Senator Robbins had blocked his admission to the Senate, it would not have helped his career, surely?'

She shrugged. 'It was an obstacle that needed to be overcome. No politician enjoys a clean run; there is always opposition.'

Amos flipped the notebook shut and put it back in his jacket pocket. 'I think that will be all for now, ma'am. I might like to speak to you again, but if I do, I would prefer to speak to you in the house. Otherwise we can do it down at the Precinct.' He tapped his forehead lightly with the tip of his index finger. 'Good day to you, ma'am.' He spun on his heel and walked down the drive.

Babs watched him go, standing by her doorstep with her arms folded until his car had pulled away from the house. Something had happened during the conversation to change the lieutenant's mind, and she couldn't figure out what it was. But something had definitely happened.

The drive from Queens down to Brooklyn where Demski lived was uneventful and gave Haman a chance to study the buildings, the traffic and the people and whatever else took his fancy from inside the reasonable comfort of the car. He made the usual comments to Demski, admitting it was his first time in New York and found it quite exciting. Demski acknowledged Haman's comments, but his mind wasn't on the eulogies tripping off Haman's tongue. All he could think of was that he was sitting next to a Nazi; one who had actually been in the bunker when Hitler and his wife, Eva Braun were shot.

His father had spoken often about the Holocaust and what it meant to be a survivor of the camps. For young Jack it was more than just a history lesson; it was a living testament to the atrocities committed against his race. Jack understood that America was controlled by a culture driven from within; a political class system that was dominated by white Anglo Saxons. They despised Blacks and Jews as well as Hispanics and any other race that did not fit their bigoted vision of what made America the country it is today, despite the powerful, Jewish presence in Congress. The irony was not lost on Jack as their driver negotiated the traffic on the beltway.

Haman, however, was now thinking of nothing other than the anticipation of meeting Isaac Demski. Even though it meant brief flashbacks to the Chancellery and his dream, he knew that soon it would be over. He will have completed his mission; his task to tell Isaac what part his mother played in the final moments of the Third Reich.

The house was in Bridgeport, overlooking the Hudson River. From the approach to the front gates the house was not clearly visible, but once inside the outer perimeter, Haman was able to marvel at its colonial elegance. It had the mark of a wealthy resident; a man of influence who would be a pillar of the community. The drive from the entrance gates to the house was only about fifty yards, but nonetheless it was impressive with its short avenue of American elms. These served to hide much of the house and grounds from the road and lend an air of privacy to the place.

The car stopped outside the tall colonnades that supported the Georgian porch. Haman glanced at the big double front doors, one of which was partially open, and saw someone standing there. He could see he was wearing a *yarmulke*, the small cloth skull cap worn by many Jewish men. As the driver of the car opened Haman's door, the man standing in the porch stepped out on to the gravel. Jack Demski walked across to him and greeted him with a kiss on both cheeks. Then he turned towards Haman and urged him to come forward.

Haman felt nervous and excited at the same time. This was the culmination of hours of searching that somehow seemed to go all the way back to the Reich Chancellery. He stopped a few feet from Jack Demski.

'Gunter, this is my father, Isaac.'

Haman felt quite emotional as he looked at the face of the man whose mother had perished in such a way, knowing that his search was finally over and that he could close the chapter on his life that he had lived with and kept secret for so many years.

Isaac Demski shook his hand. 'Shalom.'

'Guten Tag,' Haman muttered. Then he apologized. 'I'm sorry. Shalom.' He bowed his head slightly as Demski released his hand.

Demski shook his head. 'Don't worry. I speak German if it would be easier for you.'

Haman thanked him. 'That would be a great help.'

'*Willkommen*.' He turned to his son. 'Jack, take Herr Haman's case, then join us on the terrace.' He put a hand on Haman's arm. 'This way,' he told him. 'We'll have a beer or coffee or something; whatever's your poison. Then you can freshen up and we'll go out and eat.'

'Yes,' Haman mumbled, 'that sounds good. But now we have a lot to talk about.'

'When Jack is here,' Demski told him. 'I want him to hear what you have to say. He should know about these things.'

Haman shuddered mentally and hoped that his story would not be too harrowing for either Isaac Demski or his son, but he knew only time would tell. He followed Demski around the outside of the house until they reached an old, but tastefully refurbished terrace overlooking the busy waters of the Hudson River where they would talk about the terror that stalked the earth over half a century ago.

When they were settled on the terrace, and Jack Demski had joined them, his father held his hands open towards Haman.

'So, why don't you begin at the beginning?'

Haman made himself more comfortable. It was an unconscious gesture, really; a kind of nervous reaction to the story, as short as it was, that he was about to relate.

'Well, we all know what happened in the Reich Chancellery at the end of the war,' he began. 'At least, the world believes it knows what happened. But I was there.' He shrugged. 'Probably the only living witness to what took place. Hitler had been given a sedative. People believe it was poison, but they are wrong; it was a potion given to him to make him relax. His senior officers were all very nervous. His personal valet was in tears.' Haman shook his head. 'It was very emotional.'

'What about you, were you emotional?' Demski asked.

Haman smiled. 'I was barely seventeen years old. These men could have crushed me as they would an insect and think nothing of it. I was petrified just being in their company. I don't think I should have been there, but I had been ordered by my commanding officer, Hauptmann Lörenz to remain with him at all times. He told me he had a special task for me.' Haman paused for a moment and recalled the moment he had told his wife on the morning she had persuaded him to talk about the dream.

'Go on,' Demski prompted.

'Hitler was taken out of the room by his valet. I will never forget the expression on those faces; the officers in that room. When the Führer had gone, they just filed out. It was over. I didn't know what to do. Lorenz told me to wait there until he came back. So I waited on my own in the place where Hitler had conducted his war; a 17-year-old boy.'

He paused again, recalling those moments. The noise from the water traffic drifted up from the river, and he could hear the cry of the gulls as they weaved overhead. The earlier warmth from the sun had been lost behind drifting cloud and rain threatened.

'Lörenz came back,' Haman continued, 'and told me to follow him. We went up to the Chancellery garden. Hitler's body was lying face down. I didn't notice it at first. Then I heard a scuffling sound behind me and a young soldier came in with a woman. She had been blindfolded and her hands were tied behind her back. I thought it was Eva Braun.' He shook his head. 'It was probably because she was dressed in the same clothes Eva Braun had been wearing. At least, they looked the same to me. She was about the same age, same build. The soldier forced her to her knees alongside Hitler's body. He removed the cords from her wrists. Then Lörenz stepped forward and put a pistol to her head.' He shuddered and fought back the tears. 'I'm sorry. When she fell forward the soldier removed the blindfold. Then Lorenz told me to burn the bodies.'

The two men said nothing, but waited for Haman to continue. They could see he was struggling but did not want to disrupt the picture he was painting in their minds.

Haman blinked away the tears. 'There was some gasoline there. Lorenz handed me a cigarette lighter.' He chuckled. 'I can even remember at the time that I didn't smoke, so why did I need a cigarette lighter?' He shook his head. 'I sprinkled the gasoline over the two bodies and put the can on the ground beside them. Then I found some paper and rolled it into a tube and set light to it. I knew I couldn't chance lighting the gasoline directly, so I stood back and threw the burning paper on to the bodies.' He closed his eyes for a few moments and could see and smell the burning flesh. 'The curiosity of a young boy made me walk over to the flames and look. I wondered what it would be like to see human flesh burning. I remember how bad the smell was. I was almost sick. And that was when I saw the number on the woman's arm; 180328, the date of my birth.'

He stood up and turned towards the river, breathing in the fresh air as though he was trying to get the stench out of his nostrils. He looked back at Isaac Demski.

'I didn't have to try and remember that number. As shocked as I was I dismissed it as an amazing coincidence that this woman should have the date of my birth tattooed on her arm.' He sat down again. 'Can you believe that I didn't know the significance of that tattoo? Well I didn't. That was how powerful our propaganda was: the German nation didn't know. We weren't allowed to know what they were doing.'

'It was my mother, right?'

Haman nodded. 'Do you remember her?'

Demski breathed in deeply through his nose. It pinched the cheeks of his face together. He exhaled noisily. 'I was about eight years old when they took me away from her. She told me everything would be fine.' He shrugged. 'As any mother would. I only have vague memories of her.' He leaned forward in his chair. 'Why my mother?'

Haman shook his head. 'I've thought about that for some time. Your mother was "assigned" as they put it in the *Buchenwald* log. It meant they had a special purpose for removing her. They knew what they were planning to do all along. My memory of her when she was dragged into the Chancellery garden was that she was similar in height and build to Eva Braun. But she wouldn't have been like that while she was in the camp.'

'They fattened her up, is that what you're saying?'

Haman nodded. 'I guess I am. They had to because they meant to convince the world that Eva Braun had perished with Hitler.'

'So where did they take her?'

Haman shrugged. 'I don't know. And I doubt if we ever will know.'

Isaac Demski knew that the German had reached the end of his incredible story. He looked away from Haman and turned to his son. 'What do you think, Jack?'

The young Demski knew instinctively what was in his father's mind. 'I think we should find out, if it's possible.'

'Why?' his father asked him.

'Because knowledge is power, and those bastards didn't save Eva Braun because she was a pretty woman. They had a reason, and if we can find out what it was ...' He left it unsaid, but his father understood the logic behind his son's reasoning. He looked across the table at Haman.

'It would be interesting to find out why they did this, and who was behind it. I know the Nazis had a powerful group of supporters who helped them escape to South America. It might be the place to start.' He reflected on this for a while and then said to Haman, 'Perhaps you should extend your stay with us, Gunter, for a little while at least. I presume you intended to spend some time in America?'

Haman shrugged. 'I have no fixed plans, Isaac, but I don't think I would want to spend too much time away from my wife.'

Demski agreed. 'No of course not. How about a couple of days then, Gunter? It's the least we can do for you. Then you can go back to your wife and we can begin our search.'

FOUR

LIEUTENANT AMOS HAD a great deal on his mind as he drove to his office at the 7th Precinct on Hillside, just off the interstate highway. He was wondering how he was going to handle the interview with Captain Holder, the Precinct commander. John Holder was a career officer whose aim was to become police director at the head of one of America's police departments before stepping up to State. It meant a certain amount of glad-handing was required along the way with the right kind of senior figures. Amos knew that Holder was in the pocket of the Newark Mayor, Nik Pedersen, and the mayor was a close friend of Gus Mason, husband of Babs Mason. To cast suspicion on the Masons at such an early stage in the investigation would not be good for Amos's prospects. But Amos wasn't interested in bringing home results that would satisfy department targets or serving the career desires of supplicant police captains; all Amos was interested in was justice with a capital 'J'.

He pulled into a vacant lot outside the precinct building, parked, got out of the car and headed towards the front door. He threw a cheery wave at the front desk officers as he headed for the stairs which would take him to his office in the homicide division squad room on the second floor. His door was very rarely closed because he couldn't get used to the idea of shutting himself off from the officers working at the squad room desks. He liked to hear the hustle and bustle of the office around him, the sounds of the phones ringing, the gallows humour that bounced spontaneously between officers working on dreadful cases that became an everyday part of their working lives.

He worked his way through the desks which seemed to have been positioned to inflict maximum difficulty on everybody, catching a few smiles along the way. Amos was a popular officer, and most of the squad enjoyed working with him when they got the chance.

His office door was open as usual, and he could see a yellow, Post-it note stuck to his phone as he crossed the squad room. He knew what it was before he'd even peeled it off. It had the words, 'ring me' scrawled in Judith's almost indecipherable handwriting. Amos smiled and picked up the phone, dialling his wife's number.

'Hallo Judith.'

'Hallo Amos. Close the door, will you?'

He laughed softly and put the phone on his desk, then went to the door and closed it. He picked up the phone as he sat down in the swivel chair.

'OK, door's closed and I'm sitting down.'

'Amos, I've heard that the Chief Medical Examiner believes Ann Robbins died of a heart attack, right?'

Amos's wife was an assistant district attorney, which gave her access to information that she did not necessarily need to know. But the DA's office was like many offices where good and bad news spread like wildfire.

'I don't believe that,' he told her. 'She was as fit as a butcher's dog.'

'Just because people jog and look fit doesn't mean they are, Amos.'

'You gonna lecture me again?' He could almost hear her smile down the phone.

'No, Amos. Just look in a mirror from time to time.'

Same old lecture, he thought. But hell, she had his best interests at heart, which was natural; she was his wife.

'So, sweetheart, Ann Robbins did not die of a heart attack. She was murdered. Is that what you're going to tell me?'

'No, Amos, you already knew that.'

'Gut feeling,' he interrupted. 'Years of practice. So how did she die?'

'I don't know.' He could almost hear her shrug. 'Perhaps you should ask the CME.'

He chuckled. 'Like the Chief Medical Examiner is going to tell me he got his first diagnosis wrong?'

'Why not phone him? The DA's going hot on this one, Amos. Any prevarication by Doctor Robertson will not go down well with him. I thought it right to warn you. If you can't get a line on the killer—'

'If she was killed,' Amos interrupted.

'Like I was saying; if you get a line on the killer, your department will need a cast iron guarantee the senator was murdered. Did you get a toxicology report?'

Amos asked his wife to wait while he pulled the report from his desk drawer. He flipped open the folder.

'Preliminary report suggests her death could have been caused by succinylcholine poisoning; the CME found higher traces of potassium than normal. Her pulse rate and blood pressure would have been high just before she died, but that wouldn't necessarily have accounted for the levels found. The traces of the muscle relaxant were difficult to detect, but sufficient to need further tests. If the senator was murdered, then whoever killed her would have administered the sux and pushed her into the water. With enough of the stuff in her, she would have been unable to swim. She'd have sunk like a stone.'

Succinylcholine was a well known muscle relaxant used by surgeons on patients during operations. Dentists used it too. The drug was obtainable on prescription and, like any other drug, was safe to use according to medical advice. High concentrations of the chemical would induce paralysis and consequent cardiac arrest. There were antidotes to the drug, but none of these would have been available to Ann Robbins when she was murdered by the lake.

'How was it administered?' she asked.

'The report suggests that if the sux was administered involuntarily, it would have to have been injected. Trouble is the doc can't find the wound.'

'Hairline?' his wife suggested.

He shook his head into the phone. No, it's usually done intravenously. It can be administered through the cheeks of the backside, but there were no marks there, according to the report. So the next step is to open the rectum. Chances are the needle was rammed in there. If the attacker was lucky, he would have hit the anus and left no visible puncture marks.'

'You said "he", but it could have been a woman.'

'You're so clever, Judith. Have anyone in mind?' As Amos said that, he recalled his conversation with Babs Mason.

'No. Have you?'

'Not really,' he admitted. 'Clutching at straws as usual.'

'Well if I know you, honey, those straws will be your harvest.'

'You're so poetic.'

He saw Captain Holder through the windows of his office. He was standing at the far end of the squad room. He had his arm raised and was beckoning Amos. Amos looked at the framed photograph on his desk of himself, his wife and their daughter, Holly. She was eight years old.

'I've gotta go now, honey. You picking Holly up?'

'I'm on my way there now, Amos. See you tonight?'

'You bet. Big kiss sweetheart. God bless.'

He put the phone down and slid the toxicology report into a drawer, locked it and left his office, not bothering to close the door behind him.

Captain Holder was already sitting behind his desk when Amos walked in and shut the door. He nodded towards an empty chair. Amos dragged it over and sat down. Holder was leaning back with his elbows resting on the chair arms. He had his hands closed in an attitude of prayer, although prayer was the last thing on his mind. The tips of his fingers were pressed into his lips. He was in his forties, still with a good head of hair. It was cut *en brose*, which always reminded Amos of an upturned scrubbing brush, probably because the captain's hair was white.

No one in the department really liked Holder. Being a career man to his boots and fast tracked into an elevated position did little to endear him to his squad of detectives and police officers who patrolled the streets of the 7th Precinct. He was never afraid to express his opinion, popular or otherwise, and was known to hold some extreme views.

'You went to Babs Mason's house couple of days ago.' Holder had his own way of getting straight to the point.

'Yes, that's right; I did.'

'Why?'

Amos shrugged, lifting his massive shoulders. 'Just eliminating Ann Robbins's acquaintances; they're all potential suspects until then.'

'Will you be talking to Gus Mason?' Amos nodded but said nothing. 'You know he's running for office?' Again Amos nodded. 'It would not help his chances if he was seen to be part of your investigation, Amos.'

'I wouldn't be accusing him of anything, John. But I have to talk to all the senator's friends.'

'It might have repercussions; could put the department in a bad light.'

Amos could begin to see which way the conversation was heading.

'We do our job the best way we can, Captain. No one's beyond the law.'

Holder nodded quickly. 'Of course, of course, but there are times when we have to show discretion. Softly, softly.'

'Is there any other way?'

'Yes,' he said suddenly, 'I want you to put the Robbins investigation to bed.'

That caught Amos by surprise. After a slight pause he shook his head. 'Can't do that, John; investigation ain't complete yet.'

Holder lowered his hands until they were flat on his desk. 'She died of a heart attack. We know that. Bit of a shock, a fit woman like the senator, but it happens.'

Amos was surprised that Holder was talking of the cause of death as de facto, when nothing had been finally confirmed by the chief medical examiner.

'The press ain't going to let it go that easy, Captain. Besides, I believe she was murdered.'

The captain's expression didn't alter. It was a classic example of control. 'You got anything to substantiate that, Amos?'

'Reckon I have.'

'Be good to me. Tell me what you have.'

Amos gave a kind of lopsided grin. He didn't want the captain to know of the conversation he had just had with Judith. The man had a habit of feeding information to his favourite newspaper hounds in return for favours that would make him look good in the public conscience.

'Let's say that we regard the death of Senator Ann Robbins as suspicious and we are continuing with our inquiries.'

Holder leaned forward aggressively. 'Amos, don't fuck with me. I'm your captain. Tell me what you have, then find a way of putting this to bed.'

Amos pulled a face and lifted his hand to his forehead to scratch an itch. 'We believe the senator was killed by an overdose of succinylcholine.'

'Sux?'

Amos nodded.

'But you're not sure?'

'No.'

'You can get sux on prescription.' Holder was thinking out loud. 'Maybe she overdosed on that. Self-inflicted.'

Amos disagreed but it didn't seem to make any difference to the way his captain was thinking.

'If we have a murdered senator on our hands, Amos, the crap will hit the fan.' He stopped for a moment and rattled his fingers on the desk. 'We don't want some political retard running round popping off our representatives.'

Amos chuckled at this. 'No one's popping anyone off, John. I don't even think there's a political tag on this.'

Holder gave him a strange look. 'You never know, Amos. Tell you what,' he said suddenly, making up his mind. 'Give it a couple of days. If you're no further forward I want you to declare it as death by misadventure, an accident, natural causes or anything to get the press off our backs. Close the case.' He lowered his voice for effect. 'Then do a little digging on the quiet. Be discreet, Amos. Get my drift?'

Amos wanted to tell him to piss off, but he had his own way of dealing with obstacles that had less to do with solving crimes and more to do with political advancement. Holder wanted his department efficient and squeaky clean, not delving into senators' lives and lifting stones that would hurt his own advancement prospects. There was something in the captain's attitude that puzzled Amos, though. It was almost as if the captain wanted the senator's death to be declared either accidental or by natural causes. It wasn't for a police detective to do that; it was up to the coroner. What Holder was suggesting was tantamount to hiding the truth and by definition, harbouring a criminal. Was Holder protecting someone, he wondered?

He put the thought to the back of his mind, filing it away for consideration later. His next move was to delve deeper into Babs Mason and her husband, Gus, and find out why Holder appeared to be shielding them. Truth was there was little or nothing for Amos to investigate. No clues. No reliable witnesses. Nothing. It was true, though, in all police detective work, that an element of luck is often necessary to get a result. Or the perpetrator of the crime has to be unbelievably stupid and make a mistake. Even a trivial one can lead the police to the felon.

He made his excuses to Holder, said he would get on to it and try to bring the case to a close, and left. But sitting in his office later, Amos knew that the only way he was going to clamber over the obstacle Captain Holder had firmly placed in his way, was to get lucky.

Amos did get that little piece of luck, but it was a couple of months later. Had he arrived at the Precinct HQ a few minutes earlier or later than he did on that particular day, he would not have witnessed the commotion at the front desk.

Sergeant Bibby was holding fort that morning as Amos walked through the front door. The desk sergeant was being berated by a woman, about fifty years of age. She was holding what looked like a small roll of cloth in her hand.

'You should get off your fat fannies and clean up this city,' she was saying forcibly to him. 'There's enough of these damn needles about.'

Amos stopped at the bottom of the stairs and looked across at the altercation. He had a smile on his face because he could understand how patient Sergeant Bibby would have to be while being accused of being responsible for half the crime in New Jersey.

'Yes, I understand your worries, ma'am,' Bibby said carefully, 'and I do realize that there is more we can do—'

'Damn right there is!' She cut him off by slapping her hand on the counter. 'Too many of you hiding away here when you should be getting down to the lake and cleaning the damn place up. Never know when you're gonna step on a needle. I pay my taxes, you know....'

Amos walked over to the front desk and leaned forward so that he was caught in the woman's peripheral vision. She stopped haranguing Sergeant Bibby and turned towards Amos.

'And who the hell are you?'

Amos smiled at her. 'Lieutenant Amos, ma'am.'

She looked surprised. 'You ain't got no uniform.'

He shook his head. 'That's because I'm a detective, we don't need a uniform.'

She nodded her head once. 'Then you should be out there detecting.'

Amos looked at the small roll of cloth she was holding. 'Is that it?' he asked her.

The woman looked at the cloth as though she hadn't seen it before. 'Sure is.' She put it down on the counter. 'See for yourself.'

Amos unrolled the cloth gently. The syringe that the woman had wrapped was stained from spending a long time in the open.

'Where did you say you found this?'

'Down by the lake.'

'You go there often?'

'Some.'

Amos knew he was taking a chance. There were probably dozens of syringes lying about all over the place, but he was relying on his detective's gut instincts now, plus a little desperation. 'If I take you there now, could you show me exactly where you found it?'

'Sure, but I need to be back quick; got my man's lunch to cook.'

'I'll make sure you're back in plenty of time.' He took her carefully by the elbow and guided her away from the desk. 'We'll get a car. Be there and back no time at all.' He looked back at Sergeant Bibby and winked.

Bibby arched his eyebrows and looked down at his paperwork. The syringe was gone and it was no longer his problem.

Jack Demski looked out over the waters of the Hudson River and towards Long Island Sound in the distance. He thought about the events of the previous week, and the subsequent discussions that had gone on, some until the small hours of the morning. His father had said he wanted justice; for his mother's murderer to go to the chair, but Haman had told him that the killer was almost certainly beyond the law now. Jack Demski was more interested in why Eva Braun was allowed to escape, and where she had escaped to. He argued that someone would have that knowledge, and that person or persons might still be alive. He also argued that to have proof of her escape, if that was possible, would make major headlines all over the world, and that the Demski family should have ownership of that story. He told his father they could make a fortune.

Isaac Demski was more pragmatic. Being something of a realist he knew there was little chance of learning anything, but had gone along with his son's desire to at least follow up Haman's dramatic revelation. The question was: Where to start? Gunter Haman had suggested the Simon Wiesenthal organization, but Isaac thought that might be too public. The decision was made to use Jewish contacts of their own, and Jack was given the task of learning whatever he could. And all he had was one name; the one given him by Haman. It was the German officer who had shot Rosmaleen Demski.

Hauptmann Lörenz.

FIVE

BABS WAS GETTING *tired and it showed. The young writer watched as her fingers fretted more at the threads in her skirt. She had sensed Babs's irritability when pertinent questions were put to her, but she knew it was essential to get everything down on paper while she was still willing to talk about it. The whole truth had been lost in rhetoric and lies, claim and counter claim while the world clamoured for the right to know the truth of what happened that day in the Chancellery in Berlin and the single reason for it.*

'At this point you were still unaware of Demski's interest in your husband's future?' she asked.

'Of course. Had we known he would have been stopped.'

'How?'

Babs looked at the young woman. It was a brief, patronizing look. 'Die Spinne?'

The young woman looked puzzled. 'Die Spinne?' she repeated.

Babs nodded. 'Yes. The Spider; a group that came into existence to help smuggle senior Nazis out of Germany.'

'Were you a member of that group?'

Babs laughed softly and shook her head. 'Of course not, but I suppose I was considered part of the family.'

'They go back a long way, I presume?'

Babs breathed in through her nose and then exhaled with a deep sigh. 'Way back to the end of the war. They came into their own in 1945. That's when they knew the war was lost and there were a lot of Nazis clamouring to get out of Germany. They set up an under-

ground network smuggling the top brass into Switzerland and then into Italy. The SS used them to smuggle their own kind out.' She glanced quickly at the young writer and then looked away again. 'You might have heard of them as Odessa, but it was Die Spinne that supplied the false documents, the routes and the Catholic priests who were misguided enough to believe they were doing their Christian duty by shifting the Nazi thugs through their monasteries.'

'Did The Spider network dissolve after the war?'

Babs shook her head and a wry smile changed her expression. 'No, they simply spread their web all over the world.'

She looked around her cell.

'Even here in America.'

General Mort Tyler, four stars and a Vietnam veteran, stood in front of the State House in Trenton, Newark watching Gus Mason climb into a taxi. He lifted a hand to acknowledge Mason's wave and turned to Judge Henry Lawrence who was standing beside him.

'Seems like a good Republican, Henry,' he drawled with his trademark Texan accent. 'Could do with more of him on our side.'

Lawrence said nothing for a moment; just watched the taxi pull away from the State House. He then took the general's elbow and turned to lead him back inside the state legislature building.

'But he's the important one, Mort,' Lawrence told him. 'We've had to open many doors for him.'

'Perhaps I should get him up to the Pentagon.'

Lawrence laughed. 'Heaven forbid. His path is mapped out. That's why he's working in the judiciary.' This was the branch of state legislature that was the final authority on the constitutionality of the State laws. 'He's putting time in at the DA's office as well. We'll need good, solid lawmakers when the time comes.'

Lawrence acknowledged the security guard as the two men walked through the metal detector and two minutes later were seated in an office that the judge used during his working visits to the State House.

Mort Tyler settled into a leather chair and took the whiskey that Lawrence offered him. He was wearing civilian clothes because his uniform marked him out as one of the most decorated soldiers in the

American army, and such was the public's love and admiration of men in uniform, to be seen in his would attract attention immediately. It wasn't that the general shunned publicity, but this visit was private and he felt less conspicuous in a suit.

He glanced around the office as the memory of his conversation with Gus Mason drifted through his mind. The young man was a gift to the organization; an absolute diamond. With him in the White House, everything that the organization needed, both in political placement and influence, would be there for the taking.

Tyler had travelled up from the Pentagon because he wanted an update on their protégé and preferred to keep the press at arm's length, hence the suit. At other times he had been happy to be seen with Gus Mason. Not that Mason could raise the general's profile; it was the other way around. And Mason's image had to be right when he began his push for the United States Senate and eventually the White House.

'Has all the fuss died down over Senator Robbins' accident?' He laid a little emphasis on that last word.

Lawrence sat down and lifted his glass in salutation. 'Nothing to worry about,' he assured the general confidently. 'It was a tragedy caused by heart failure. The coroner was quite firm on that.'

'The road seems clear, then.'

Lawrence nodded. 'It's down to Mason now and the public. We've lifted his profile and he's in demand. That's the important thing. We've improved his technique. He's more at ease now with whoever he meets, and they are at ease with him, whether Democrat or Republican, white, black. He appeals to everybody. The women love him. His wife is an absolute doll of a woman.' He shrugged. 'There's no one else in their marriage. They're loyal. They appear to love each other.' He laughed gruffly. 'Hey, I'd make him president tomorrow if I could. No question.'

Tyler lifted his glass. 'So here's to you, Henry. King-maker.'

Lawrence shook his head. 'To us,' he responded. 'And to the America we will prepare for the true Americans.'

Doctor Hal Robertson, chief medical examiner at the county coroner's office did not normally feel out of place sitting in a police car alongside Lieutenant Amos, but this time it was different. Robertson's Lexus was parked fifty yards away in Old Short Hills Road. They were just by South Mountain Reserve, about six miles from the city centre. It was Robertson who had made the call and suggested a discreet meeting with Amos, who was reluctant at first until the doctor mentioned Senator Ann Robbins. Amos had pulled one of the unmarked squad cars from the parking lot and driven over to where Robertson had asked him to meet. It was early evening but the light was already fading. It was why the doctor had chosen that particular time of day.

The moment Amos had stopped his car, he saw Robertson leave his parked Lexus and hurry across the road towards him. His pace was quick and furtive, which both surprised and encouraged the detective. Years of experience told Amos that this was to be no ordinary meeting.

Robertson clambered into the front seat beside Amos and said nothing for a few moments. His breathing was a little harsh but it sounded to Amos more like hypertension than lack of exercise.

'So why did you ask for this meeting, Doc?' Amos asked him after a while.

Robertson didn't answer immediately but nervously picked at his fingernails. Amos waited patiently.

'It's about Senator Ann Robbins,' the doctor told him, his voice faint.

Amos settled back in his chair. 'You told me,' he said a little impatiently. The senator had been dead about three months now and Amos had not been able to move the investigation forward because of Captain Holder's insistence that the case was closed. He waited. 'So what is it you want to tell me about her?'

'She didn't die of a heart attack.'

The statement was simple and straightforward. At least, it would have been if this hadn't been the man who had signed the death certificate.

Amos felt his pulse rate go up a little. Immediately his mind was racing ahead and he didn't like what he was thinking. He reined his detective's brain in and waited.

'She died of an overdose of succinylcholine.'

Robertson mumbled so quietly that Amos had difficulty hearing him. He thought about the woman who had found the syringe.

'So why did you lie? You knew the cause of her death was because of the drug, but you pulled the autopsy report. Why?'

Robertson's head dropped. His chin pressed against the collar of his shirt. 'It was what I believed then and what I knew to be true, but I had to change my diagnosis because I was afraid.'

'Afraid of what?'

'What they would do to my daughter.' His voice was barely audible.

'Who are "they"?'

The doctor glanced quickly at Amos and then directed his gaze out through the windscreen of the car. He shook his head. 'I don't know.'

Amos knew he would have to be patient. He had dealt with people like Robertson before. They come to you wanting to get something off their chest or to confess to some awful crime, or involvement in a crime, but usually they clam up and forget it was them who contacted you first. You had to ease the confession out of them, treat them with kid gloves.

'Why did you think something was going to happen to your daughter?'

The doctor raised his head and took a deep breath. He looked at Amos and then turned away.

Amos wondered if the doctor was feeling shame or guilt, but knew it was really fear that had put the man in this situation. The shame and guilt would always be there, whatever the outcome.

The light was almost lost and the interior of the car was quite dark now. Amos felt it was helping the doctor in some way, but until he came clean on why he wanted this visit, the fading light was all the help he was likely to get.

'My daughter is eleven years old,' the doctor began. 'She has lovely, blonde hair. It's natural. Her mother brushes it every night before she goes to bed. One evening, a couple of months after the senator was found dead, my wife noticed a piece of our daughter's hair had been cut off. Just a small piece,' he added and drew an imaginary line in front of him. 'Her hair curves neatly like this. But there was a chunk missing.' He made a straight, incisive line with his finger. 'Naturally my wife asked her what had happened, but my daughter didn't know. We decided it must have happened at school. You know, kids playing around.' He shrugged. 'Anyway, we let it drop; thought no more about it.'

Amos began to feel uncomfortable. It was not a physical discomfort, but a mental one. He had an absolute certainty in his mind of where this was going to end up. And he didn't like it.

'The following morning,' Robertson went on, 'I went to work in the normal way. Thought no more of it, naturally. But when I got to my office, there was an envelope on my desk. It was a white one,' he said, and held his fingers about six inches apart. 'About that big. It had my name on it. No address; just my name.'

He sat there for a while gazing out through the windscreen into the late evening. Although Amos couldn't see his expression, he guessed it would have looked wistful, probably philosophical. He'd committed a crime and was unburdening himself. Owning up.

'I opened the envelope. It opened quite easily.' It was an unnecessary statement but Amos knew the doctor was struggling and ignored it. 'There was a lock of my daughter's hair inside.' He turned quickly, and for a moment Amos thought the doctor was going to break down. 'I didn't know what to do or what to think. For a while I thought it was some kind of silly joke.' He settled back in the seat. 'I thought of phoning my wife but decided not to. Then about five minutes after I had picked up the envelope, my phone rang.'

'The person who cut off your daughter's hair?'

'Yes!' The doctor looked quite surprised in the gloom. 'You know?'

Amos shook his head. 'No, I'm a little ahead of you, Doc.'

The doctor nodded as he realized that the lieutenant's experience would be opening the story for him. 'It was a warning. Change the autopsy report or my daughter would suffer.' He opened the palms of his hands in an empty gesture. 'That was it.'

'Why didn't you come to us?' Amos asked. The question was obvious, but it had to be asked. And Amos knew exactly what the doctor would say.

'How could I? As much as I respect the police, Lieutenant, my daughter was under threat. They had taken a lock of her hair without her even knowing. Just imagine what else they could do.'

Amos thought of the lethal injection the senator had received while out jogging. It didn't bare thinking about.

'We could have taken your daughter into protective custody. It would have given us time to track down the person who attacked her.'

'You have a daughter, Amos, right?'

Amos nodded. 'Holly. She's eight years old.'

'And what would you do if your daughter was threatened?'

Amos's expression changed. 'I'd beat the shit out of the guy who threatened her.'

Robertson laughed. It was more like an explosive cough. 'You'd have to identify him first. Not easy when you are dealing with the kind of people who threatened me.'

'Why do you say that?'

'A couple of days after that phone call, my wife was on her way to pick up our daughter from school. She was involved in a minor collision. Nothing serious. Once the paperwork had been dealt with, my wife was about to get back in her car when my daughter turned up. She'd been brought there from her school by a policeman in a patrol car. Naturally my wife was grateful, surprised even. But with the trauma of the collision it never occurred to her to ask our daughter how come the policeman knew about the accident and that my daughter was at school.' He turned towards Amos then as though he was about to make a forceful point. 'My wife did not phone the school. Neither did our daughter receive any calls. But the policeman turned up in a patrol car and told my wife that the head of the school had contacted the precinct and asked for someone to pick our daughter up and take her home. It all seemed above board of course, but we found out later that the school head knew nothing of it. Now you see why I couldn't ask the police to take my daughter into protective custody. I can't trust them.'

'And if you had done, they could have threatened your wife.'

The doctor nodded. 'The cause of the senator's death was of small consequence alongside the safety of my daughter, so I changed the death certificate.'

The two men sat in silence for a while. Amos had all manner of things buzzing around in his brain, but most importantly he now knew, had irrefutable proof if you like, that Senator Ann Robbins had been murdered.

'Did your wife take all the necessary details when the accident happened?' he asked the doctor.

'Of course, but they were false.'

'Was the driver of the other car a man or woman?'

'Woman.'

'And would your wife know her again if she saw her?'

The doctor shook his head. 'Probably not. And it's been such a long time now, I doubt if she ever would recognize her.'

'They were telling you that they could lift your daughter at any time.'

'It's like having your pocket picked,' the doctor said. 'You know you've been touched but have no idea how or by whom.' He shuddered. 'And you know they can do it to you whenever they want.'

Amos considered his next step, living in hope that something could be developed from this. 'You couldn't have conducted the autopsy on your own, so who was with you?'

Robertson drew a deep breath. 'Young doctor. It was his first.' He shook his head. 'He didn't stand up too well. I told him to take a break; leave it to me.'

He turned and looked at Amos with a philosophical look on his face. 'You can tell them anything, you know. They have an inordinate fear of seniority for some reason.'

'So why did you wait until now to tell me?'

'It's been on my conscience too long. I needed to unburden myself. I've known you a long time, Amos. I know I can trust you.' He put a hand on Amos's arm. 'I don't want the truth to come out. If it does, I will go to prison.'

'If the truth comes out, Doc.'

Robertson shook his head. 'I hope not. But I was protecting my daughter and my wife as any father and husband would, and I'm not ashamed of that.'

'OK, Doc. I'll keep tabs on the case. It's officially closed, but I'll see what I can come up with.' He turned the ignition key and started the car. 'You go home now and don't worry; I'll think of something, but whatever you do, don't talk to anyone about this.'

Robertson thanked him and slid out of the car. Amos watched him hurry across to the Lexus and wondered how the hell he was going to find the senator's killer without revealing the doctor's complicity in the case. He pulled the small, digital voice recorder from his pocket and switched it off. Then he put the car into gear and pulled out on to the highway.

Gus Mason pulled up outside his father's house just as Bill Mason was coming off the porch to greet him. He thought his father looked in pretty good shape for a man who had turned seventy and subconsciously wished that he had his father's genes. People often remarked that he didn't look at all like him.

Bill Mason's ranch had known better days when his wife was alive. The ranch, or spread, as he liked to call, it covered about four hundred acres. His wife had bred horses there, but that had been her passion, not Bill's. He supported her financially but was not much good when it came to horses. Now his wife was gone, so too were the horses. All sold. The ranch had been left to nature over most of the acreage, but Mason kept the immediate area around the house and his stables in good condition.

Bill Mason put his hand up as Gus stepped out of the car. 'You're looking good, Gus. They keeping you busy in the legislature?' His shoes crunched on the gravel as he walked towards his son.

Mason shook his hand and put his arm on his father's shoulder as they walked towards the house.

'Can't grumble, Dad. This is what I've wanted for a long while now. Most of what I do is committee work. Get to meet a lot of influential people. All hoping we can make the city a better place between us. I'm doing good.'

Bill Mason was noticeably taller than his son. In their stockinged feet, Mason's father was probably six or seven inches taller. Gus Mason was a creditable five feet ten inches, which gave him a small advantage over others, but not over his towering father.

'I hear you're chairing one of the judicial committees.'

Mason smiled at his dad. 'Sounds important, eh? But it's a load of baloney in most cases. Just catching up with work others don't want to do.'

'If it's to do with the law, Gus, it's important.'

They walked into the lounge and Bill Mason offered his son a drink.

'Soda will do fine, Dad.'

Mason senior grinned. 'Never did like the hard stuff, did you?' He didn't wait for a reply. 'I'm having bourbon.'

'Straight, no doubt,' Gus Mason called out, but his father didn't appear to hear. Gus knew his father liked a drink, and did worry about his state of health, but there was no stopping the old boy.

He slumped into a soft chair and picked up a copy of the car magazine, *Classic American*. His father was an adherent to classic cars, particularly those of his youth, and was extremely proud of his 1947 Buick Super Convertible. He spent most of his waking hours lavishing all kinds of attention on it and if he drove the car into Hutton, the local town, it was washed and dried lovingly once he had returned home. Any time he wanted to drive into Newark, his father would use his Toyota Land Cruiser. The irony was that he would always drive along the old, dirt road into Hutton with the Buick, but took the modern highway when driving the Toyota to the city.

Bill Mason returned with the drinks. Gus looked up at the clock. It was in the shape of an old '57 Buick, naturally. It was a little after 4.30; too early for a hard drink, but his father was carrying a good measure in his whiskey glass. He said nothing as he took his soda.

'How long do you plan to stay in the Senate?' Bill Mason asked as he took a seat.

Gus made a small, waving motion with his free hand. 'No more than a year I hope.'

'So I guess its Congress you're after?' His son nodded. 'When?'

Gus shrugged. He looked a little coy. 'We're hoping to cut some corners. Maybe get into Congress earlier than planned.'

'We?'

'My supporters, Dad,' he answered drily. 'We all need them.'

Bill Mason's eyebrows lifted. 'Seems a mite quick to me, Gus. You'll need some powerful backers, not just supporters. Got any in your pocket yet?'

Mason laughed. 'I don't call it like that. I have people who will back me, put it that way.'

'Good Republicans?'

'Powerful Republicans.'

Bill Mason put his glass on the small table beside him. Gus knew he usually did that when he was about to make a point.

'Et tu, Bruté? Beware the Ides of March.'

Gus grimaced and shook his head. The quotation from Shakespeare's *Julius Caesar* about being knifed in the back often rang true in the seedy world of politics.

'They are not plotters; just people who want what's best for America.'

'And you believe you're the man to give the Americans what they want?'

Mason dipped his head. 'Sure do.'

His father shifted forward in his chair. 'Remember this, Gus; a politician's career ends in failure one way or another. Stay too long and you're thrown out. Stay too briefly and you haven't been successful enough. The guys who back you are the faceless ones. They will get what they want from you simply by putting you where you think you want to go.'

'But I know where I want to go. I want to be president.'

Bill Mason relaxed and settled back in his chair. 'So do a million other Americans.' He picked up his glass. 'I wish you luck, but watch your back.'

Lieutenant Amos opened his desk drawer and looked at the syringe for about the tenth time that day. It had been in his drawer for about a year now. He used to look at it most days and wished he could use it as evidence, but the case was closed and he knew he would have one helluva job persuading Captain Holder to reopen it. Holder was just about confirmed as the new police director of the New Jersey State Police Department, and the last thing he was about to do was allow Amos to jeopardize his future.

The syringe was retractable. It had a needle that withdrew into the body of the syringe after use. This was to prevent accidental spiking and reduce the risk of contamination. Ordinarily, the syringe would have been discarded in the proper receptacle after use, but it was not always the case, particularly when drug addicts had used them. Amos knew who manufactured this particular syringe and that it was distributed all over the United States, so there was little chance of tracking down the destination to which a consignment of them would have been sent. But he did know that the large, pharmaceutical firm, Corr Chemicals who were based in Newark, had employed Babs Mason in their chemical engineering department.

Once again, Amos was using gut instinct to reach a conclusion on which there was little but circumstantial evidence, but everything pointed to Babs Mason. He had irrefutable proof that this syringe had been used to administer succinylcholine because the DNA of Senator Ann Robbins had been found on the needle. The fact that the needle had been retracted meant that the sample had not been washed off by rain, or destroyed by the weather as it had lain, undetected in the undergrowth about thirty yards from where the senator had been murdered. Babs Mason had admitted to seeing the senator the same morning although denied having a conversation with her, despite a not very reliable witness statement to the contrary. And during the one and only interview he had conducted with her, Babs Mason had said that Ann Robbins's objection to her husband being voted into the state legislature was 'an obstacle that had to be overcome'.

Reluctantly, Amos closed the drawer and locked it. Time would tell whether he would ever be able to bring Babs Mason to justice. At the rate her husband was climbing the political ladder, and while people like Captain Holder were in place, he doubted it.

The phone rang and broke into Amos's train of thought. He picked it up and grunted into the handset. A squad officer across the other side of the room lifted his hand up to attract Amos's attention. He glanced out of his open door.

'What is it, Jeff?'

'Got a report coming in, Amos. Body found in a burnt out Lexus. It's a homicide. Looks like it's Doc Robertson, the chief medical examiner.'

SIX

MARION ROBERTSON'S FACE was a picture of death, almost. Her skin was ashen and her cheeks seemed to shrink into her cheekbones. She was sitting on the edge of a leather armchair, her legs drawn close so that her knees were touching. In her hand she held a small handkerchief that was now wet with her tears. She was quite a demure woman, not big in stature and had aged considerably since being told of her husband's death barely a week ago.

Her daughter, Nicole sat beside her. The girl's face was puffed and swollen through crying. She had her arm linked through her mother's and kept her gaze fixed on her mother's face. The two of them looked forlorn and pathetic, torn from the comfort of a life that held so much promise but that had now been ripped apart by violence.

Amos tried to frame his questions with as much sensitivity as he could muster, but the anger in him wanted to bully some kind of truth and explanation from Doc Robertson's widow. He had no right to feel that way, except the right one might expect from certain knowledge that he alone held.

Amos could see a sinister pattern emerging, although the structure of that pattern had yet to reveal itself. He knew there had to be a link between the death of Senator Ann Robbins and the murder of Doctor Robertson, and his experience was opening up avenues that he knew he needed to follow, but avenues that could lead to disaster.

'Had your husband's manner changed at all lately?' he asked.

Marion Robertson shook her head in a sharp, quick movement, finishing almost before it had started. Her daughter looked up at her and Amos caught the nuance of that upward glance.

'Any new friends or acquaintances in his life?'

Again the short, sharp, silent reply.

'Did your husband have an illness that might have been troubling him?'

This time he was met with a patronizing stare.

'Look, could we talk without your daughter here?' he asked.

Nicole's mother looked down at her daughter. She seemed to think about it briefly. Then suddenly she unhooked the little girl's arm from hers and whispered softly to her.

'Go and get a soda in the kitchen, sweetheart,' she told her. 'Wait for me there until the detective has gone.'

Amos waited until they were alone.

'Your husband came to see me,' he began. 'It was quite a while back. Told me how your daughter had a piece of her hair cut off.'

It was intended to shock the doctor's widow and shake her out of herself. Her eyes widened as she took in exactly what Amos was telling her.

'He told you that?'

Amos nodded. 'He was scared. Had no one he could trust. No one he could turn to except me. So tell me; what did your daughter think of all this?'

Robertson shook her head. 'We kept it from her; the things that had happened that she wouldn't have known about. She knew about her hair being cut, of course.' She paused for a moment, and then her expression changed. 'Are you saying this is connected?'

'Difficult to say,' he lied. 'But there's a possibility your husband was being intimidated by someone for some reason. Your daughter's hair and your husband's death may not be connected, but we have to keep an open mind on it at the moment.'

She put her handkerchief to her face, thought better of it and stood up. Amos watched as she walked across to a sideboard and took some tissues from a drawer. She came back to the armchair and sat down.

'He told me everything. Why he had been to see you. How scared he was.' The tissue went up to her eyes again. Amos waited. 'He couldn't trust the police, except you, of course, so he went to Judge Lawrence.'

Amos stiffened at this revelation. 'I told him not to talk to anyone.'

'Oh, it's all right for you,' she snapped suddenly. 'You weren't frightened out of your wits when you told him to keep quiet. He knew your hands were tied, although he couldn't understand why. He felt the police had let him down. It played on his mind for months. That's why he went to the judge.'

'How long ago was this?'

She shook her head. 'Two months ago, I think.'

'No contact since?' There was no reply so Amos asked her again. 'Did your husband have any contact with Judge Lawrence after he had seen him that first time?'

She looked up. 'Couple of weeks ago. He was on his way to see the judge when he was murdered.'

Amos had met Judge Lawrence several times in the course of his police duties and often when he found himself in court giving police evidence during a case. So it was something of a surprise to him when the judge refused to see him for almost a week. He didn't see the delay as prevarication on the judge's part, only that Lawrence was genuinely too busy, even though Amos had informed him that he was investigating the death of the chief medical examiner.

Amos was ushered into the judge's office by a court official and sat in the comfortable, leather chair facing the desk. Lawrence appeared within a couple of minutes and apologized for the lengthy delay in getting round to seeing him.

'Would you like a coffee?' Lawrence asked as he settled himself in his large, leather chair.

Amos shook his head. 'Thank you, Judge, but no thanks.'

'Right,' Lawrence began with the one word, clutching his hands together and placing them on the desk blotter in front of him. 'Sad business, Doc Robertson.' He shook his head solemnly. 'I can't believe it,' he said as he arched his eyebrows and looked directly at Amos.

'He came to see you on the day he was murdered.'

Lawrence looked genuinely surprised. 'Did he? My word.' He shook his head again and cast his eyes down. 'I can't remember. But then, I did see quite a lot of the doctor.'

'Can you recall anything of that meeting?'

Lawrence opened the large diary that graced his desk. He thumbed through it, turning the pages back until he found the entry he was looking for.

'Let me see; two weeks ago.' He laid the tip of his finger on an entry. 'Yes.' The word slid out of his mouth. 'I was in court at ten. Had the doctor pencilled in at twelve. Then I chaired the ...' He paused. 'Helps me to remember if I see what I've been up to,' he explained. 'But I'm damned if I can remember what it was the doctor wanted to see me about.'

'Can you remember how he was that day?' Amos asked him. 'Was he confused, nervous? Was it a medical matter? Perhaps an autopsy report?'

The judge leaned back in his chair and fixed a spot somewhere above Amos's head. He looked as though he was racking his brains to recall something about the meeting. Eventually he gave up.

'No, I'm sorry Lieutenant, I can't remember.'

His expression conveyed to Amos that there was little to be gained by continuing, but Amos wasn't to be denied.

'Did he say anything about the death of Senator Ann Robbins?' The judge's expression altered a little and he shook his head. Amos went on. 'He wasn't happy with the autopsy report he had signed.'

Lawrence frowned. 'I don't understand. Why should he be unhappy about a straightforward death by heart attack? After all, he carried out the autopsy.'

'He didn't think she had suffered a heart attack; he believed she had been murdered.'

Lawrence sniffed. 'How?'

'By lethal injection.'

'How do you know this, Lieutenant?'

'I have the syringe in my office that was used to kill Senator Robbins.'

The judge sat motionless, his eyes fixed on Amos. The large, expansive room seemed to close in on him. The sounds that drifted in from beyond the double glazed windows invaded the office.

'I don't think you should be telling me this, Lieutenant. If you have evidence that can prove the senator was murdered, why haven't you produced it?'

'I can't explain that, Judge,' Amos admitted, 'not yet, anyway. The case has been closed and filed away. But the chief medical examiner signed the autopsy report knowing that the senator had been murdered. I really need to know why he came to see you because it might be possible that he had this on his mind. He might have even confided in you.'

Lawrence glared at him. There was a malevolence in the man's expression, which didn't surprise Amos at all. In some respects it unsettled him.

'That would make me an accessory,' Lawrence said after a silence filled with menace. 'Doctor Robertson was an exceptional man; a brilliant doctor. He wouldn't have missed something like that. I think you are mistaken, Lieutenant; Doctor Robertson would never have conspired to forge an autopsy report either. When he spoke to you he must have been,' he shrugged, 'well, I don't know. I find it impossible to believe.'

'Well, I must ask you again,' Amos pressed, 'can you recall anything about the meeting you had with him that day?'

'No, I'm sorry, Lieutenant; I really can't.'

Amos breathed in deeply and eased himself up out of the chair. 'Well, Judge, thanks for your time. If you do think of anything, you will let me know, won't you?'

Lawrence came round the desk and shook Amos by the hand. He seemed relaxed; relieved that the conversation was at an end.

'I'll show you out and yes, if I think of anything, I'll let you know.' He opened the office door. 'I hope you catch his killers, Lieutenant.'

Amos looked straight into the judge's eyes. 'I intend to, Judge. I intend to.'

Lawrence closed the door and Amos walked along the corridor, wondering how Judge Lawrence knew that Doctor Robertson had spoken to him. After all, he hadn't told him that he had met with the doctor. And why did the judge assume the doctor had been murdered by more than one killer?

It was another little piece of Amos's own private jigsaw that he hoped would build into a picture of high powered collaboration on a murderous scale.

He took the steps two at a time and hurried out to his car. With little thought for safe and controlled driving, Amos pulled away from the parking lot and sped off down the main street looking for a drug store. What he had in his mind had no basis in logic, but his inherent instinct as a law officer gave him an insight into the criminal mind and he needed to do something that could trap a killer. Or at least point him to the man responsible.

He pulled up outside a shopping mall and went inside to find a pharmacy. It was getting late and the mall was still filled with shoppers. It took Amos a while to find a drug store. When he did he purchased a pack of syringes. A couple of minutes later he was back in his car and heading for the precinct HQ.

The front desk sergeant looked up as Amos waved an arm at him in greeting. Despite his bulk, Amos took the stairs two at a time. If his wife had seen him, she would have been mortified, but Amos had something on his mind and he needed to get to his desk as soon as he possibly could.

The squad room officers took little notice of Amos as he hurried through to his office, not even wondering why he closed his door behind him; something he rarely did. He slumped into the chair behind his desk, his breathing pretty laboured, and unlocked the drawer containing the syringe. He took it out, still wrapped in the evidence bag, and slipped it into his pocket. Then he removed the syringes he had purchased from the drug store and cleaned one with his handkerchief. Satisfied he had removed all trace of fingerprints, not that there should have been any, he slipped the syringe into a clean evidence bag, marked it very discreetly and put it into the open drawer. He then arranged the contents of the drawer in such a way that he would know if anything had been disturbed. Then he closed the drawer and locked it.

Amos sat in his chair for a few moments composing his thoughts. If he had misinterpreted the signs, and misunderstood his own gut feeling, he knew he would never trap the person who was responsible for the deaths of Senator Robbins and Doctor Robertson. He also understood the reality of getting too close. It could become extremely dangerous. He thought of the doctor's young daughter, Nicole, and how she had been used to persuade her father to change the autopsy report. Then he thought of his own young daughter, Holly.

He stood up, took the new syringes from his desk and shovelled them into his pocket and walked out of his office, leaving the door open behind him. None of the squad officers acknowledged him as he made his way out of the squad room and out of the building. He climbed into his car and motored away from the precinct house in a more sedate fashion than the one in which he had arrived.

Amos lived out at Madison, about a twenty minute drive from the precinct on a good day. Today, traffic was light so he made it home without too many problems. All the while he kept thinking about his wife and his daughter, Holly. As a police officer, he lived with the fear that some retard would seek some kind of vengeance on his family. It was an ever present thought and one that he, like most officers he knew, tried to keep at the back of his mind. He had known some who couldn't live with it and abandoned policing. He knew of one officer whose family had been attacked by the criminal who was the prime suspect in the officer's case. He also knew of one detective whose wife had been kidnapped, raped and murdered simply because he was getting too close to the gang he was investigating. And he thought of Doctor Robertson and his daughter Nicole.

He swung into his driveway and could see the lights were on in the house. He killed the engine and shoved the gear stick into 'Park'. He clambered out of the car and immediately saw his daughter's bicycle lying on its side beside his prize, sculpted privet bush. He smiled and picked up the bicycle, wheeling it towards the side entrance into the rear garden.

Amos could hear music coming from the kitchen window as he walked round to the rear of the house and propped the bicycle up against the wall. He pushed open the door and stepped into the kitchen. His wife turned as he closed the door behind him.

'Hallo Amos, you're late.'

He walked up to his wife and wrapped his arms around her, planting a kiss on her lips. 'Hallo sweetheart,' he said softly, pulling away. 'Where's my other favourite girl?'

Judith leaned to one side and called out over Amos's shoulder.

'Holly! Daddy's home.'

There was a short silence followed by a high pitched squeal, then the sound of running feet as their daughter burst into the kitchen.

'Daddy!' she screamed in delight and launched herself at her father.

Amos saw this lovely bundle of olive-skinned delight come racing into the kitchen, her eyes wide with joy and her toothy grin spread all over her face as he scooped her into his arms and gave her as strong a cuddle as he dared, while Holly closed her arms around his neck and tried to squeeze the living daylights out of him. And in that moment, Amos felt an unsettling moment of fear, and didn't want to let his daughter go.

He put Holly down and knelt beside her. 'What's my little darling been up to?' he asked.

'I'm writing my poetry,' she told him. 'It's about you and Mummy.'

He kissed her on the cheek. 'Good girl. Now, you run along and get on with your poetry, and I'll talk to your ma.'

She hugged him and took herself off to her room. Amos watched as she disappeared and tried to shrug off the uncomfortable feeling that assailed him.

It was a week later when Amos discovered the syringe had been moved. In fact, it had been switched. He had opened the drawer of his desk and seen immediately that the marker he had left had been disturbed. The syringe was still there in the evidence bag, or so it looked until he checked to see if the mark he had made on the evidence bag was still there. It wasn't. He knew there could only be one answer. Doctor Robertson had told him how he could no longer trust the police. But now Amos knew he could no longer trust people like Judge Lawrence.

He sighed and shook his head, closing the drawer slowly. As he looked up he caught sight of the photograph on his desk of his wife and daughter. The uncomfortable feeling he was experiencing so much more of late crept back, and he began to feel afraid for his little girl.

Bill Mason was putting the finishing touches to the regular polish of his beloved Buick Convertible when he heard the sound of a car pull up. He straightened and tossed the cloth on to his workbench, then walked out of the barn into the sunlight.

He could see Babs Mason's Red Rubicon Jeep with the prominent bull bar on the front bumper parked out the back of his ranch house.

Babs was about to step up on to the back porch when she saw Mason coming across the yard towards her.

'Still driving that piece of tin?' he called out to her.

'Yes,' she replied. 'Still polishing yours?'

They both laughed because it was a standing joke between the two of them. Mason had no time for the huge four-by-four vehicles that many of the high rollers drove. They were never ever likely to encounter the kind of terrain the cars were designed for, and were more of a status symbol; a kind of 'in your face' oversize bauble that cost the earth to maintain and the earth to run. It never occurred to him that his '47 Buick Convertible could arguably fall into the same category.

He kissed Babs lightly on the cheek, recalling distant memories of when their kisses were more passionate. Now their friendship was more affected; something Mason regretted, although keeping each other at arm's length did seem to be a problem for both of them.

'So what brings you here, Babs?' he asked, taking her arm and walking with her into the house.

'I had business in Hutton and thought I'd drop by.' She hitched herself up on to a stool beside the breakfast bar, unconsciously allowing her skirt to ride up above her knees.

'Want a coffee?' he asked, feasting his eyes on Babs's shapely legs.

'Sure. Black.'

Mason walked over to the other side of the kitchen. 'What can I do for you, Babs?'

'I need to talk to you about Gus,' she told him.

He glanced over at her as he pulled two mugs towards him. 'Why, what's he been up to?'

She shook her head. 'Nothing; just wants to run for president.'

Mason laughed. The sound rolled out of his throat like someone who had just found something that had been lost. He poured coffee into the cups and handed one to Babs.

'I knew he wanted to run, but not yet; he needs time.'

She took the coffee from him. 'It's never too soon, Bill. He's going for it.'

He leaned up against the breakfast bar. 'It's a big gamble. If he loses this he will not get another chance.'

She sipped the hot coffee and put the mug down. 'He has powerful backers, but he'll need your support too.'

Mason agreed with the fact that his son would need his support, but he wasn't sure he was happy to give it. 'I'm not convinced it's a good idea. I'd be nothing more than an appendage; something to be brought out of the closet for a bit of window dressing.'

'You'd be helping Gus.'

'But would it help me?'

Babs frowned. 'How do you mean, would it help you?'

He opened his hands and looked down at them as though he had suddenly discovered there was something wrong with them.

'These are all I have to protect me. Up to now, they are all I've needed.'

Babs shifted her position. 'You're not making sense, Bill. What have your hands got to do with Gus?'

'It's the metaphor, isn't it?' He laughed. 'With these hands I built this and that. The Pharaohs built great pyramids, although they didn't, did they? I'm on my own, I make out OK. I look after myself, no one bothers me.' He looked at her sharply, letting his hands fall down to his side. 'But they would if Gus becomes a serious candidate for the presidency. And if he made it, I'd have the secret service crawling all over this place.' He shook his head. 'I don't want it.'

He didn't say any more but picked up his mug and took a mouthful of coffee.

'It isn't about what you want, Bill,' Babs told him gently. 'It's about Gus, what he wants. And what the American people want.'

'The American people don't know me, Babs, and I like it that way,' he came back at her. 'But they soon damn would if Gus started running for the presidency.'

Babs slid off her stool. Her skirt remained hitched up before slipping down. 'Bill, you have had your career. You're now in the autumn of your years, as they say. Gus still has a long way to go. Don't deny him your support.' She made it sound like he was reaching that time in his life when old age shrinks a man. But even as she said it, Babs thought how remarkable he looked and her heart raced a little.

'And what about you, Babs?' he asked. 'Is this what you want?'

Her eyes hooded over briefly. 'Of course. It's natural for a wife to want the best for her husband.'

'There would be a great deal in it for you too, am I right?'

She shrugged. 'Well, naturally. I can't deny that.'

He looked away for a moment, and Babs could tell there was something else on his mind.

'But could you deny that we had an affair?' he said at last.

She lifted her chin and her shoulders came up as drew herself up to her full height. 'We'd have to, for Gus's sake,' she admitted. 'Even though it's common knowledge, really, Bill.'

He gave her a bewildered look. 'Hell, Babs, you didn't even know Gus when we got together.'

She shook her head sharply. 'That won't make any difference to the press; that's why we have to deny it, or at least make little of it. The press would soon get tired of trying to expose our little secret.'

'And suppose I don't want to deny it, Babs?' he put to her. 'Hell, you're a pretty fine woman.' He stepped forward until he was standing in front of her. 'It would put my stock up in the neighbourhood if they knew I'd bedded you.'

Babs stepped forward and slapped him hard. He winced and rode the blow, bringing his hand up to his cheek.

'You always were a feisty one, Babs, I'll give you that.'

Babs's expression had hardened and her face was tinged with a reddening hue as though it was she who had received the blow and not Bill Mason. But the colour in her face was because of the fire that had been awakened in her belly. Suddenly she lunged forward and kissed him hard on the mouth. Mason responded immediately and drew her in to him by throwing his arms around her. Then they began tearing at each other's clothing until they rolled naked on the kitchen floor. Mason rode her like one of the stallions he used to breed, while Babs responded with cries of sheer pleasure, digging her fingers into his back and drawing deep wheals on his flesh.

Soon their lovemaking subsided and Mason rolled off her. The two of them lay side by side on the kitchen floor. Babs started to giggle.

'Don't you ever, ever say that again.' Her voice had a soft edge to it. 'We could be anywhere.'

Mason laughed. 'I wish!' Then he propped himself up on one arm and leaned towards her. He ran his eyes over her naked body, knowing how often he had wanted to look upon her lovely form again. 'I don't think I ever stopped loving you, Babs.'

She turned her face towards him. 'You're pretty remarkable for a man of your age.'

'Give me five minutes and I'll show you just how remarkable I can be.'

Babs laughed and slapped him on the face. Then she leapt up and ran through to the bedroom.

Mason smiled and gathered up their scattered clothing. Somehow, he thought, this was going to be a long, but wonderful day.

SEVEN

BABS MASON HADN'T *slept well, which was to be expected because of her circumstances and the fact that she was reliving the nightmare. Although her head ached and her body felt like it had been in a car crash, Babs faced the young writer and prepared herself for the questions that were to come.*

'So you restarted your affair with Bill Mason?'

Babs was philosophical about it. 'I don't think I ever stopped loving him. He was a handsome man; far more warm and responsive than my husband.'

'But you kept it secret.'

'Naturally.'

The young woman jotted something on her pad and changed the subject.

'There was very little evidence to convict anybody over the senator's death, but Lieutenant Amos was beginning to build up a picture and connect people, wasn't he?'

Babs reflected on the statement and wondered why the State of New Jersey had been blessed with such a dogged police detective.

'I remember him talking about gut instinct at the trial,' Babs recalled. 'Nothing on which to base a case, but with the experience of several years with the precinct he knew it was well worth pursuing.'

'There was a lull, wasn't there?' the young writer asked. 'After Lieutenant Amos had spoken to Judge Lawrence about Doctor Robertson?'

Babs nodded and a smile tugged at the corner of her mouth. 'You could call it that, I suppose, but it was more than a lull. We all thought we were in the clear.' She dipped her head slightly and glanced at the young woman. 'Nothing more happened. It must have been four years. We heard very little about the investigations into Ann Robbins' death, and Doctor Robertson; they had been filed as cold cases. Gus was doing well; he was elected into Congress.' She chuckled and threw her head back. 'We had a wonderful party that night. All the big guns were there, powerful men. Fools really, I suppose.' She shook her head forlornly. 'Men of vision, men of power and men of violence. Can you differentiate?'

'So what went wrong?'

Babs looked a little condescendingly at her. 'Wrong? Demski,' she said bitterly, 'that's what went wrong. We hadn't counted him at all. We didn't even know about him. Turns out he had been making inquiries through his Jewish friends about his grandmother's death in the camps. It was a very slow process, but while Gus was canvassing for votes, Demski was looking for Heinrich Lörenz.'

'The Nazi officer?'

Babs nodded.

'But you had no knowledge at the time.' She changed her tack. 'None of this was relevant to your husband. Or at least, no one would have connected the two parallels; your husband making it to Congress, and Demski searching for answers to his grandmother's death in the camps.'

'Exactly.' She hunched her shoulders and laughed mirthlessly. 'God, the things that turn round and bite you.'

PART TWO

EIGHT

Four years later

JACK DEMSKI HAD never liked the Germans. The fact that he was with one now, Gunter Haman was expediency; he needed him. He loathed the German nation with a passion. Not because he had experienced any harm from them, but because of his father, Isaac, and his grandmother, Rosmaleen.

It had taken Jack a long, long time to drag the truth from his father after Haman's visit. Isaac fed his son the stories piecemeal. He had never wanted to talk about the camps. He had never wanted to relive the moment he was dragged away from his mother and put on to a train where he was pressed in with other weeping children.

Isaac Demski had wanted his son, Jack, to live the American dream and not know the fear of persecution, of slavery and of terror and death. For that reason he had tried to keep the horrors from him. But Jack knew he was entitled to know the truth; it was his heritage. And so his father responded more fully. The more Jack learned of what the Nazis had done, of the bestial things they had visited upon the Jewish nation, the more he loathed them. Although his father had tried to disabuse him of the idea that not all Germans were Nazis, the more Jack despised them. And although Jack had come to trust Gunter Haman, and found that he was a civil and charming man, he could not rid himself of that sense of betrayal; of how the Germans had betrayed the human race.

Haman had left America to return home to Germany after bringing his story to Isaac Demski. That was four years ago. Jack

Demski's desire to search for the truth about his grandmother's murder, and to locate the final whereabouts of Heinrich Lörenz, had burned away at him for some considerable time. His father had urged him to let sleeping dogs lie, and it was because of his father's urging that he allowed the thought to sleep. But it was because of a call from Haman in Germany that the urge had returned: Haman had tracked down Franz Weber, the driver who had taken Eva Braun away from the Reich Chancellery under Heinrich Lörenz's orders.

The two men arrived at the small town of Arsdorf, several miles south of Munich just as the evening sun was setting. The town nestled in the foothills a few miles from the border with Austria. The green fields and hillsides were losing their verdant characteristics as evening shadows began to cloak them in darkness, but the lingering trace of picture postcard quality was still evident in the sloping farmland around them.

Haman had driven the Mercedes hire car with the comfortable reassurance of someone in his own country. The drive from Munich airport had been uneventful although Haman lost no opportunity in relating to Demski the beauty of his beloved homeland. Demski tried to show some interest, but the dislike of his father's persecutors left no room for sentiment, and even the charm of the German countryside failed to move him.

Haman turned off the main road and followed the sign to Arsdorf. The road followed a small stream and curved into the outer reaches of the town, passing the open entrance to a farm, which seemed to announce the fact that they were in the heart of farming country.

The influence of Austrian architecture was not lost on Haman as he slowed the car on entering the main square. It was not difficult to spot the hotel they had booked because it was the only one there. A few cars were parked in the parking area along the side of the building, and Haman swung the Mercedes into a vacant lot.

'Good, we are here,' he announced.

Demski said nothing as he opened the door and stepped out on to the tarmac. He stretched and pushed his hands into the small of his back. Then he turned towards Haman who was opening the boot.

'I bring the bags, Haman,' he said as he hefted the two medium-sized cases from the back of the car. He slammed the lid and nodded towards the front of the hotel. 'We go in now.'

Demski smiled inwardly at Haman's inverted English and followed him towards the hotel. But before stepping through the open doorway, he turned and looked around the square. The street lamps were flickering into life and most of the shop windows were adding their brightness to the shadows. For a brief moment, Demski took his mind back to the vivid images portrayed by his father and he imagined this town under the polished jackboot of the Nazi thugs. Suddenly the brightness seemed to fade. He turned swiftly and walked into the welcoming lobby of the hotel.

The two men looked up at the old street name on the corner of the main road through the town. *Im Winkel* was little more than a farm track. On one side was open meadow, on the other the beginnings of what looked like farm buildings. Demski thought they looked old enough to have been around at the turn of the nineteenth century. They followed the track for about fifty metres until they reached a high gate, about five metres in length. Beyond it was a gravel area that led into a patch surrounded on three sides by low, almost derelict buildings. One looked like an old stone barn while the other, which was a continuation, looked like it doubled as a store or equipment shed. It was impossible to see beyond the small windows of these sheds. On the left, still a continuation of the other two was what appeared to be the farmhouse. Haman reached for the bell pull and gave it a sharp tug. Somewhere a bell rang.

A few minutes later a young woman appeared. She was wearing a nurse's uniform. She stopped at the gate but didn't open it.

'Can I help you?' she asked the two men.

'Fraulein, I am Gunter Haman, and this is my colleague Herr Demski,' he replied, pointing at Demski. 'We are here to see Herr Weber.'

'Do you have an appointment?'

Haman shook his head. 'No, but Herr Demski has travelled all the way from America, and we do need to see him.'

'I'm sorry, but Herr Weber will not see anybody without an

appointment. He is very sick, and very old.'

Haman smiled. 'Fraulein, as you can see, I too am old. I was with Franz Weber in 1945 in Berlin. If you tell him my name, I'm sure he will remember. I'm sure he will see us.'

The woman gave them both a deprecating look. 'Wait here.' She turned and went back into the farmhouse.

'You told me you didn't know anybody who was there when it happened.'

Haman turned and looked at Demski. 'And that is true. But since we learned about Herr Weber, it would be true to say I knew him. After all, it was a fleeting glimpse, but he was there.'

The nurse returned and opened the gate. She stepped aside as the two men walked into the yard. She closed the gate and locked it, then led the men into the house.

For Gunter Haman it was like stepping into a time warp and being transported back to the war years. The door opened into a bare, quarry-tiled hall that had very little in the way of decoration on the walls. They were painted white, but the colour had faded and become stained over the years. An old, metal lamp hung from the ceiling, and up against one wall was a black framed mirror that was crazed and dirty. It was dark in the hall, the only light coming from the door and from somewhere above the poorly lit staircase that led up from the hall.

They were led across the small hall and into a kitchen. On their left was an old wood burning stove that served as a cooking range and heating for the room. The black stove pipe reared up from the back of the stove and into the ceiling above it. There was a table to one side, covered in an old, plastic cloth. A sink stood beneath a small, shuttered window, and to the left was a work surface on which stood a small oven. The smell in the room was a mixture of pine wood and cooking oil.

The nurse took them through a door into a small lounge. A window, similar to the one in the kitchen was the only source of daylight. On one side of the room was a small bed. At the far end was an open fire in which a few logs smoked and threw out a tremendous heat. Near the fire, sat in a high-backed armchair, his legs covered in an ageing blanket, was the man they had come to see.

'Try not to tax him,' the young woman asked them. 'I will come back in fifteen minutes. Then you must leave.'

Haman thanked her and waited until she had left the room before he introduced himself and Demski to the old man.

Franz Weber looked frightfully old and decrepit. Haman had never known the man, although he did see him briefly on that fateful day in the Chancellery, so it was difficult to put an age on him. He was sitting close to the log fire that was throwing out a tremendous heat. He seemed oblivious to it even though it was quite warm in the room. His body was hunched forward. His hair, what there was of it was wispy and white. His scalp was covered in flaking skin and dotted with the tell-tale brown spots of age. He looked up at the two men through red rimmed eyes.

'Guten Tag,' he said quietly.

Haman stopped beside the chair and offered his hand. Weber ignored it.

'Herr Weber,' Haman began. 'Thank you for agreeing to see us. My name is Gunter Haman. This is my friend, Jacob Demski.' Weber showed no reaction. 'We would like to talk to you about the end of the war in Germany.' Weber's eyes widened a little. 'In 1945, in the bunker.' Haman looked around the room quickly. 'May we sit down?'

Weber nodded. 'Why do you want to know about Berlin?'

Haman and Demski found themselves a couple of old, dining chairs that were pushed up against a small table.

'Can you remember much about that day?' Haman asked as he settled himself in front of the old man.

Weber shook his head. 'It was a terrible day for us. A terrible day.'

'So you do remember some of it?'

Weber's face brightened a little. 'It is difficult to unlock the doors of a memory that has faded, but sometimes we are encouraged to remember pieces of it.'

Haman leaned a little closer to the old boy. 'Can you recall bringing a woman into the bunker? A Jewess?'

Haman had taken many, many months to track down Franz Weber. Through Jewish and German organizations that were dedicated to tracing any Nazis who had escaped the Nuremberg War

Crimes Commission, he was able to get on to Weber's trail. He wasn't a Nazi, but a soldier like Haman who had been doing his duty; a junior rank who simply followed orders. Weber had been a driver assigned to Hauptmann Lörenz. The Simon Wiesenthal Organization and others like it had uncovered mountains of evidence as to the way in which the senior Nazis had fled Germany. These men and women used an organization known as *Die Spinne, The Spider*. The group was often referred to as *Odessa*, but by whatever name they were called, the Nazis were smuggled out of Germany by this group. They came into their own in '45 when they knew the war was lost and there were a lot of Nazis clamouring to get out of Germany. They set up an underground network smuggling the top brass into Switzerland and then into Italy. The SS used them to smuggle their own kind out. They supplied the false documents, the routes and the Catholic priests who were misguided enough to believe they were doing their Christian duty by shifting the Nazi thugs through their monasteries. The Spider network did not dissolve after the war either, but simply spread their web all over the world. Even to America.

Haman had discovered Weber's name in among the mountains of files he had searched through. It was because Weber had fled along with his commanding officer, Hauptmann Lörenz, that he had been listed as a wanted criminal. In his absence he had been sentenced to ten years in prison, but that was suspended on appeal because the commission realized that he was after all, a minion in the service of the Nazi butchers.

Haman recognized Lörenz's name and realized that the driver listed as an accomplice was indeed the man who had brought the struggling Jewess into the Reich Chancellery.

A thin smile crossed Weber's lips. 'I've never been asked that question before.'

'Do you remember?'

His eyes moved from Haman to Demski. They could see he was questioning them and probably coming to a conclusion over something. 'How do you know this?' he asked eventually.

Haman's head lifted. 'I was there.'

Weber's mouth opened. Then he shook his head as he tried to

recall what he saw in that room. Then he lifted his hand and pointed a thin, skeletal finger at Haman.

'There was a young boy there.' He peered at Haman. 'It was you?'

Haman glanced at Demski and then back at Weber. He nodded. 'That was me.'

Weber laughed. It was a dry cackle. Then he stopped as quickly as he had started. Something had struck him. He jabbed the finger again.

'So you and me.' He stopped as though he wanted to make sure that his facts were right, that he hadn't forgotten anything. 'You and me must be the only two people left in the world who were there that day?'

Haman's head bobbed up and down slowly. 'Hitler was dead. Eva Braun had been taken out of the room. I was there when you came in dragging a Jewess with you. Hauptmann Lörenz was there as well.'

Weber's mouth opened wide. 'I remember. Fraulein Braun was in the car. She was scared. We all were. Berlin was thick with Allied soldiers. The Russians were there.' He shook his head. 'We all feared the Russians. Brutes!'

Haman wondered how a German could refer to the Russians as brutes. It was a savage irony indeed.

'Why was the woman taken there?' Haman asked. 'Why was she chosen?'

Weber shook his head and lifted his thin shoulders in a weak shrug. 'I don't know. I was only following my orders.'

'Did you know she was going to be shot?'

Weber looked genuinely surprised. 'No. Why should I?'

It was true; there was no reason why he would have been told of the murderous plan to swap Eva Braun with Rosmaleen Demski.

'Hauptmann Lörenz shot the Jewess.' Haman turned and pointed at Demski. 'The woman was this man's grandmother.'

Weber's head turned and his eyes widened a little more. It was obvious that he was hearing this news for the first time.

'Oh my God.' His voice came out in a faint whisper.

'Where did you take Fraulein Braun?'

Weber looked confused now. 'Take her?' His head dropped and he gazed at his thin, bony hands. 'There was nowhere to go. Too many soldiers.' He began to weep. 'I drove to an airfield, a strip of grass. I don't know, somewhere.' He looked up at Haman. 'I'm sorry, I cannot remember.'

He began muttering something when they heard the sound of footsteps. The nurse came into the room. She ignored the two men and walked straight up to Weber. She leaned over him and dabbed a handkerchief on his face to wipe away the tears.

'You must go now,' she told Haman. 'You have distressed Herr Weber enough. Please, go.'

Haman knew it would be pointless arguing with her. He stood up and looked at Demski who had been aware of what had been exchanged between Haman and the old man, but because of his infrequent use of the German language, his father's first language, he had allowed Haman to lead the conversation. He knew, though, that it was time to leave.

Suddenly the old man reached out and grabbed the nurse's arm. 'Please, let them come back tomorrow.' His eyes switched to Haman. 'We have so much to talk about. So much.'

The nurse looked cross with the old boy but finally agreed.

'You can call back tomorrow,' she told the two men, 'but only if he is well enough. Is that clear?'

Haman said he understood and thanked her. He then reached down to Weber and shook his thin, cold hand. 'I will return tomorrow,' he promised. 'And we will talk again.

That evening, Haman and Demski talked over the prospect of extracting more information from the old man. Demski had used the time at the farmhouse to observe the surroundings and watch the body language of the nurse. He came away with the feeling that something was too contrived about the apparent arrangement with the nurse and Weber: something he couldn't quite put his finger on. His experience of subterfuge and deceit gave him a reason to suspect that whatever it might be, they would never learn the truth by direct questioning. Any secrets Weber had, he believed, would have to be hidden somewhere.

It was well past midnight when Demski closed the door of his room behind him and walked quietly down the stairs and out of the hotel. The main street of the town was well lit, but his route took him the short walk to the darker edges of the hamlet and to *Im Winkel*.

His shoes crunched on the gravel so he walked up on the balls of his feet. When he reached the gate he wasted no time but clambered over the top and dropped softly down on to the other side.

He approached the old front door that they had passed through that morning and began working on the lock as noiselessly as he could, using a tool that was shaped like a retractable biro with a thin blade. It was a legacy of Demski's youth; a burglar's tool for picking door locks. He always carried it with him.

By working the small, steel blade vigorously, Demski was able to move the inner pin tumblers and compress the small springs against the outer pins. He pushed a small, thin flat key with no shape into the open lock and twisted. He felt the door lock move and then pushed down on the handle. The door swung open without any noise.

He stepped into the room and pushed the door back but didn't close it because he knew it would lock again. Raising himself up on to the balls of his feet, he headed towards the small lounge where Haman had spoken to Weber that morning. Looking carefully into the room he could see the old man's shape beneath the bed clothes on the small, single bed that was pushed up against one wall.

He turned away and crossed the kitchen, heading for the stairs and paused there, listening carefully. There were no sounds coming from the rooms above, so he went back to where Weber was sleeping. He began to cast around, looking for something like a small box or case that might contain a clue to Weber's past. The small torch he had with him threw a round beam against the grimy walls; picking out precious little that he could see would be of any worth to him.

He turned back and studied the bed, wondering if the old man kept his most precious belongings with him. He walked up to the side of the bed and crouched down, sliding his arm beneath the bed frame. His hand struck a square object which he pulled towards him. For a moment he thought he had struck gold. But when he opened the box, he could only see a few letters and some old postcards. He ignored these and pushed the box back beneath the bed.

And that's when he noticed that Weber wasn't breathing.

He straightened and looked at the white face and the bullet hole drilled neatly into the forehead. Weber's pillow was covered in blood.

Demski stood up and switched the torch off. He had seen many bloody corpses in his time; often the result of a gangland killing. What he was looking at now was an execution.

He thought of the nurse and turned towards the open door. He automatically cast his eyes up towards the ceiling and sensed that what he would find up there would not be pretty.

Without too much caution, Demski scaled the stairs two at a time and pushed open the first door he came to. Lying on the bed was the nurse. She had been shot through the head.

In that moment, Demski knew what had happened. And he knew now what was going to happen if he didn't hurry. He wasted no time in thinking about being able to search the house uninterrupted, but ran back downstairs and went into the front room. He bent down beside the bed and pulled Weber's box out. Then he emptied the few bits that were in there into his hands and rammed them into his jacket pocket.

He fled from the house and ran back through the town to the hotel. He ignored the night porter's stare and hurried up to Haman's room. It took a while to rouse the German from his slumber, but when he finally made it to the door and opened it, Demski pushed past him.

'Weber and his nurse are dead, Gunter,' he said breathlessly. 'And we'll be next. Get your gear. We're leaving.'

Haman started to protest but Demski shut him up. 'Five minutes, no more, or we're dead. Do it now, Gunter!'

He left the German standing there in his underwear, speechless. But five minutes later the two men were in the Mercedes hire car and heading fast towards the Austrian border and God knows where.

The city of Innsbruck was waking up to a fresh, sunny day with the early morning dew vanishing as quickly as a misty breath. The noise of the rush hour filled the streets, and people hurried by, their minds fixed on journey's end, or the day's diary. The trams stopped and deposited passengers into the busy street, filled up and moved on again. Early street vendors plied their trade into the waiting arms of those who wished to buy their wares, while cafés welcomed them into the relative calm of a coffee laden atmosphere. Sitting in one of the cafés that dotted the pavements near the railway station were Demski and Haman.

Their car was parked at the station and they had crossed the street to find an unobtrusive café where they could talk in relative safety. The drive from Arsdorf had been mostly silent as Haman let the full impact of Weber's death sink in. Demski's strident voice had lanced his brain like a knife at the hotel, and it was several minutes after fleeing the small town before the danger they were in began to have an effect on his sanity.

Haman had come up with many questions, but Demski had shut him up because he needed time to think. He sensed that the German was close to breaking point because the poor man had never been in such a terrifying position before. It was the stuff of high drama he was used to seeing at the cinema; not experiencing it in real life. Demski had taken over the drive and hurried through the early morning light through the hills and eventually into Austria.

Haman pushed a plate of half eaten meat and cheese away, his appetite lost. He rolled his empty coffee cup between his thumb and finger and glanced inquiringly at Demski.

'What now?' he asked simply.

'What now? We split up; it's all we can do.'

Haman's complexion and pallor was lifeless. The fear that had visited itself upon the man was now clearly evident in his demeanour.

'Why?'

Demski sighed deeply. 'They're after the two of us, Gunter. By going our separate ways, we stand a better chance.'

'But I don't understand why they are after us. What have we done?'

It was naïve to say the least, but Demski could understand why he had asked the question. 'Our crime, from their point of view, was speaking to Weber.'

Haman leaned forward. 'But that's insane. What's the harm in talking to an old man about the war?'

'We don't know yet,' Demski admitted. 'But whatever it is, it was important enough to murder two people.'

'But what did we do?' Haman persisted. 'We didn't steal anything. We didn't hurt anyone.'

Demski jabbed a finger at him. 'Just stop there, Gunter.' He shifted in his chair, moving a little closer. 'Whatever it was we did or didn't do, it was enough. We didn't know which way our inquiry was going to take us, but wherever it might have been, someone doesn't want us to find out.'

'But who are these people? What right have they to do this?'

'Who are they?' Demski frowned as he posed the question. 'They're Nazis, Gunter. And they don't need to have a "right", as you put it, to do anything; they do what they want.'

Haman's face twisted into a snarl. 'They have no right,' he spat out. 'Why should they pick on an old man and his nurse? And why should they want to kill me? I haven't done anything.'

Demski regarded him with a look of pity. 'Neither did six million Jews.'

That stopped Haman in his tracks. It was like a blow to the face. He knew what Demski meant. The Jews hadn't done anything either, except be Jewish. So what right did his countrymen have in deciding to erase an entire nation just because they didn't approve of them, or had some twisted idea that the Jews were the cause of all their problems.

'*Die Spinne*,' he said eventually as it dawned on him who was behind the murders.

Demski nodded. 'Exactly. The Nazi thugs are alive and well, and they're hiding something important. Important enough to kill.'

Haman stared into his empty cup as though he might find an answer there.

'How did they find out we had spoken to Herr Weber?'

Demski thought the question was naïve. 'His nurse must have reported our visit. Poor woman signed her own death warrant.'

'So what can we do?'

Demski reflected for a while. 'Split up,' he said eventually. 'You go home to your wife. Take her away for a while; just to be on the safe side.'

'What about you?'

'I'll stay in Europe, carry on looking. If I leave a trail, they'll come after me, leave you alone.'

Haman shook his head vigorously. 'No way! Absolutely not! We shall go to the police.'

Demski reached across the table and grabbed his arm. 'And announce to those Nazi bastards where we are? Don't be stupid.'

'But if you leave a trail, won't you be announcing your whereabouts to them?'

Demski relaxed and took his hand from Haman's arm. 'I can look after myself, Gunter. I can deal with these people. I'm used to watching my back, believe me.'

Haman gave it some thought. 'What about the car? Should I take that, or do you want it?'

Demski shook his head. 'No. Phone the hire company, report it stolen. Leave it at the station and get the train home. You got enough cash for a train ticket?'

Haman took his wallet from his jacket pocket and flicked through the notes. 'I may have enough.' He shoved the wallet back into his pocket. 'I can use my card,' he said.

Demski shook his head and took his own wallet out of his pocket. He peeled off some notes and handed them to Haman.

'Take this. Might not be a good idea to use a card; it will announce your presence.'

'What about you?' Haman asked, genuinely concerned.

Demski smiled. 'I can manage, Gunter. I promise.'

'So what will you do now?'

Demski decided not to tell him, working on the old saying about the least said the better.

'Don't you worry about me; I'll be fine. Now, go.'

Haman stood up and took a card from his wallet. 'You will let me know when you get back to America, won't you?' He put the wallet back in his pocket and shook Demski's hand.

Demski nodded. 'Sure thing; as soon as I'm back.'

Haman let his hand go and sighed deeply, shaking his head. 'Good luck.'

He walked away from the table without looking back. Demski

watched him go until he was no longer in sight. He then got up and walked across to the counter and paid the bill. He had no idea then where he would go, but before he made up his mind, Demski had to make a phone call.

NINE

'WHEN DO YOU *think it all began to go wrong?' the young writer asked.*

Babs was tired now. All the memories, the hurt and the fear seemed to drain her. But she knew she had to continue.

'It was the night of the banquet. I didn't know what Bill had seen at first. If I had, he wouldn't have left the banquet alive.' She sighed. 'I can't believe I almost came to hate him that night.' She looked sharply at the young writer. 'Not for myself but for Gus. But then I came to hate Gus!'

'Love is a strong emotion, but so is hate. We all know how easy it is to switch feelings.'

Babs studied the backs of her hands. They were lined and wrinkled; the hands of an old woman. But she wasn't old. Not yet.

'I had a feeling Bill knew something that could give the organization a real problem.' She looked up. 'Trouble was I didn't know that and I had to find out.'

'Why you?'

Babs managed a smile. 'I was the only one who could get close to him.'

'So what did you do?'

'Nothing at first. I thought it might be better to let Gus handle it.' She sat up and leaned back, stretching her shoulder muscles. 'But Demski was our biggest problem, and I thought the organization was handling that too.' She laughed. 'We underestimated him. And I think we overestimated ourselves.'

*

Oakwood Park Country Estate in the New Jersey countryside was a throwback to the days when America had thrown off the yoke of British rule and replaced the empire builders with its own men of vision and strength. Elegant in its heyday and dripping with power, it had now lost the charisma that had once fortified its mystical eloquence, but its tired facade hid a more sinister truth.

General Mort Tyler, its owner and custodian of values that were no longer part of modern America, was playing host to some formidable people in the world of global economics. Added to Mort Tyler's guest list were men who played a key role in the American judiciary and in the industrial heartlands of this great country.

None of the men who attended Mort Tyler's splendid banquet would have missed it for the world. It wasn't because the man was popular, but because of the date. It was 20 April, Adolf Hitler's birthday.

The only members of the press who attended were those whose affiliation and affection to the cause was indisputable. Other branches of the media were excluded, and any member of the paparazzi who tried, foolishly, to gain access was dealt with summarily.

Mort Tyler coveted his role in the organization and moved heaven and earth to ensure the absolute privacy of all those attending. He was helped in this endeavour by having Chief of Police John Holder in his pocket. Four years earlier, Holder had been captain of detectives at the 7th Precinct in Newark. His accelerated promotion had been helped by the organization's control on the levers of power in New York State, and it was under Holder's authority that the police cordon around the huge estate was operating.

One other guest at the function, and another reason the big hitters had assembled, was Gus Mason. They were there to honour Mason's meteoric rise in the world of politics, and the fact that he was about to be chosen as the Republican candidate for the office of President of the United States of America.

With Gus was his father, Bill Mason, something of a reluctant guest, but his son had been very persuasive, pointing out that only as a family could he show the strength that could be found in a trusted, family unit. Babs was there too, her looks and glamour a massive attraction to many of the priapic men who harboured hopes of a liaison but knew their hopes were, in reality, a lost cause.

After the meal, the speeches and demanding shouts of, 'Give us Gus!', it was the turn of Gus Mason to rise and give the speech of his life to those people who would do anything to lift him to the highest pinnacle of the American dream.

Bill Mason listened to his son's speech, at first with a moderate approval. He found it strident in places and contrived, sometimes disconcerting, but he realized it would be music to the ears of those who were assembled in the eloquent banqueting hall. Those seated at the top table looked on with smug satisfaction. The longer his son's speech went on, the more worried Bill Mason became. There was an element of rebellion in the lines, a hint of anti-Americanism, although these men were all hardcore Yanks; old school empire builders. There was also a subtle hint of totalitarianism which Bill Mason found worrying, and wondered if he was the only one in the hall who saw something sinister in all this.

When Gus Mason sat down, the glad-handing began. First, Judge Henry Lawrence shook his hand vigorously, followed by Mort Tyler. Babs Mason looked on as all the power brokers clamoured to rub shoulders with the man who they believed would be the next president. If there was stardust to fall from his shoulders, they wanted a sprinkling. After all, they were funding the campaign and would almost certainly expect it to pay dividends. But how? Babs found it a little disconcerting.

Bill Mason got up from the table and took his unfinished drink with him. He had no idea what he wanted to do just then, but felt the need to stretch his legs. So he wandered around, nodding at the few faces he recognized in the room. He noticed too, that some of the top table diners were making their way to a door at the far end of the room. It looked to him as though it was being done discreetly; as though they didn't want to appear rude to the guests in the room. He couldn't see Gus.

His curiosity began to surface and he started making tracks towards the door when someone touched his arm. It was Babs. He raised his eyebrows in delight because they had hardly been able to exchange two words since the beginning of the evening.

'Hey, how are you?'

Babs smiled. 'I'm fine. What did you think of the speech?'

'Do I have to answer that, Babs? Do I really?'

She stood in front of him. 'I take it you didn't approve?'

'I imagine that the majority of Americans wouldn't approve either.'

The smile left her face. 'Gus needs you on his side, Bill.'

'Gus?' He pointed around the hall. 'Don't you mean everyone here, or is it just those on the top table?' He lifted the glass to his lips. As he sipped the amber liquid, he couldn't take his eyes of Babs. She was gorgeous; a catch for any man. He knew the American public already loved her and that admiration was growing. 'They're the ones backing him, aren't they?'

She turned, looking in the direction of the top table. 'They're powerful men, Bill,' she said over her shoulder. She swivelled. 'And you can be part of it.'

He shook his head. 'I'll bale out this time if you don't mind, Babs.' He lowered his head a little. 'I'll catch up with you later?' He didn't wait for an answer but began to walk away from her.

Babs grabbed his arm. 'Bill, why don't we get a few minutes alone?'

He gave her a puzzled look, not quite sure what her intentions were. His expression softened and he stepped a little closer to her. 'Here?' His eyebrows arched and he glanced upwards. When she nodded he felt a reaction gathering in his loins. 'Where?'

'We can use my room. Give me ten minutes.'

'I don't know where your room is,' he told her.

Babs smiled. 'That's not like you, Bill.' She reached forward and brushed his cheek lightly with her lips. Her perfume wrapped itself around him. 'Just go up to the first floor. I'll find you.'

He gave her hand a squeeze as he pulled away. 'Ten minutes?' Babs nodded and he walked away.

She watched him go, knowing there was something he was holding back, and she needed to find out what it was. And find out soon.

Mason wandered off. He had been bored and with that came curiosity. He made his way towards the opposite end of the room and went through an open door. He found himself in a fairly large hallway with stairs leading to the upper floor. There were a few people there talking, but none of them took any notice of him. He put his glass down on a convenient table and walked up the stairs as though he had every right to be doing so. At the top he took a right turn and stood for a while to get his bearings, wondering where he should be so that Babs could find him.

A corridor with windows overlooking the large acreage at the rear of the house led away from where he was standing. He ambled along it expecting it would take him somewhere above the end of the banqueting hall. He listened carefully for any sounds that might tell him where his son had gone with the others who had left the top table, not wanting to come across any of them before he had finished his liaison with Babs. It was still fairly quiet, but he soon heard the muffled sounds of men's voices. There was laughter too and in the air was the distinct fragrance of cigar smoke.

Getting closer to where he believed the men were, Mason stopped and wondered what to do. Whatever Judge Lawrence and the others who had filed out of the room with Gus and Mort Tyler were up to, it was probably none of his business. He thought about a plausible reason for being up there, but could not come up with one. Being nosey was hardly an excuse and he certainly couldn't tell them the real reason.

As these thoughts ran through Mason's mind, he heard the sound of footsteps coming from the far end of the landing on which he was standing. Beside him was a door which almost certainly led into a bedroom. He took a chance and opened the door, stepped into the room and closed the door behind him.

The first thing he saw was a large double bed. Lying on top of the bed was a suit of clothes, a shirt, tie and a pair of socks. Placed carefully beside the bed was a polished pair of evening shoes.

He looked around the room, expecting to see somebody or perhaps hear them in the bathroom taking a shower or getting changed. Then he looked across to the other side of the room where a pair of double doors were half open. He could see that these were connecting doors which would have been opened wide to turn the bedroom into a small apartment. As he looked, the doors opened a little further as someone on the other side took hold of them, and before the doors could be pulled shut, Mason caught a glimpse of what was in the other room.

He saw about eight men. They were all looking at Judge Henry Lawrence who was standing beside General Mort Tyler. And then he understood the fear he had about the speech his son had made and the body language of the men who had sat and watched him with an overt reverence.

Judge Henry Lawrence and General Mort Tyler were dressed in the steel grey uniforms of the Nazi SS.

Isaac Demski listened to his son as he explained to him over the phone the predicament he found himself in. He told his father that he and Haman had had to part company.

'I need cash. I daren't use a credit card.'

'You think the organization is tracking you that way?' his father asked.

'It has to be; there's no other explanation for it. That's why I need cash.'

'I can get some to you,' Isaac reassured him. 'It will have to be delivered personally so it might take some time.'

'I'll hide up somewhere, find a cheap motel.'

'Where will you go when I get the money to you?'

'Switzerland.'

Isaac frowned. 'Why Switzerland?'

'It's the postcards; those I found in Weber's place. I can't explain. Too complicated.'

Isaac wasn't happy with the arrangement, but his son was in trouble and needed help. 'Listen, Jack. Let me know where your motel is once you're there. I'll give you a phone number. The cash will be there.'

Jack thanked his father and hung up. He then walked out of the station and found a taxi. He asked the driver to take him to an out of town motel. Thirty minutes later he was sitting in a fairly standard room – one bed, one bathroom, one phone and a piece of carpet. And spread out over the bed were the postcards.

What had intrigued Demski when he had first looked through

them in the car was the fact that the old man had kept the postcards like a forlorn lover might keep letters from a long lost love. They were all old, well fingered as though they had been studied and admired many times. There were a few photographs among the postcards, but the curious thing was that they were all of the same place; a small village in Switzerland.

At first the postcards bore very little information, and what struck Demski was that they were addressed to *Fraulein Gretchen Mayer*. The message wasn't signed but finished with two initials: F.W. Demski assumed this was Franz Weber, the old man. After a short while, the postcards stopped. There was a lengthy gap, then a photograph of a young man and a woman. On the back of the photo were the names *Franz and Gretchen*. Then the words: *Piva 1948*.

It wasn't difficult for Demski to build a timeline through the postcards and the photographs. Gretchen Meyer was Franz Weber's fiancée at first. Then they became man and wife and, for some reason, took their holidays at Piva, a small village in Switzerland. They always stayed at the same hotel, evident from the photos, and usually twice a year. All Demski had to do now was to find out why and what the connection was between that and the murder of his grandmother, Rosmaleen. He hadn't a clue how he was going to go about it, but he knew he was going to have a good try.

Babs Mason and her husband left the party in a hurry, determined to find some way of stopping Bill Mason and his threat to expose that 'fucking Nazi bunch', as he had put it. Babs had been mortified when he had grabbed her by the elbow and literally dragged her out of the main room, away from the prying eyes and ears of the people assembled there.

They had a furious argument once he had got her out into the grounds of the mansion. Mason insisted that his son was not going to be a puppet to the Nazi thugs, and he was going to stop them. Babs knew that if a hint of what had gone on behind closed doors at Mort Tyler's mansion was leaked to the press by Bill Mason, the campaign to get Gus elected as president would fail. Babs found herself torn between what was right, and her husband's chance of success. For some reason, she felt that failure for Gus would mean his resentment would fall on her. But she still loved Bill Mason, and didn't want to see him hurt either. She had no alternative but to stop Mason from risking his neck by exposing Tyler and Lawrence and the organization of Nazis that they intended leading into power.

It was about five o'clock in the morning when Babs and her husband saw Mason pull up outside his ranch house in the Buick. They hadn't been able to speak to him at Mort Tyler's place once he had argued with Babs because he had literally disappeared. They had arrived a couple of hours earlier hoping to find him in the house and try to persuade him from carrying out his threat to go to the press. There was no one in the house so they waited in the Jeep behind the barn in which Mason always kept his old Buick.

Mason clambered out of his car and hurried into the house. Babs and Gus wondered where he might have gone after leaving Mort Tyler's place in such a temper, but it was something they had to forget about and think on how they were going to deal with the problem of stopping him.

They were still talking about the best way to deal with the problem, and were still wrestling with the dilemma when they saw Mason come out of the house and climb into his Buick. He pulled away from the house and turned towards the old, dirt road that led into town. Gus Mason told Babs to get out of the driver's seat and switch places. He started the motor and followed, keeping the lights off because he didn't want Mason to know they were behind him. Gus kept an eye on his father's tail lights and with the thin, early dawn light seeping into the sky, was able to concentrate on the Buick and not worry about the state of the road.

Suddenly Mason's stop lights blazed out in the gloom, and Gus knew he had reached the beginning of a treacherous curve and a drop in the road that ran alongside a deep gully. He pushed his foot down on the throttle and felt the Jeep lurch forward. The speed increased until they were almost behind the Buick. Gus saw his father's head turn and glance back over his shoulder. As he did, his car bucked and swerved. Gus pushed forward and smashed into the back of the Buick.

They both felt the impact of the bull bars as they hit the rear fender of the Buick. Babs was flung forward, striking her head on the hard edge of the sun visor. The Buick fishtailed wildly as Mason lost control and his car disappeared over the edge of the road, dropping twenty feet into the bottom of the gully.

Gus hit the brakes and brought the Jeep to a slithering stop. He glanced across at Babs who sat there trembling. She put her hand to her forehead and could feel the blood. She wiped it away and looked at her husband with an expression of horror on her face. He clambered out of the jeep and ran over towards the gully. Babs followed him, but as soon as she reached the edge, Gus grabbed hold of her arm.

'Nothing we can do,' he told her. 'Come on.' He pulled her away, but Babs resisted.

'Aren't you going to see if he's all right?' she screamed at him.

He said nothing at first as he dragged her away, but she kept fighting him and trying to break free from his iron grip.

'Gus!' she screamed. 'For God's sake, he's your father!'

He got her to the car and bundled her in through the open door. He slammed it shut and pointed at her through the closed window. 'Stay there!'

Babs watched him run round to the other side and climb in. She was almost speechless now as the horror of what had happened, and what Gus was planning, dawned on her.

'You're going to leave him,' she said with shock in her voice. 'Your own father and you're going to leave him.' She grabbed the handle of the door and was about to open it when Gus slapped her hard around the face.

'Don't you dare, Babs,' he warned her with a hard edge to his voice.

Babs felt the stinging blow and almost passed out. She put her hand to her face and the image of her husband's demonic face was lost as tears flooded into her eyes.

Gus turned away and rammed the gear lever forward. The car jerked as the wheels spun on the dirt. Then he turned and said, 'Nothing must stop us, Babs. Nothing.'

Demski had to wait twenty-four hours for his money. When it came there were no identity checks, no histrionics; simply one man handing over a package to another. After the courier had left, Demski opened the envelope and found 2,000 Euros, 2,000 Swiss Francs and 5,000 American dollars. It was enough; more than enough, in fact. He gathered up the postcards, put the money in a money belt that he always carried and paid his bill at the reception desk. After scribbling his signature, he went out looking for a taxi.

Demski was banking on the people who were almost certainly after him and Haman expecting them to try the main exits to leave the country. Working on that theory and the fact that Haman was no longer with him, he felt comfortable enough using the railway to get from Austria into Switzerland. He arrived in Bern the following day and booked into a small hotel. He used the time to refresh himself with a well-earned shower and a few hours' sleep, but all the while he was thinking of his next move.

Demski knew he would have to head for Piva, but if there was a distinct, solid connection between that small town and Franz Weber, he was sure the people who murdered the old man and his nurse would be there waiting for him to turn up. There was little doubt in his mind that the group responsible for Weber's death were the Neo Nazis. As a Jew he had every reason to loathe them with a passion, and knew that the feeling would be reciprocated. He had to be on his guard, simple as that.

He arrived in Piva the following day and found a small hotel. He didn't wait around too long, but as soon as he had arranged his room in such a way that he would know if anyone had broken in, he pushed the postcards into his pocket and went off in search of the landmarks he had seen in Weber's postcard memories.

The small hamlet of Piva nestled in a lush, green valley. A backdrop of hills in the distance and the mountains beyond lent an ambience of tranquillity. A church spire rose above the town to dominate it due to its position on higher ground. Beyond the church were a scattering of houses that eventually gave way to the canopy of green that sloped gently upwards towards the lower slopes of the hills. There were cattle grazing in one area, and the sound of their bells could be heard quite clearly, tinkling down the slopes.

Demski took this all in as he stood in the road outside the one inn that he recognized from Weber's photograph. The inn was called Der

Jäger, *The Hunter*. It was an apt description. It had been built on the very edge of the town and afforded a spectacular view across the valley. It had taken Demski about an hour to locate the place, and now that he was there, he thought it best to have a snack, a coffee and to ask a few questions.

'I'm looking for my grandmother,' he told the owner of the inn after finishing his meal. 'I believe she used to come here when she was a young woman.' He fished the photograph from his pocket; the one showing Weber standing outside the front of the inn. He looked about twenty years of age in the picture.

Demski then showed the man a second photo. It was of Weber with his wife. The owner's eyebrows lifted and he began to nod his head.

'When I was a little boy, I remember two people who came here often.' His head continued to bob up and down. 'It could be them. My father would know,' he said after a pause. 'I'll get him.'

Demski left the photos on the table and waited until the owner returned with his father. He introduced him as Gerd. He was well into his seventies but looked very fit for his age. Demski showed him the pictures.

'They came here twice a year, sometimes three.'

'Do you know why?' Demski asked.

He shook his head. 'Is that your grandmother?' he asked, pointing at the photo.

'No,' Demski admitted. 'But I believe this man knew her. If I could find him or the lady in this picture....' He left the rest unsaid.

The man sat down at the table. He leaned forward, his arms laying folded flat across the tablecloth. 'This was a long time ago, yes?' Demski nodded. Gerd carried on. 'Just after the war?' There was no response from Demski. He didn't have to wait long for an answer. 'Many people came this way after the war. Many of them were Germans. Nazis. But some of them were Jews.' His eyes pierced Demski's silence. 'You're not a German,' he said at last, shaking his head.

'Is it that obvious?'

He laughed. 'Don't worry, I hated the Nazis too. So, your grandmother, she was fleeing from them?'

Demski nodded. 'I think this man may have helped her, but I need to talk to him if he's still alive.' It sounded right even though Demski had seen Weber with a bullet in his head just a few days earlier.

Gerd shook his head forlornly. 'Probably not now, but you never know.'

Demski tried a long shot. 'Do you keep records of guests who have stayed here?'

Gerd smiled. 'Only about as far back as a couple of years.' He stopped suddenly as though something had occurred to him. 'There is one thing, though. I remember a man who came to see them. It was about five years after the war. They travelled up to the sanatorium together.' He stopped and leaned back in his chair.

'You think perhaps my grandmother could have been in the sanatorium?'

Gerd shrugged. 'I don't know. It's possible, but you would have to ask them. If they have a guest list, I'm sure it would go back quite a way.'

'Where is this sanatorium?'

Gerd leaned away from the table and pointed to the window. 'You can just about see it up on the slope. Most of it is hidden by trees.'

Demski got up from the table and looked out through the window. He could see the rooftop of what looked like a long building, but the treeline obscured most of it from view. He felt a frisson of excitement welling up in him. If this was where they had taken Eva Braun he might be closer to learning the truth.

If it was true, then he understood why the Nazis were prepared to murder to keep it a secret; he intended to find out.

Although the sanatorium was just about in view from the inn, Demski was told that it was too far to walk, as pretty as the walk appeared, so he took a cab. The climb up the hill lasted about ten minutes. As the driver approached the entrance, Demski leaned forward and tapped him on the shoulder.

'I think I will walk from here,' he told him.

He paid the driver and watched the cab turn round and disappear back down the winding road.

The walk up to the gate into the sanatorium was about a hundred metres. On one side was a high wall that looked as though it had been built as a retaining wall. Mounted high on the stone was a sign with the words, *Schwestern des Friedens*, Sisters of Peace, and an arrow pointing towards the gatehouse. Demski wondered what secrets the Sisters of Peace might be hiding. He nodded briefly and made his way up the slope.

To his surprise, the gatehouse was empty. He walked through the pedestrian gate which looked as though it had never been closed and followed the road as it curved to the right beneath a canopy of trees. He paused at a small cottage, not much bigger than the hotel bedrooms he had been used to. There was a date etched into a plaque on the side of the cottage and an explanation that it was the original dwelling place of Sister Anselma, the founder of the sanatorium. The date was 1820.

He didn't stay too long, but was now aware of a kind of peacefulness coming over him. It was hard not to feel a sense of tranquillity settling gently on his shoulders. He continued walking and followed the road as it curved and dropped into an area that had a shop and a small café. There were a few people sitting outside who waved at him as he walked by. He acknowledged them but didn't stop because he could see just beyond the small, commercial area, and beyond an expansive car park, what appeared to be the main building.

It was three storeys high and about a hundred metres in length. It was painted white, perhaps to give it an air of peace and tranquillity. He crossed the car park and walked into the main entrance, allowing the doors to swing shut behind him.

On one side of the large hall was a reception desk. A nun was seated behind the desk. She looked up as Demski walked in and smiled.

'Good morning. Can I help you?'

Demski listened for other noises in the background, but there seemed to be an amazing silence.

'I hope so,' he answered pleasantly as he approached the desk. 'This may sound odd; but I'm trying to trace my grandmother.' The lie fell easily from his lips.

'I see. You think she may be here?'

'Well not exactly. She may even be dead.'

The nun's mouth fell open. Demski put his hand up. 'Let me explain,' he said, and went on to tell of Eva Braun's apparent escape from Berlin, but substituting his grandmother's name, Rosmaleen Demski. It was something that Demski had come up with while he was trying to figure out the reason for the postcards. If, he reasoned, Eva Braun was fleeing from Germany, it would have made sense to have adopted a Jewish name. So why not the name of the woman who had been murdered in her place?

'We would have to check our records,' she told him. 'But you would have to speak to Sister Maria.' She picked up the phone and pushed a button. After a short while she spoke to somebody rapidly in French. She put the phone down and asked Demski to wait.

'Sister Maria is French?' he asked.

The nun nodded. 'Yes. She is also very old and very deaf.'

'I'll try to remember that,' he promised and walked over to an armchair. He sat down and picked up a magazine from a side table. He flicked through the pages, not reading but just looking at the pictures until he heard footsteps and the voice of a gentle soul.

'Mr Demski, I am sorry to keep you waiting.'

Demski quickly closed the magazine and stood up. The woman he saw coming towards him was dressed in white. She was well advanced in years and walked with a stoop.

She shook his hand. 'How can I help you?'

He repeated what he had told the nun sitting at the reception desk, but was careful to speak loudly and clearly.

'We can try,' she replied. 'Do you have any identification; something that will confirm your connection with Rosmaleen Demski?'

It didn't surprise him that he had been asked. He took his passport from his pocket and handed it over to her. 'I have this.'

She opened the passport and looked at the photograph and name. Then she closed it and handed it back. 'Well, it says you are Jacob Demski, but we do have to be careful, you understand.' Demski said he did. 'This way.' She pointed a finger towards the other side of the entrance hall.

They walked through the hall to a door that opened into a large square. It was well maintained with shrubs and flowers, and there were benches and chairs scattered around for visitors and patients. There was also a fountain, and the sound of the running water added a wonderful calm to the place.

Demski could now see that the main building of the sanatorium was in fact a square built around a quadrangle. It still retained its pristine whiteness even though he guessed it was many years old. Sister Maria unlocked a small door at one end of the building, producing the key from an enormous key ring that was hanging beneath her apron.

It was quite chilly inside the room. She turned the overhead light on revealing two old filing cabinets against one wall. There was a desk in the room on which was a computer and a telephone.

'Modern accoutrements,' she told Demski, pointing at the computer. 'But I can't use them. Too old,' she added with wry humour. 'Now, when did you say your grandmother arrived at the sanatorium?'

He watched her walk over to the filing cabinets. 'I believe it was about April, 1945.'

Once again she fished beneath her apron and pulled out the set of keys she carried there and opened one of the filing cabinets. Pulling out a box file, she opened it and began thumbing through the ledgers inside. With a little cry of triumph, she pulled out one of the ledgers and laid it on top of the files. She opened the book and tossed the pages until she came to the page she was looking for.

Demski watched as she ran her finger down the page and then stopped. There was a discernible change in her demeanour as she read the entry. As small and as frail as she looked, Sister Maria seemed to shrink inside her habit. Demski thought for a moment she was going to collapse, but then she regained some measure of control and closed the book. After a while, she turned and looked over at him. There was a definite change in her manner; a sadness almost.

'The record shows that a Rosmaleen Demski came to the sanatorium in May, 1945.' She paused for a moment. 'I'm sorry to have to tell you that she died in childbirth. It was in October of that year.' She shook her head. 'I am so sorry.'

For a moment, Demski was stunned. It really was as though he had uncovered a terrible tragedy in his life. Although he knew his grandmother had died in the bunker, this small piece of information had its own kind of tragedy. He recovered his composure quickly enough to look a little sad.

'That is terrible,' he muttered, then sighed. 'That's it, then; I suppose that's the end of my search.'

Sister Maria was shaking her head. 'It's life. In the midst of it we are in death.' She put the ledger back into the filing cabinet and closed the drawer. 'I expect you would like to visit your grandmother's grave?'

It caught Demski off guard for a moment. 'Well, of course. Pay my last respects, naturally. Is she buried here?'

She pointed somewhere beyond the small window. 'We have a small cemetery at the top of the hill. We sometimes have need of it, particularly when one of our patients passes on and there are no relatives. It's the least we can do,' she added.

'Can I go up there now?' Demski wasn't really the least bit interested in visiting the grave, but he thought it would look better for the sake of appearances if he made some effort.

'Of course. I'm afraid I can't come with you, but if you go out of the rear door of the sanatorium, you'll find some steps that lead up to a small road. Just follow that.'

Demski thanked her as profusely as he thought fitting and made his way up the small road to the cemetery. The road was lined with tall cypress trees, which added an unusual solemnity to the short walk.

At the gates a small plaque declared that the cemetery was only open during the hours of daylight. Demski shrugged and walked through into an area that was well tended. Small shrubs edged the tarmac roadway that meandered around the perimeter, forming a loop that came back to the gates.

He began checking the lines of headstones when he heard someone call out.

'Can I help you?'

He turned in the direction of the voice and saw an old man with an armful of dead flowers and twigs standing beside a rubbish bin. He smiled and put up a hand in acknowledgement. 'I'm looking for my grandmother's grave,' he called back.

The old man dropped the waste into the bin and walked over to him. He walked with a limp and leaned forward with the gait so common in old people.

'What was her name?' he asked as he came up beside Demski.

'Rosmaleen Demski.'

The old boy squeezed his lips together and half closed his eyes as he tried to recall the name. Then he lifted his hand and pointed a gnarled, crooked finger at Demski.

'Strange thing.' It was all he said as he turned and walked away. Demski followed until the old man stopped beside a grave. 'I wondered when someone might come.'

Demski thought it odd that the old man should say something like that. Then he noticed the writing etched into the headstone. *E.B. and child. 1945.*

'Wrong grave,' he told him. 'My grandmother's initials are R.D.'

The old boy stared at him through watery eyes and shook his head. 'I was a young man when I came to work here. Dug most of these graves,' he added unnecessarily. 'Dug this one. Weren't no money then, so no headstone. Poor woman had nothing except a dead infant.' He shook his head sadly and pulled a screwed up handkerchief from his pocket and blew his nose. 'It was like that for a long time. Used to be a young fellow, German lad, would come here couple of times a year and tidy the grave up. Not that it needed tidying. He'd put some flowers on it. Then he would give me a few Swiss francs for more flowers and go away for a while. Never said much.' The old man stopped and looked at Demski quite suddenly. 'One of yours, maybe?' When he saw Demski shake his head, he carried on.

'Then about five years after we buried the poor woman, a stranger came. Tall man. He came with the young chap. He had a wife now; the young chap, not the stranger. He paid for a headstone. Said we should put *E.B. and child* on it. I told him it wasn't this E.B. woman, but he wouldn't listen; insisted we did as he bid.' He straightened up and turned towards Demski. 'So there's your reason why.'

'Who was the tall man?'

The old boy shook his head. 'The young man always called him Heinrich, same name as me, but he was much older than the young man.' He coughed and blew his nose into his handkerchief. 'I've got to go now. I can't tell you any more, but if you need any more help, don't be afraid to ask.'

Demski said he would and watched the old boy wander away to the gates of the cemetery. He found it hard to believe what he was thinking, but it looked as though Eva Braun had given birth to a child here at the sanatorium. It was almost certainly stillborn, but there was no way to prove this had happened. No way at all. The whole thing was preposterous, he decided. The world would laugh at such a suggestion. But the irony was that somewhere out there were people who were prepared to murder to keep this secret.

And Demski wanted to know why.

TEN

LIEUTENANT AMOS STUDIED the wreckage of Bill Mason's old Buick. The car was a total write-off. They found Mason's body about fifty yards away. Amos turned his head and shoulders, looking back up at the point in the road, about twenty feet above the gully in which he was now standing, and imagined the car roaring over the edge and cartwheeling towards its final resting place. If Mason had not been thrown out of the car, he would have been crushed by the impact. Not that it mattered; he was dead anyway.

He looked back at the Buick and began a slow walk around the twisted metal. The forensics team had already been there and cordoned the area off, but Amos was wearing his one-piece, sterile bunny suit so was able to get quite close. He had with him Sergeant Phil Moyes, the local sergeant from Hutton who had put a call through to Amos's desk.

'He liked a drink, Amos.'

Amos grunted. 'Had he been drinking?'

'We don't know yet, but he was at Mort Tyler's place night before last. Big party there.'

Amos grunted again. They all knew about General Tyler's penchant for a gathering of like-minded Republicans.

'What do you think?'

'I'd put money on it,' Moyes told him.

Amos scratched his head and continued walking round the wreckage. He stopped when he got to the rear end. It was well damaged and covered in huge scratches and dents, plus a mixture of dirt and grass stains where it had bounced along the ground. Pretty much like the rest of the body.

He noticed something on what was left of the rear bumper and leaned forward for a closer look. He straightened and turned to Moyes.

'He was pretty fond of his old Buick, right?'

Moyes nodded. 'They were joined at the hip. Always kept it immaculate.'

Amos bent forward and studied a small section of the bumper again. He could see a red smear on the coachwork. But the Buick was red too. He couldn't be sure if it was part of the primer or undercoat that had been brought to the surface as a result of the battering the car had taken.

'When do you plan to take the car away?'

'Soon as forensics have finished with it. We'll take it down to the pound.'

Amos noticed something else; something that did not look like crash damage. He puffed his cheeks out as he straightened up.

'Did Mason always take his car to the same garage?'

Moyes nodded. 'Sure did. Wouldn't have anybody but Old Tom touch it.'

Amos brightened. 'Really?' He gave this some thought. 'Where would I find Old Tom?'

'Old Tom's Panel Shop. It's in Hutton.' He gave Amos a curious stare. 'Why, what's on your mind?'

Amos shrugged. 'Oh, it's just a thought. I want to know a little more about Bill Mason; how much he cared for his car.' There was a moment's silence. 'I'd like another look at this when you get it into the pound,' he told Moyes before the sergeant could ask any more questions. 'Probably call in tomorrow.'

He turned round and ducked underneath the police tape, then peeled off his paper suit, throwing it into a bin provided. He then clambered up the slope, using a rope that had been fixed there by the local firemen and headed towards his car. Next stop for Amos was the town of Hutton and Old Tom's Panel Shop.

Amos soon found out that Old Tom was not old at all. In fact he was quite young, about mid thirties and a handsome sort of guy. His name was Jeff Clooney and he had inherited Old Tom's shop from his grandfather.

'You heard about the crash?' Amos asked him after the introductions were completed.

Clooney wiped his hands on a piece of old rag. Amos noticed that he did it habitually.

'Crying shame.' He shook his head. 'Lovely old Buick like that.'

Amos noticed that Clooney seemed to care more about the car than the fact someone had died in the accident.

'Did Mason bring the car here many times?'

He nodded. 'Sometimes I think it spent more time in here than it did up at Bill's place.'

Amos frowned. 'Why's that?'

Clooney looked around quickly, almost conspiratorially. 'Well, I don't like to speak ill of the dead, but he used to scrape it a lot. Everybody knew he liked a drink,' he said in way of mitigation.

'So he wouldn't have left any marks on his car for too long?'

Clooney laughed. 'I've known the old boy to get here before I opened up in the morning because he'd put a scratch on the fender.'

'Good customer then?'

Brad nodded boldly. 'Damn good.'

'You'll be sorry to lose him then?'

'Darn right I will.'

Amos put his hand out. 'Well, thanks Jeff. You've been a big help. I may want to talk to you again, would you mind?'

'No problem, Lieutenant. No problem at all.'

Amos thanked him again and left the garage. He had a picture forming in his mind and that old police instinct of his was kicking in as he climbed into his car and headed back to the 7th Precinct.

Amos watched the funeral from a distance. It reminded him of some of the mafia funerals he had attended in the past. All the bosses would be there from out of state; men who controlled gambling, prostitution, drugs, the protection rackets. The family members would be the centre of attention. Homilies would be paid, promises made, guarantees assured. How different was this one, he wondered?

Bill Mason was the father of the man who would almost certainly be the next president of the United States of America, but Mason wasn't the important one; it was his son, Gus Mason. Looking suitably mournful, but with a disarmingly attractive presence, he looked the perfect partner alongside his beautiful wife, Babs Mason. She carried herself elegantly and managed to look so chic in black. Amos had noticed a small plaster just beneath the rim of her dark glasses. He wondered about that.

The cemetery had been cordoned off from the general public, but not to the television cameras and national press. This was a big vote catcher for Gus Mason and the party he represented. With the nominations for Republican candidate now whittled down to two people, Gus was winning the support of the waverers without effort. Any undecided votes would now surely swing in his direction.

Security was tight as well because of the number of high profile people who had gathered to pay their last respects. Police Chief Holder was prominent among them and of course, General Mort Tyler and Judge Lawrence. There were others there from industry, from Wall Street and the local state legislature. But what seemed to stand out to Amos, and probably no one else, was that these people were there, not to mourn Bill Mason, but to be seen with Gus Mason.

Amos wanted to get close to Babs Mason, not to offer his condolences, but to get a look at that sticking plaster. Not that he could do anything about it, but his senses were on alert and he couldn't help putting two and two together. He shook his head slowly as she was helped into the limousine by her husband. The line of cars moved out slowly, and soon the presence of some of the most powerful people in America was no longer invading the solemnity of the graveyard.

Amos walked out to where he had parked his police car and climbed into the driver's seat. His mind was buzzing with the feeling that there was far more to Bill Mason's death than was apparent. It had been declared as death by misadventure; a tragic accident. Nothing had been mentioned of the excess of alcohol found in Mason's blood, which could have been a contributing factor. It looked as though the investigation into the accident had been peremptory and hurried. He thought of the death of Senator Ann Robbins and how her death had been accepted as a heart attack.

He pulled out of the car park and headed off towards Hutton. He wanted to see Clooney at Old Tom's Panel Shop, and he wanted another look at Bill Mason's Buick. What was left of it.

An hour later, Amos was standing in the police pound with Clooney. They were studying the effects of the accident on the Buick. Amos said nothing of the paint marks he had noticed, preferring to wait and see if Clooney would spot the difference too.

The young mechanic crouched down beside the rear fender and began running his finger over the damaged section. Amos instinctively looked around to see if anybody else was watching. It unsettled him to think that he was getting overly suspicious of any police officer who might be watching, but he had learned to be distrustful about anything to do with the Masons or Judge Lawrence.

'He's had a scrape here,' Clooney observed, shaking his head. 'Wouldn't have left it like that; he'd have brought it in straightaway.'

'Do you think it's recent?'

Clooney looked up at him. 'It wasn't there a week ago.'

Amos suspected that Clooney would have a very close knowledge of Mason's old Buick. 'Could you tell what kind of car Mason could have scraped?'

Clooney squinted in the sunlight and a puzzled look came over his face. 'What are you up to, Lieutenant?'

Amos dropped to one knee and leaned in close. 'Listen, Jeff, there's a reason I want to know what happened but I can't explain. I'm not on the case, but it's important I find out the truth.'

'Why?'

Amos shook his head quickly. 'Trust me on this, and don't, whatever you do, tell anybody that I've been nosing around.'

Clooney jerked his head in the direction of the office. 'They know you're here.'

Amos nodded. 'I told them I've asked you to make an assessment; see if you can rebuild the car.'

Clooney studied him in silence for a while. Then he took a small, Swiss Army knife from his pocket, opened a blade and dug it deep into the fender. He sliced off a short length of the paint and then put the sliver into his handkerchief. He closed the knife and slipped it back into his pocket.

'Give me a week,' he said, 'and I'll have something for you. It'll cost.'

Amos agreed. 'Whatever, but this is just between you and me. OK?'

Clooney nodded his understanding and the two men left the pound.

Isaac Demski shook the newspaper to straighten it out and continued reading the article that had caught his eye. He was sitting at the kitchen table where he had eaten breakfast. His son Jack had returned from Europe and had spoken to his father about the strange events that had taken place. Neither of them could come up with a plausible reason why the Neo Nazis would resort to murder to keep Eva Braun's demise a secret. As far as the world was concerned, she had died with Hitler in the Reich Chancellery in 1945.

Isaac chuckled. 'Boy, that Gus Mason is going to walk into the White House.'

Jack looked up. 'Why's that?'

Isaac tapped the newspaper with his finger. 'His old pa was buried yesterday. Big funeral. All the big hitters were there.'

'His old man was important then?'

Isaac shrugged. 'Maybe he was, I dunno. But Gus Mason was the feature, right? Won't do his election chances any harm at all.'

'So what did his father do? I've never heard of him.'

Isaac scanned down the article. 'Not a lot really. Seems he was something in SOE during the war.'

'What, did he fight in Europe?'

Isaac shook his head. 'No. He worked for the SOE in Switzerland. It's where he met his wife. She's dead now; been dead a few years.' He read on. 'It says here that that was where Gus Mason was born; some clinic near Bern.' He looked over the top of his newspaper at Jack. 'What was the name of that clinic you went to?'

Jack had only been taking an idle interest in what his father had been telling him. Now he sat forward, paying full attention.

'Sisters of Peace.'

Isaac shook his head. There was no mention of the clinic's name in the newspaper article. 'What was the name of the village?'

'Piva.'

His father scanned the article, and then suddenly lifted his head in triumph. 'Same damn clinic, Jack.'

'What year was it?'

Isaac looked back at the newspaper. 'Forty-five.'

Jack slumped back in his chair. His mind went racing back to the moment Sister Maria had opened the filing cabinet and pulled out the ledger. He thought she had reacted to the entry in the book quite unnaturally. But then she had regained her composure, or at least; she seemed to. After all, she was bound to be saddened at the thought of a young woman dying as she gave birth to a stillborn child.

Isaac looked at his son. 'What's the problem, Jack?'

'I think I should go back.'

Isaac regarded his son quite sternly. 'Why?'

Jack shook his head. 'I can't explain, but I've got to go back.'

Amos was back at Old Tom's Panel Shop after phoning Jeff Clooney. It was one week since his previous visit. Clooney greeted him as soon as he pulled up outside the garage and took him through to his office. It was typical of many small town repair shops; filled with all manner of clutter, pin-up pictures of scantily clad girls, a couple of calendars, time sheets, receipts bunched beneath a bulldog clip, and the inevitable, grease-stained swivel chair.

'Know much about paint?' Clooney asked him as he threw himself into the chair.

Amos shook his head. 'No.'

Clooney opened a drawer and pulled out a thin folder. He laid it on the desk and flicked it open. There were a couple of single sheets there, the top one of which he lifted and studied for a while.

'You know, before 1985, most domestic cars only had a single stage paint job. It meant that the paint had to contain the pigment, the resin and the solvent. In the case of metallic paints, it had to contain the metallic element too. Every time Bill Mason brought his Buick in for a touch up, I had to remove the old, damaged paint and try to match it with new.' He shifted in the chair and laid the report on the desk. 'Trouble is, Amos, old paint fades over time. When you try to match it, you have all kind of problems. There's a difference in paint shades, depending on where the car was manufactured. West coast cars with the same colour as East coast cars would look a different shade standing side by side. The difference in shade could be as much as five per cent. So when I did a paint job on Mason's Buick, I had a head start because I knew exactly how I wanted the paint mixed.'

'What about the other colour we found?'

'Well, the lab I use told me that was a bit tricky, but eventually they came up with Chrysler. They did a pigment analysis using UV spectrophotometry and narrowed it down to a Dodge, a Plymouth or a Jeep.'

Amos wanted to shout and punch the air, but he kept his lips pressed tight together. This was not the time for jubilation or histrionics; he needed a clear, level head. Clooney's detailed explanation was pointing the finger at a high profile suspect. He had to be careful.

'How much did the report cost you?'

'Hundred bucks.'

Amos took his wallet out and peeled off a hundred dollars. He handed it over to Clooney.

'Whatever you do, Jeff, don't let anyone know about this.'

Clooney closed his fist around the money. 'Is this a murder investigation?' he asked.

Amos shook his head. 'Best you don't know. But for now, this is private.' He stood up and pointed at the report. 'May I?'

Clooney laughed. 'Sure thing, Amos. You paid for it.'

Amos took the report and shook Clooney's hand. 'I'll be in touch.'

He left the panel shop and thought about how he was going to push this investigation along. But first of all, Amos knew he needed to get a look at Babs Mason's Rubicon Jeep.

Gunter Haman picked up the phone on the third ring. His mind was elsewhere, still dwelling on what he had learned by surfing the Internet, which he had been doing a lot lately, particularly since he had returned from Austria after parting from Jack Demski. He had been looking for newspaper reports about the slaying of Franz Weber and his nurse, but all that he could dig up was that the police were not looking for anybody; they believed Weber's nurse murdered Weber and then took her own life. It was a totally absurd notion, but it reinforced the fear he had that the Neo Nazis had infiltrated the police in Germany to such an extent that they were able to manipulate the evidence and the facts. It was a truly frightening prospect.

'Gunter Haman.'

'Hallo Gunter, this is Jack Demski.'

Haman's eyes widened in surprise. 'Hallo Jack. I didn't expect to hear from you again.'

'I didn't expect to contact you again either.'

'So why the call?'

'I need to see you. It's important.'

'Where are you now?'

'In Germany. I can be at your place in a couple of hours. Will that be OK?'

Haman found himself nodding. 'Sure, Jack. Couple of hours.'

The phone went dead. Haman looked at the receiver and hung up.

It was a little more than two hours, but it mattered not to Haman, except that his burning curiosity had been trying his patience. He hurried to the door when Demski arrived and showed him through to a well-appointed lounge. Haman's wife had prepared a snack for their guest and after being introduced by Haman, she told the two men she would be in the other room if they needed anything.

Haman urged Demski to eat the food his wife had prepared before talking about the reason for his unexpected visit. Demski enjoyed the sandwiches and coffee, but turned down the offer of a beer.

'I'm all ears, Jack,' Haman told him. 'So what's happened?'

Demski reached into his pocket and took out the postcards and photographs he had taken from Weber's house. He laid them out on the table and explained the timeline he had worked out. He also told Haman that Eva Braun had died giving birth to a baby boy.

'Do you recognize the guy in this photo?' he asked, showing him the one of Weber as a young man in front of the inn at Piva.

Haman, still shaken by the revelation of Eva Braun's demise, studied the black and white picture carefully. He nodded slowly and eventually handed the picture back to Demski.

'It certainly looks like the man who came into the Chancellery,' he admitted. 'The one who took Eva Braun away.'

'The driver, Franz Weber?'

Haman nodded. 'I'd seen him a few times before that day. He was Hauptmann Lörenz's driver.'

'What about this one. It's with his wife.'

Haman nodded more positively. 'Yes, I think this is he.'

Demski then showed him the photograph with the second man in it. 'Who is this?'

Haman seemed to reel back in shock. 'Hauptmann Lörenz. So he escaped.'

Demski took the photograph back. 'What was his first name?'

Haman stared at the table top for a while. Then he lifted his head. 'Heinrich.'

'That's it,' exclaimed Demski. 'That's the guy who visited the cemetery at the sanatorium; the one who had the headstone put in.'

'So Eva Braun died in childbirth and he wanted her to have a proper headstone?'

Demski's head bobbed up and down. 'Looks that way.'

'But why turn up after five years and do that?'

Demski had wrestled with the conundrum for a good many hours. 'I can only think that he was in love with her. He wanted to keep her memory alive.'

'But where did he go after that?' Haman asked. 'It was unlikely he would remain in Europe. After all, the Nuremberg trials were under way. He would have been scooped up into the net.'

'South America, I would imagine,' Demski said quietly. 'Most of the Nazi bastards ended up there.'

'If you could get a look at the *Odessa* files, you might learn where he went,' Haman suggested.

Demski shook his head. 'Wouldn't do any good; he's probably dead now anyway.'

'Which means his secret died with him.' Haman picked up his cup and drained it. He put the empty cup back on the coffee table. 'Which also means there is little point in you carrying on with this.'

Demski had been sitting forward rather rigidly. He relaxed a little and leaned back in his chair.

Suddenly the front window shattered as a hail of bullets came crashing through it, followed by a Molotov cocktail. As the bottle smashed on the wall of the lounge, the burning petrol cascaded over the walls like the tail of a strutting peacock. The two men dived for cover as the sound of machine-gun fire continued over the roar of the flames and everything in the room seemed to explode into a thousand fragments. Then the shooting stopped and the sound of an escaping motorbike could be heard mingling with the screams of Haman's wife as she burst into the room.

Amos couldn't think of a reason, a good reason to get a look at Babs Mason's Jeep. He had driven past the house a few times over a couple of days but the Jeep was never there. He had even tried the ruse of phoning from a public call box and pretending he was cold calling, selling life insurance. This was just to ensure Babs was at home. He had disguised his voice as best he could, which was pretty difficult for a man of his ancestry. When Babs had replied and cut him short, he was quite happy because it meant she was at home, and it meant he could drive past her house and check on that Jeep. But it wasn't there.

In desperation he phoned Jeff Clooney and asked him if he knew of any garages where Babs was likely to take the car for a repair. Clooney said he didn't, but he came up with something that gave Amos some encouragement.

'If the bull bars were wrecked, they would need replacing,' Clooney told him. 'The only place I reckon the garage would get the replacement from would be Mitchell and Hayes. They supply most of the garages in and around these parts. Why not ask them. Make it official, like?'

Amos liked the man's guile and thanked him. His next move was to drive into Newark and find the company trading as Mitchell and Hayes.

The place was quite large, covering a full block on an industrial estate out near Harvey Field, east of the city. Amos walked into the front office and showed the receptionist his police badge.

'Good morning. I'm Lieutenant Amos, Newark Police Department.'

The young woman glanced at the badge.

'Morning. Lieutenant. What can I do for you?'

Amos put his ID away. 'I'd like to speak to the dispatcher, guy who handles the orders.'

'That will be Charlie Price. If you wait a moment, I'll give him a call.'

Two minutes later Charlie Price came into the office. He was in his late fifties and looked busy.

'Morning Lieutenant, what can I do for you?'

'I'd like to know if you've had an order in lately for a set of bull bars for a Rubicon Jeep.'

Price stood there and looked like he was thinking. It wasn't unusual for men like him to have an almost encyclopaedic knowledge of everything that went in and out of Mitchell and Hayes.

'Reckon I did,' he nodded with some degree of satisfaction. 'Come through to the office.'

Amos followed him through to his office. Price took a folder from one of the shelves that seemed to lean over with an overload of arch lever files. He opened the file and sprung the clip. He flicked through the invoices and came to the one he was looking for.

'Yep, delivered a set of bull bars to Cutlers out at Coopersville.'

'When was that?'

'Couple of days ago.'

'Got a map?'

Price closed the folder and put it back on the shelf. Then he opened a drawer in his desk and pulled out a local atlas. He flipped open the page and pointed to Coopersville. Amos looked over his shoulder. It was about ten miles away from Hutton. Ten miles from where Bill Mason died.

Jack Demski cursed as he pulled Haman from the edge of the flames and dragged him out of the room by the scruff of his neck. Haman's wife was standing in the open doorway, her hands squeezing the sides of her face as she continued to scream. Demski threw an arm round her waist and lifted her bodily into the short hallway. It seemed to startle her and bring her to her senses. She could see that Jack was struggling with her husband and mouthing words at her, but she could make no sense of what he was saying.

The roar of the flames was terrifying and the heat seemed to roll out of the burning room like liquid, searing her flesh. She looked down at her husband and was appalled to see the black scorch marks over his clothes. His hair had burned away and she could feel her own hair melting under the intense heat.

Demski's jacket was on fire and he let Haman drop to the floor as he struggled to slap at the flames. He managed to get the jacket off and rolled it into a ball, which he jammed beneath his arm. Then he hooked his fingers beneath Haman's collar again and shouted at his wife.

'Get the front door open. Now!'

His angry, commanding voice shocked her and brought her out of herself. She shook her head suddenly as though something had startled her and ran to the front door, pulling it open. Demski carried Haman through into the cool, evening air and out on to the street where he laid the injured man on the pavement. His wife came running up behind him and almost fell on her husband, sobbing and uttering soothing words.

Already a small crowd of neighbours had appeared from their houses and were gathering in the street by the burning house. Little more than two minutes had passed since the house was fire-bombed, but already the flames had taken hold and it was obvious that there would be nothing left.

Demski took hold of Haman's wife by the elbow and pulled at it quickly. He managed to get her attention, distracting her from her natural concern for her husband. When he was sure she was listening, he whispered coarsely in her ear.

'Make sure you get your husband police protection if he has to stay in hospital.'

She snapped her head away and gave him a puzzled look. 'Why? What on earth for?'

He shook his head. 'Listen, it's important you and your husband are under guard. If you can, get Gunter away from here. Miles away. Don't contact anybody.'

Demski didn't want to frighten her any more than she had already been, but he knew they wouldn't survive if another attack was planned. Whoever had thrown the petrol bomb and raked the house with gunfire were probably poor amateurs. If the Nazis had another go, Haman and his wife would be dead.

'What about you, what are you going to do?'

'I'm going. If anybody asks what happened in there, tell them your husband had a journalist in who was doing a write-up about the war.' He squeezed her arm. 'It's close to the truth. But whatever you do, don't tell them my name or anything about me. Understand?'

She nodded and then turned back to her husband.

'One day,' Demski told her, 'I'll be in touch.'

He left her there, bent over Haman, and slipped away under the cover of darkness. The next stop for Demski was the sanatorium in Switzerland.

ELEVEN

LIEUTENANT AMOS ENJOYED this time of the day more often than not. It was a chance to sit and talk to Judith before going into work. Breakfast was eaten leisurely and with pleasure. He always wanted more but his wife would remind him of his need to lose weight and refuse his pleas. He would look at Holly, his daughter, now almost thirteen years of age. Every time she heard her mother refuse Amos that extra slice of bacon or an extra waffle, she would arch her eyebrows and smile wickedly and knowingly at him. Amos always returned her impish reaction with a wink.

Once he had left the house, there was no telling what time he would get back. Often Holly would be in bed and Judith would be watching the TV or curled up on the sofa with a book. Sometimes she would be asleep and the book would be lying on the carpet where it fell. She would never go to bed until she knew Amos was home safe and sound.

He finished his breakfast and drained his coffee cup. Then he got up from the table, lifted Holly from her chair and gave her a massive hug.

'Who's my favourite girl?'

Holly squealed. 'Mummy is.'

Amos shook his head and looked into her huge, brown eyes. 'No, Mummy is Mummy. You're my favourite; especially when you write those lovely stories.' He gave her kiss on the side of her face and put her down gently. Then he walked across to his wife and put his arms around her waist. She was standing with her back to him and he whispered softly in her ear.

'You're my favourite, really.'

She turned in his arms and planted a kiss on his lips. 'Liar. Don't tell Holly that; she might get jealous.'

He laughed and let her go. Then he lifted his jacket off the back of the chair and headed for the back door.

'I'll try and get home early so's we can go bowling,' he called as he stepped through the open door. 'Love you!'

The door closed and Judith looked at it with a kind of resignation in her face.

'One day,' she said quietly.

Amos pulled out of the drive and headed out of town for Cutlers, the garage that had taken delivery of the bull bars. It was a fine day and traffic was normal, so the journey out to Coopersville was uneventful. He thought a great deal about Babs Mason and her husband while he was driving. It seemed such a long time ago that he had questioned Babs about the death of Senator Ann Robbins and wondered about the death of Doctor Robertson. The trail, what there was of it, had gone cold and it looked as though someone would get away with the perfect murder. Gus Mason's rise through the ranks was meteoric, almost unknown in career politics. He had an uncanny knack of being in the right place at the right time. Obstacles that might have thwarted any other ambitious politician had melted away, and he looked destined for the top.

But now Amos was looking into the death of Bill Mason, and he couldn't shake himself from the conviction that Babs Mason was involved. But there was something else nagging away at his brain that he couldn't pin down; something that was even more sinister. The devil of it was that he had no idea what had put this conviction in his heart, but once again that old gut instinct of his was telling him that the case had not gone cold; the death of Bill Mason had opened the door.

He pulled up outside Cutler's garage. It had the appearance of a business that was doing well. The front showrooms were displaying the latest, gleaming models; while on the forecourt were a row of used cars that looked as though they had just come from the factory. Very impressive.

He walked through the doorway leading to the workshop and stood beside the reception desk waiting for someone to notice him. Pretty soon a young woman asked if she could help him.

Amos smiled at her. 'Sure. I'd like to speak to the chief mechanic.'

She got up from behind the desk. 'That will be Wayne Ryland. I'll get him for you.'

Two minutes later she was back with a man in his forties. Tall, well-built and probably a bit of a ladies' man.

'Can I help you, sir?'

Amos pulled his badge from his pocket. 'Lieutenant Amos, Newark Police Department. I'd like to ask you a couple of questions.'

The young woman looked up at Ryland with an inquiring expression on her face. Ryland pointed towards an office. 'We'll go in there.'

Amos followed him through to the office and sat down in the chair offered to him. Then Ryland settled himself behind his desk.

'So how can I help you, Lieutenant?'

'You had a set of bull bars delivered here a week or so back. I'd like to know what car you fitted them to and who the owner was.'

Ryland fidgeted for a moment. 'Not sure I can tell you that.'

'Can't or won't?' Amos asked him.

Ryland said nothing for a while. 'Is this an official investigation?' he asked eventually.

Amos couldn't tell him that he was doing this on his own, without the knowledge of his captain.

'That depends,' he answered cryptically, 'on how much you're prepared to tell me.'

'We fit a lot of add-ons here,' Ryland said by way of an answer. 'Sometimes the guys do a little after hours work, off the record of course.' He shrugged. 'We turn a blind eye to it, so long as they don't overdo it.'

Amos could see that Ryland was hedging, playing for time, or maybe looking for a good reason not to say too much.

'You saying one of your mechanics could have done a job fitting bull bars without your knowledge?'

Ryland sat forward a little too quickly. 'No, not saying that. They pay for the spare parts; we just let them use the workshop. So we would know who's doing what.'

'So who took delivery of the bull bars and who fitted them?'

Ryland spun round in his chair and positioned himself in front of a computer screen. He tapped a few keys and eventually came up with the information Amos wanted.

'We fitted a set of bull bars to a Jeep last week.'

'Owner?'

Ryland looked back at the screen again. 'A Mr Mason.'

Amos wanted to clap his hands. He was a lot closer now. 'You want to print that invoice out for me?'

Ryland hit the print button and immediately a printer sprang into life across the room. He got up from the desk and picked up the printout which he handed to Amos.

Amos took it and folded it into his pocket. 'Thanks. I'll be in touch.' He walked out of the office feeling a lot taller than when he walked in.

Ryland watched until he saw him climb into his car and pull out of the parking lot. Then he picked up the phone and tapped in a number.

Babs Mason was driving along the interstate highway when her cell phone rang. She picked it up from its holder on the dash.

'Babs Mason.' She listened carefully and thanked Ryland for the information. She switched the phone off and hurled it on to the front passenger seat beside her.

'Damn you, Amos! Damn you!'

She put her foot down hard on the throttle in anger and wondered how on earth they were going to get the detective off their backs.

Demski had to buy a new jacket and a pair of trousers after discovering that his had suffered scorching in the fire. He didn't feel too bad in himself, happy that he had escaped the inferno intact. But after a long soak in a bath and fresh clothes, he felt much better outwardly. Inside he was still raging over the brutal attack on Gunter Haman and himself. It didn't take much to figure out that he had been a bit naïve in thinking he was safe from the Nazi thugs who had murdered Franz Weber and his nurse. They had obviously infiltrated much of the German security services and border police; otherwise they would never have known he had returned to Germany. He knew that he had to be on his guard and finish his business as quickly as he could and get back to the States.

He decided to keep the hire car he had and dump it later if necessary. His immediate thought now was to get out of the hotel and head for Switzerland, remembering to keep one step ahead of anyone who might be tailing him.

The drive to the sanatorium took about eight hours. He had set off very early in the morning and arrived late afternoon. After parking the car, he went through to the main entrance and asked to see Sister Maria. It was the same nun who had been at the desk on his one and only visit. She phoned through and within a few minutes, Sister Maria appeared.

Although it had only been a week or so since he had last seen her, Demski thought she looked a lot older. The moment she laid eyes on him, her demeanour seemed to change. It was as though she was about to face the inevitable and the only way to deal with it was to adopt a fatalistic approach.

'Mr Demski,' she began as he shook her hand, 'I wondered if I should see you again.'

'Is there somewhere we can talk?' he asked.

She lifted her hand and gestured towards a door on the other side of the hall. 'There is a private room in there.'

Demski followed her into a small, adequately furnished room. A plain window allowed natural light in and helped to brighten the dullness of the plain furniture. She indicated an upholstered dining chair. It matched one other that was positioned on the opposite side of a small table. There was a settee in the room, but Sister Maria chose to ignore it.

'How can I help you?' she asked once she was settled. Her voice showed signs of tension.

Demski wondered how he should begin. What he was about to tell her was something he knew to be true, but not whether this elderly nun had any knowledge of it. But he knew that two people had died because of his and Gunter Haman's investigation, and an attempt had been made on their lives back in Germany. He could think of only one way.

'The woman who is buried in my grandmother's grave is not my grandmother.'

If Demski expected to see Sister Maria reel back in shock, he had another think coming. She merely acknowledged his statement with a philosophical movement of her shoulders and a small change in her expression.

'Since your visit,' she began, 'I have had sleepless nights.' Her eyes were cast down, and now she lifted them and looked straight into his. 'I wanted to take my burden to the Holy Mother, to ask God for forgiveness.' She shook her head, her eyes beginning to glisten with tears. 'But I had committed no sin other than a childish error of judgement.'

'Why, what happened?'

She took in a deep breath to steady herself. It finished almost in a sob. 'The woman who is buried in that grave came to us in 1945. She had papers identifying herself as Rosmaleen Demski. She lived quietly in one of the private rooms, on her own. From time to time she would have a visitor, but most of the time she carried her baby without any support other than what we could give her.'

'She was pregnant?'

Sister Maria nodded. 'It wasn't obvious at first, but her condition soon became very clear. We wondered why her husband rarely visited, but we decided it was none of our business; she was in good hands here.' She stopped suddenly, her face brightening. 'Oh, I'm sorry. How very rude of me; I should have offered you a coffee or a cold drink.'

Demski put his hand up and shook his head. 'No, nothing thank you. Please go on.'

He could see that simply by beginning to unburden herself, Sister Maria's tension was ebbing away.

'By the time the young woman had reached the end of her pregnancy, it was obvious there would be a problem. We wanted to transfer her to the hospital in Bern, but ...' she shrugged. 'The war had brought so many casualties fleeing from Germany. People were sick with disease, starvation and all manner of illnesses. Our hospitals were overwhelmed. We couldn't contact her husband because we had no idea of his whereabouts or even who he was. She would only ever refer to him as Heinrich. So there was no way we could ask him to bring some pressure on the hospital to admit her.' Sister Maria's eyes clouded over for a moment and she looked forlornly at Demski. 'She died giving birth to a beautiful baby boy.'

Demski immediately thought of the inscription on the headstone: *E.B. and Child*. He knew there was more to come.

'It left us with a major problem,' Sister Maria was saying. 'The young infant would need to be taken care of while we disposed of his poor, dead mother. There were no relatives to hand him over to, so it meant that we would have to care for the child until the authorities could take him off our hands.'

She paused again and studied the backs of her hands. They were thin and bony. 'I delivered that baby with these hands,' she told him. 'I was a novice at the time. I thought it was my fault that the mother had died.' She looked up at the window, recalling the events in her mind's eye. Outside the wind rustled through the trees in gentle gusts. She looked back at Demski.

'Then something remarkable happened; something quite extraordinary. A young American woman gave birth to a stillborn infant at the same time. The birth had been quite traumatic and the poor woman went into a coma. She had no idea that her child was dead. Even though I was a novice, I could see that there was a way to solve the problem that had been thrust upon us by the death of a young mother and the stillborn infant.' Her expression changed and became quite stern. 'You must understand that my actions were those of an inadequate novice who was innocent enough to speak her mind.' She allowed herself a small chuckle. 'I hadn't had discipline hammered into me; too young.'

Demski smiled too. He said nothing and waited for Sister Maria to carry on.

'We switched babies,' she said.

Amos arrived home late in the afternoon. It was getting dark. As he pulled into his drive he could see his daughter's pink bicycle lying on the front lawn. It was her new bike; one he had bought her for her birthday. He made up his mind to warn her about leaving her possessions lying around for others to steal.

He climbed out of the car, weary from his mental exertions during the day and from the daunting task of building a case against Babs

Mason, who he was convinced was up to her neck in the death of Bill Mason. Trouble was he had no hard evidence and precious little support he could rely on from the precinct officers. This was because of his conviction that Mason's backers had infiltrated the police department.

There were no lights on in the house. He locked the car and wondered why the house appeared empty. Little alarm bells began ringing in his head. He tried to ignore them but found his foot-steps quickening as he walked round to the back of the house. His heart starting beating faster; trip hammers sounding in his chest.

He pushed the back door open and stepped inside the kitchen. It was in darkness, and the only sound he could hear was from his daughter's television which was permanently on in her bedroom. He dropped his briefcase on to the table and went through into the lounge and called out.

'Judith!'

There was no answer.

'Judith!'

He went upstairs two at a time and flew into his daughter's bedroom. 'Holly?'

The TV set flickered away at him in the corner. On her small writing table were the open pages of the little story she was working on for her school project. But there was no sign of his daughter. He turned quickly and went downstairs again, his heart now racing and his breathing beginning to rasp in his throat.

'Judith! Holly!'

Still no answer. He rushed outside and ran to the bottom of the garden where he had a shed. He knew it was pointless looking, but he had to. There was no one there. He went back to the house and reached for the phone, dreading the thought of what he was about to report in to the Precinct HQ. He could feel his hand shaking.

'Amos, you're home early.'

He spun round as his wife came through the back door followed by his daughter.

'Where've you been?' he asked, the fear still hanging in his voice.

'We were next door.'

Holly ran round her mother and threw herself at Amos. 'Hallo

Daddy!'

He looked down at his daughter as though he wondered where she had come from. Then it all fell into place and he scooped his daughter up into his arms. The fear that had crawled its way into his body was now being pushed out as relief flooded into his bones.

'Hallo sweetheart,' he said as his little girl tried to squeeze the life out of him; something she always did. His wife turned the kitchen light on and came over to him.

'Amos, you look shattered. Want a beer?'

She kissed him and he felt as though he was going to burst into tears. He was thankful that he had his daughter's little frame to hide behind. He let her down and kissed his wife.

'Yeah, thanks Judith. I'd love a beer.'

And suddenly his family was complete again and he was able to put his fears away. But it had frightened him and made him realize how paranoid he was getting. Amos had never forgotten the time he had sat in his car and listened to Doctor Robertson telling him how his daughter had been threatened.

He took the beer from his wife and promised himself he would say nothing. Having one paranoid family member in the house was quite enough, he decided, without frightening his wife.

It was a simple statement, spoken with an open simplicity; or at least, the simplicity that had put the thought into a novice's mind. But the repercussions of that act were probably going to have enormous consequences because of who the surviving child's father was.

'Just like that?' Demski asked with utter disbelief in his voice.

She shook her head. 'At first the Sisters were horrified, but soon they began to see how they could prevent a mother from the anguish of knowing her child had been stillborn, and also give the other child a mother.'

'But it couldn't have been that easy, surely?'

Again she shook her head. 'Sister Francesca, she's dead now; been dead years. She took the woman's husband into a side room and explained that his wife had given birth to a stillborn child. She went on to explain that because of her condition, that she was in a coma, there was every chance that once she woke, she would not be able to withstand the shock of knowing she had lost her son. She could suffer a trauma from which she may never recover.'

Demski frowned at her. 'Is that true?'

She smiled. 'Probably not, but it was up to the husband to make the decision. He was only young, about twenty; just a boy really. His wife was about the same age. You must understand that a man would not grieve for a stillborn son in the same way as the mother. Men are very stoic about these things. Or at least, they were,' she added tightly. 'He could see that there was no need for his wife to suffer. He could bear the loss much easier than she would have done. So for the sake of his wife, and for the sake of the motherless infant, he agreed.'

'He was an American, right?' Sister Maria nodded. 'So what was he doing in Switzerland?'

'Oh, something to do with the SOE; the Special Operations Executive,' she told him. 'They were based in Switzerland so they could manage their spies from a neutral country. Very convenient.'

'So the baby would have been registered here as the son of this couple. And no doubt he would have been registered with the consulate to the embassy as an American.'

She nodded. 'Yes, of course, that was the way.'

Demski had been leaning forward. He hadn't realized it either, and as he relaxed he settled back in the chair. Now it was very clear; Bill Mason had agreed to accept the son of Eva Braun as his own. But the question that now puzzled Demski was whether Mason had known the identity of the baby's mother. He asked Sister Maria.

'Oh no,' she replied, shaking her head vigorously. 'It wouldn't have done to release any of that information. It wouldn't have helped anybody.'

'Do you know, or did you know the identity of the woman who called herself Rosmaleen Demski?' he asked.

'No. As far as I was concerned, that was her real name.'

'So nobody knew?'

She shook her head.

'And no records were kept of this?'

Sister Maria straightened up in the chair. 'Sister Francesca was a stickler for keeping accurate records. It's all recorded, but has never been made public.'

'That's tempting fate, isn't it?' he suggested.

She smiled sweetly. 'We don't believe in fate.'

Demski accepted that. 'Of course you don't. But if someone came across those records, it would become public knowledge.'

'No one is likely too,' she told him. 'I'm the only one who knows where they are.'

He almost felt sorry for her. Her naïvety was staggering. He had managed to get this far without too much effort beyond instinct and deduction. The Nazi thugs who tried to murder him and Gunter Haman may not have had that knowledge, but it was certain that their leaders knew. And that was the reason they were willing to kill to keep it secret.

Now Demski knew what, but he didn't know why.

TWELVE

BABS YAWNED, NOT *from boredom, but from tiredness. The effort of recollecting such a traumatic period in her life seemed to be depleting her strength. The young writer was not bullying her into revealing personal and private moments because those moments were virtually public property. She had been drawn willingly into a plot to destabilize American foreign policy, re-write the Constitution and rid the American way of life of what her evil cohorts often referred to as the cancerous underbelly of the American nation. They meant the Jews and the Blacks, and anybody else who did not fit in with their zealous ideology.*

'What do you think was the reason it changed?'

Babs covered her mouth as she finished yawning. 'Two things, I should think. One was when Demski uncovered the facts about my husband's birth, and the other was when a Jewish police officer was appointed captain at the 7th Precinct.'

'Why would a Jewish policeman's appointment have affected the organization's plans?'

Babs looked at her as though she was stupid. 'It meant Lieutenant Amos had an ally. When Captain Holder was running the precinct, they had control, and people like Amos could not achieve anything that ran counter to the way the operation was proceeding.'

'You mean Captain Holder could screw up any investigation he chose?'

'What you have to realize is that my husband's elevation was absolutely paramount to Die Spinne; if we had lived in California that is where their key strategy would have been implemented. They

had Newark running like a Swiss watch; complete control. Other states were being drawn in slowly, but Newark was the key. They couldn't have a police investigation drawing attention to them; it would have stopped the organization in its tracks.'

'But the Nazis were prepared to stop others in their tracks?'

'They had too!' Babs gave her a withering look, then turned her face away and studied the far wall of her cell. 'An ordinary cop and a Jewish gangster; who would have thought it?' She glanced back at the young writer. 'It should have been easy, but it wasn't.'

Amos was behind his desk wondering how he could bring his investigation out into the open when his new captain knocked on the door jamb.

'Got a minute, Lieutenant?'

Amos got up from his chair and nodded. 'Sure thing Captain.'

Captain Paul Dubrovski was a young, career policeman. Amos had not been impressed when he had been introduced to the precinct by the former chief of detectives, John Holder, now chief of police. He thought Dubrovski was a Holder clone, and would only be impressed by targets, discipline and subservience to his position in the precinct house. Amos had never aspired to rise any higher than the rank of lieutenant, even though he believed he would make a damn fine chief of detectives, and he couldn't see any good coming of Dubrovski's placement in the 7th Precinct.

The young captain asked Amos to sit down. He closed the door and settled himself behind his desk, facing Amos.

'We haven't had a great deal of time to talk, have we?' he began.

Amos pushed out his bottom lip and gave a shrug in acknowledgement. 'Been busy, Captain,' was all he said.

Dubrovski hunched forward. 'Tell you what; how about, when that door's closed, I call you Amos and you call me Paul?'

Amos's eyebrows lifted in surprise. 'Sure thing, Paul; if that's what you want.'

Dubrovski nodded vigorously. 'It might not make us friends, Amos, but it sure is a hell of a lot more comfortable. You want a coffee?'

Amos was thinking carefully, not wanting to be drawn into a cosy, contrived relationship that might impact on his police work and his ability to work without preconditions.

'I'll take a rain check on the coffee, Paul. I've just had one,' he lied.

'Fair enough. Now,' he said with the manner of someone keen on getting down to business. 'What case are you working on, Amos?'

Amos wondered where this was going. It was a strange question. 'A couple of homicides, an arson attack, a hold up at a drug store.' He opened his hands in an empty gesture. 'Plenty of cases around.'

Dubrovski's head bobbed up and down in small, rapid movements. 'But what about the ...' He paused and lifted his chin slightly, giving him a thoughtful look. 'What about the special case you're working on?'

Amos felt the skin on his face tighten. 'Special case?'

'Yeah, you know; Bill Mason's accident.'

Dubrovski had thrown him a curved ball. He hadn't seen it coming. 'Just clearing up a few loose ends,' he muttered unconvincingly. 'Nothing special, really.'

'You want to tell me about it?'

Amos shrugged. 'Not a lot to tell, really. It was an accident and somebody got killed. It's standard procedure to follow it up.'

'By a lieutenant? Couldn't uniform handle that?'

Amos felt he was being painted into a corner. 'They are. I was just poking around. Probably shouldn't have been, but sometimes you get a gut feeling about these things.'

'And?'

'And what?'

'Your gut feeling, Amos. What does it tell you?'

Amos didn't know where or how far to take this. He could try and make up a weak excuse and wriggle out of it, or he could come clean with the captain. If Dubrovski was indeed a Holder clone, then he would be in the chief's pocket, and Amos's investigation would be dead in the water. He knew that the Masons had powerful friends and he was convinced they were involved in the deaths of Senator Ann Robbins, Bill Mason and the chief medical examiner for the county. He had no proof and only circumstantial evidence which would never hold up in a court of law. So how could he expect Dubrovski to sanction his own, private investigation? He decided to bite the bullet and see how far Dubrovski would run with it.

'I believe Bill Mason was murdered.'

Dubrovski didn't show any reaction other than a slight change in his facial expression. Then he said, 'What makes you think that?'

So Amos told him about the smear of paint and the bull bars. 'Why didn't you point that out to the investigating officer at the time?'

Amos shrugged. He couldn't tell Dubrovski the truth that he couldn't trust anybody in the police department when investigating anything to do with the Masons.

'Amos,' the captain went on, 'you've either got to trust me or not work here at all.'

Amos decided to try a different tactic. 'How well do you know Chief Holder?' he asked.

'Fine officer, credit to the force, could do with more like him,' he replied. Then he added: 'And all that bullshit.'

Amos put his head down and laughed quietly to himself.

'I know you've been conducting an investigation into Mason's murder.'

Amos looked up sharply. 'How...?' The unfinished questioned died on his lips as Dubrovski held up his hand.

'I wouldn't be any good at my job if I didn't know what my officers were up to.'

Amos stared across the desk at his captain whose facial expression was like granite. There was a hardness there that belied the captain's young years. Amos thought he recognized a kinship in that face.

'My inquiry into Senator Ann Robbins death was terminated pretty quickly,' he told Dubrovski. 'I knew she'd been murdered but Captain Holder pushed for a verdict of natural causes. Heart attack, something like that. The chief medical examiner came up with the right report, of course, but not until he'd been persuaded into it.'

'How do you mean?'

So Amos told him about Doctor Robertson's daughter and the clip of hair.

'Shit!' Dubrovski let out the expletive and looked genuinely aggrieved as he tossed his head back. 'Then he committed suicide, right, Amos? Wasn't that what the report said?'

'It was rumoured that he couldn't live with his own deceit. He spoke to me about it and said he wanted to come clean but he feared for his daughter's life. We couldn't prove he was murdered.'

Dubrovski shook his head sadly. 'Corrupt bastards.' A thought struck him. 'Is this why you've been keeping your investigation under wraps?'

Amos told him about the syringe and how he had planted the information in Judge Lawrence's mind. 'Took them less than a couple of hours, I reckon, to switch the syringes.'

'You still got the original?'

'In my deep freeze at home.' Suddenly Amos had an overwhelming feeling of doom and wished he'd never said it, but Dubrovski managed to read his downcast expression and reassured him.

'Don't worry, Amos, I'm not about to raid your freezer.'

Amos smiled and felt a little better. 'I hope not.'

Dubrovski leaned forward, an earnest look about him. 'I want you to trust me, Amos. I want you to carry on with this investigation and I want a full report on your progress every couple of days. Believe me, I know a little more than you do and I know there's something going on; just can't nail it, though.'

'Well I don't know what they're up to, Paul,' Amos admitted. 'It doesn't seem right; just to get a guy elected.'

'It's political corruption, Amos. And if it's worth money and power, it's worth killing for. World never changes,' he added, shaking his head.

Then he stood up suddenly and pushed his chair back. Amos realized the interview was over and took Dubrovski's offered hand. At last he felt he had an ally in the Precinct. He would be putting that to the test now because his next move was to interview Babs Mason.

Isaac Demski stepped from the cab outside the offices of the American Jewish Council on Fifth Avenue in New York, his mind still dealing with his son Jack's call from Switzerland. He couldn't come to terms with the fact that the Nazis were still active and were resorting to their traditional methods of intimidation and murder. What soured him the most was the fact that Jack believed that the thugs were operating not only in Europe, but in the United States as well.

Isaac had contacted an old friend of his who had worked with the Simon Wiesenthal Organization in the hunt for Nazis who had fled Germany at the end of the war. He had passed on a name and hoped his friends could come up with any information that would help the Jewish community to discredit the Neo Nazis in America.

Jack had called a week ago with an incredible story about the baby switch at the sanatorium in Switzerland. He had given Isaac a name and then said he would be travelling back to Germany to find out how Gunter Haman was. He told his father that he would be in touch but for now he wanted to keep his head down.

The cab pulled away from the kerb and was lost in the flow of traffic as Isaac walked through the double doors of the impressive looking entrance at ground floor level. He walked up to the reception desk and produced his card, telling the young woman behind the desk that he had an appointment to see Maria Jankowski.

Maria Jankowski had arrived in America about the same time as Isaac. They had grown up together in the Bronx. Many of their friends believed they would marry and spend the rest of their lives together. But Maria had suffered terrible abuse at the hands of the Nazi prison guards, even though she had been a child, and had never recovered from the horror inflicted on her by sexually enraged men. As much as she liked or even loved Isaac, she had been turned off ardent, physical contact with men and remained single all her adult life. And Isaac's chosen lifestyle did not help either.

Maria welcomed Isaac into her office, accepting his kiss on her cheek and the traditional greeting of 'Shalom', genuinely pleased to see him.

'Thank you for agreeing to help me, Maria,' Isaac said to her as he released her from his gentle embrace.

'We don't see each other enough, Isaac,' she told him. 'And helping you is something I enjoy doing.'

She pointed to a leather armchair. Isaac walked over to it and made himself comfortable. Maria sat in a similar chair that had been placed at an angle, separated by a low coffee table.

'Would you like a drink?' she asked.

He shook his head. 'Thank you, no. I'm fine.' He looked around the office. It was well appointed and reflected the position Maria had become entitled to, working within the Jewish community. 'You've done well, Maria. It's good to see.'

She didn't blush, but felt a little self-conscious as Isaac paid the compliment. 'We've both come a long way, Isaac,' she reminded him. 'Thank God. Now, I do have some information for you, but you promised to tell me something that you couldn't tell me over the phone.'

He nodded. 'My boy Jack has uncovered something extremely disturbing. It's the reason I asked you to trace Heinrich Lörenz.' He began by telling her about Gunter Haman and the recurring dream, and his search for the truth about Rosmaleen Demski, Isaac's mother. 'I assumed, quite naturally that she had died in *Buchenwald*, but the SS brought her to Berlin, to the Reich Chancellery, in '45.' He knew that what he was about to say would not shock Maria, because she was beyond being shocked by anything the Nazis were capable of. 'She had been chosen, because of her age and her size, to die beside Adolf Hitler in place of Eva Braun.' He went on to explain briefly what had happened. 'Rosmaleen Demski was taken to the Chancellery by Hauptmann Heinrich Lörenz and his driver, Franz Weber. Gunter Haman was there. He was a boy soldier; Hitler Youth. Naturally he was unaware of what was about to happen. He told me that merely being in the presence of powerful Nazis frightened the life out of him. But what he saw ...' He paused, allowing compelling images of his mother to fill his mind. He felt incredibly sad at that moment, remembering what his mother looked like before they were dragged away to become part of the planned slaughter in the camps. He shook his head and his breath caught in his throat. He put a hand up. 'I'm sorry, Maria, even now I am overwhelmed by the memory of my poor mother.' He took a deep breath to compose himself. 'After my mother had been murdered, Gunter was ordered to burn the bodies. He followed orders, naturally, and eventually was able to live his life without thinking too much about what he had done. But when the dreams started it all came flooding back to him.'

'So he went in search of your mother's family,' Maria interrupted, stating the obvious.

Isaac gave a lopsided smile. 'He doubted that she had any family left, but he wanted to do it. He found me. I didn't think there was any more we could do, but it was Jacob, that's my son, Jack,' he explained, 'who wanted to know why Eva Braun had been spirited away from the Bunker and my mother selected to die in her place. He went to Germany to see Haman.' He thought of what he was about to reveal to Maria, and how incredible it seemed. 'They found the driver, Franz Weber, the man who took Eva Braun away from the Chancellery with Hauptmann Lörenz. He was being cared for by a nurse. He was quite old and infirm. They didn't get too much out of the old boy, but Jack went back to his house that night and found the two of them had been murdered.'

Maria's hand flew to her face. She certainly hadn't been expecting the dramatic change in events. 'Murdered?' she repeated.

Isaac nodded. 'Jack is convinced it was the Neo Nazis. He believes the old man was murdered to prevent him telling more than he already had. But Jack discovered that Weber and Lörenz had taken Eva Braun to a sanatorium in Switzerland. He found postcards and photos in Weber's home. He went to the sanatorium and learned about something that is absolutely incredible.' He then told her about the baby switch.

Maria had been listening with growing amazement at Isaac's account of Eva Braun's demise. Once he had finished, she stood up and walked across to the window. She stood there for a while, looking down at the traffic running along Fifth Avenue and the pedestrian hordes flowing like worker ants along the sidewalks. How many of them, she wondered, harboured secrets such as she had just heard that would rock the world? Precious few, she decided. But how many men in positions of power in the United States were privy to such a truth; a truth that they would use to change the course of American politics and the destiny of a nation?

She turned round. 'So the baby was handed over to Bill Mason?' He nodded. 'And now his son, Gus who is, in fact, Adolf Hitler's son, is set to become the next president of the United States?' He nodded again. She came over to him, her expression full of concern. It wasn't concern for Isaac or herself, but for all Jews who believed that the Nazi terror was past.

'You wanted to know about Hauptmann Lörenz. Well, he's dead of course, but I don't think that surprises you. It wasn't difficult to trace him; it's a matter of public record; just a case of knowing where to look. He was cleared of war crimes and was granted permission to settle here in America. He changed his name. He anglicized it and called himself Henry Lawrence. He married and had one son. That son carries the same name as his father. He is Judge Henry Lawrence of the Newark Judiciary. He's also a major player in Gus Mason's race for the White House, and when Mason becomes president, he is bound to appoint Judge Lawrence to the Supreme Court.'

'And all his other cronies,' Isaac lamented.

'Which means that the Neo Nazis will be in a position to dictate and change American policy against Jews and any other race of whom they disapprove. And with the son of Adolf Hitler at the head of the most powerful nation on earth, it will be a prolific rallying call to all the Nazi thugs who hide behind the freedom won by the deaths of millions.'

She sagged into the chair beside Isaac and took his hand. 'God help us, Isaac, but Mason has to be stopped.'

The conference room of the Zuckerman hotel on Eighth Street overlooked the New York skyline. It was of little interest to the five men who sat around the oval table discussing business that would have been of interest to the NYPD, even though officers of the New York Police Department were aware the meeting was taking place.

The air conditioning worked continuously to remove the fog of cigar smoke that permeated the room. The five men seemed unaware of the almost toxic conditions having spent many hours in smoke filled rooms talking over the fiefdoms that they ran.

Between them they controlled one of the biggest crime syndicates in America, second only to the Italian Mafia. These were the top men of the Jewish Brethren whose empire covered most of the states in America. Their big operations were concentrated mainly along the East Coast, the southern states and California.

There were no notes taken at this meeting and no recordings. The room had been swept for electronic bugs and none of the men carried any weapons. To all intents and purposes, this was a legitimate, but informal business meeting.

Sitting at the head of the table was Isaac Demski. He was the head of the organization; top man. When Isaac called a meeting, which happened about every six months, his opposite numbers all made the effort to attend. Usually they all knew what the meeting would be about and always made sure they were up to date with facts and figures that Isaac, or any of them for that matter might be asked for.

But today, this meeting was unexpected and had been called in a hurry. The previous hour had been spent in discussing sundry matters because they had been told that nothing could be concluded until Isaac's son, Jack turned up. They were all curious, but none of them complained about the wait.

Eventually there was a knock at the door and Jack Demski came in. He was carrying a folder which he dropped on the table in front of his father. He kissed him lightly on both cheeks.

'Shalom.'

He acknowledged the other men in the room and took his seat beside Isaac.

'I'm sorry I've had to keep you all waiting,' Isaac began. He glanced quickly at his son. 'Most of you have met Jack. He has just returned from a trip to Europe. It wasn't a vacation either; it was business. He has learned something that could have repercussions in America, particularly among the Jewish people here.'

Jack waited until his father had finished before addressing the men sat around the table.

'You all know my father's history. Some of you have suffered in the same way at the hands of the Nazis. Some time ago, we were contacted by a German national called Gunter Haman. He had an amazing story to tell us. As a result of that we invited him over here to talk about it and subsequently I went to Germany with him and learned something quite incredible.' He then related to them the whole story and the bizarre truth he had uncovered.

'My father and I understand that Gus Mason is the baby that was switched. It means that he is Eva Braun's son; Hitler's progeny. As you know he is almost certain to be elected as the Republican nomination for the presidency. The way things are, he will become the next president of the United States.' He could sense a feeling of horror running round the table. 'He has powerful supporters in the judiciary and the military, and he has many leading industrialists eating out of his hand. We also know of the backing he has received from the Klan.' This was the Ku Klux Klan. 'We believe that once he is in power, he will elevate several of those men into important positions of power with the intention of changing domestic and foreign policy. And we've got to stop him.'

He picked up the folder and opened it. 'My father had a meeting with Maria Jankowski at the Jewish Congress. They talked a great deal about the baby switch and what it could mean to America.' He looked down at the folder. 'In here are some details of the men who could be elevated into key places once Mason is president. I'll read them out.

'General Mort Tyler. He is one of Mason's main sponsors. He joined the Army in 1968 while still a member of the Young National Socialists in Texas.' He glanced up at the men. 'A euphemism for Nazis.' He went on. 'He had to relinquish all contact with the movement, but retained his beliefs and support for extreme right wing groups. Highly decorated, he is about the most popular soldier since Eisenhower. We believe he would become head of national security.

'Judge Henry Lawrence of the Newark legislature. He is the son of Hauptmann Heinrich Lörenz, the man who took Eva Braun to Switzerland. Hauptmann Lörenz avoided prosecution by the Nuremberg War Crimes Commission and settled here in America. He changed his name to Henry Lawrence and named his son after him. Lawrence backed Mason when he first entered politics and would almost certainly be elevated to the Supreme Court once Mason is in power.

'Chief of Police, John Holder; a Mason lackey. His rise up the ladder has been swift and supported by Lawrence. Most likely to figure highly in Mason's government, possibly as White House Chief of Staff or perhaps holding a key position alongside Mort Tyler.

'These appointments are all presidential, but each man will bring with him a second in command in their own particular chain of command. They will certainly be able to wield influence in key areas of policy.'

'So why should we worry about these three guys?' someone asked.

Jack looked across the table at Zeek Davidoff. He was the West

Coast boss. Born in Poland, he was named Ezekiel by his parents, but on settling in America he had to get used to the local boys calling him Zeek.

'We are looking in to all of Judge Lawrence's known associates, and those of Mort Tyler. We know they have very influential backers in industry, particularly weapons manufacture and communication, but naturally they will always remain faceless. And if Lawrence's organization is working from a position of strength, we have to assume they have other men in place that would bend the knee, so to speak.'

'That's a lot of people in a lot of states,' Davidoff observed.

Jack acknowledged that. 'I agree, Zeek, but it depends what they are offered.'

'So what are you and your father afraid of?'

'Zeek, the last time the Bill of Rights was questioned publicly, it was in 1944 by President Roosevelt. Now, most Americans would consider the Bill of Rights to be sacrosanct. It gives them the freedom men and women have died for. But nothing is permanent in this world, and it would not be beyond a powerful, right wing government to modify it.'

'That's shit, Jack, and you know it.'

Jack shook his head. 'So why did the Nazis murder an old man and his nurse, and why did they try to eliminate me and Gunter Haman if they didn't have something they believed was worth protecting?' Nobody answered. Jack went on. 'We have to make sure that their plans, whatever they are, do not see the light of day.' He sat down.

There were murmurings of discontent around the table. Isaac put his hand up and waited until the noise had subsided.

'You guys have to look out for the lunatics in your own neighbourhood. Bring some pressure on them.'

A big man known as Levi lit a cigar and shook the match until it went out. He then waved the smoke away from his face. He was a union man, big name in the trucker's union.

'You want these guys taken out, Isaac?'

Isaac shook his head. 'Not yet, Levi; first off we gotta make life difficult for them. Get them to see things differently.'

'Which they won't,' Levi said, casting a look up and down the men assembled there.

A taut smile crossed Isaac's face. 'Precisely, but we're going to give them a chance.'

'Which they never gave our folks,' someone lamented.

'Life won't be worth living if those Nazi bastards get in power.'

'We gotta be hard,' came a voice. 'We gotta look after ourselves.'

Isaac put up his hands. 'Gentlemen, if these idiots can do it, they'll change the American Constitution and we'll all be in the shit.'

'So we take them out!'

Isaac knew Levi would have loved to turn his men out armed to the teeth, but he didn't want it that way; the Nazis had a great deal of power on their side.

'No Levi,' he said sternly. 'We need a little more subtlety.'

'Why not make it public knowledge?' someone asked.

Isaac shook his head. 'We'd be made a laughing stock. There's no proof, other than that of an old nun. No, these guys will use Mason as a rallying point. They'll make it known once he's in power that he is Hitler's son. Then all the nutters in America will flock to their cause. Our only chance is to stop Mason before he becomes president.'

Babs Mason had been persuaded to take an office on the floor of the Tyler building, named after its owner, General Mort Tyler. The Republican Party occupied the top floor below Mort Tyler's penthouse suite. Babs had been reluctant at first because it 'politicized' her life and removed her sense of independence. She believed it was essential that a candidate's wife supported him but showed no strident, political leanings.

It was over a month since Bill Mason had been buried and the sense of shock still hadn't left her. Gus Mason's behaviour, on the other hand, was frightening and he seemed unaffected by his father's death. From time to time Babs would find herself thinking about Bill Mason and their lovemaking. It had been almost like a rebirth to her, and despite Mason's age, Babs had found him wonderful, loving and certainly energetic. It saddened her deeply that he was gone.

She found herself wondering about the relationship between her husband and his father; how there seemed to be little love lost between them. Mason's fatherly affection for his son had sometimes looked a little contrived; something which Babs put down to a man's inability to show outward affection to another man. There were occasions too, when Gus Mason seemed ambivalent about his father.

Babs was still dwelling on these thoughts when her phone rang. She picked it up. It was reception.

'Hi, Mrs Mason, we have a Lieutenant Amos here, says he would like to speak to you.'

Babs groaned inwardly. 'Can he come back another day?'

'He says not.'

Babs shook her head. 'OK, Jennifer, send him up.'

Five minutes later, Amos was ushered into Babs's office. He looked round at the trappings of success and wondered how someone like Babs Mason could endure what was a facsimile of hard earned rewards knowing that she had done nothing to achieve it. In his opinion it was all pretentious nonsense. Nevertheless, he greeted her cordially.

'Good afternoon, ma'am.'

Babs pointed to an upright chair that faced her desk. 'Good afternoon, Lieutenant.' She hadn't bothered to stand up when Amos had been shown in, and her manner showed a smidgeon of irritation. 'How can I help you?'

Amos came straight to the point. He knew he would waste precious time with any preamble. 'I'm investigating the accident in which Bill Mason died.'

Babs showed no emotion although Mason's death had affected her deeply, particularly knowing how it had happened as well. 'It was very sad,' she said.

'I have evidence that your Jeep was involved in a collision with Mason's Buick,' he told her. 'And I know that new bull bars were ordered and fitted to your car a couple of days after the accident. Would you like to tell me how that happened?'

Babs shrugged, showing colossal indifference. 'I crashed into Bill's car a couple of days before he died. There's nothing sinister about it. Why?' This was the way in which her husband had insisted the 'accident' would be explained.

'We've examined the scene of the accident quite thoroughly and believe that Mason's car was pushed off the road, probably by your Jeep.'

Babs pulled a face. 'You can believe what you like, Lieutenant, but I can assure you that is simply not the case.'

'Were there any witnesses to your shunt with Mason's car?'

She shook her head. 'No. It happened at Bill's place. We were just about to leave for Hutton. Bill normally takes the dirt road, but that particular morning he chose to take the main road into town. It caught me by surprise because I was behind him.'

'So you weren't on the dirt road into Hutton?'

Babs shook her head. 'No, I've just told you; we were on the main road. I've no idea why he decided to drive back along the dirt road; I'd left by then.'

'It happened very early in the morning,' Amos reminded her. 'What were you doing at his ranch that early?'

Babs looked perplexed. 'I don't see that is any of your business, Lieutenant, but since you ask, I followed Bill home after the banquet at Mort Tyler's place. I wanted to make sure he got home in one piece.'

'Was he drunk?'

'Why, does it matter now?

Amos conceded that point.

'Why did you wait until after Mason's death before taking your car in for repair?'

'Too busy.'

Amos always knew it would be a struggle. There was no way the woman was going to admit knocking Mason off the road. Her story was virtually water-tight, and he couldn't see a way of catching her out. Not yet.

'We've questioned the catering company who supplied the staff for Mort Tyler's function the evening before your father-in-law died. One of them recalls seeing you and Bill Mason having an argument. Would you like to comment on that?'

She shook her head. 'No.'

Amos watched her carefully, looking for some sign of nerves. 'When Bill Mason left Mort Tyler's place, he drove into Hutton. He went to see the editor of the *Hutton Chronicle*, got him out of bed at three o'clock in the morning. Told the man that he'd seen your husband, Judge Lawrence and Mort Tyler wearing Nazi uniforms? He insisted that the story should appear in the morning editions. Naturally the editor refused; said he needed something more solid than Mason's pretty weak testimony.'

'I know nothing about that,' Babs told him purposefully.

Amos arched his eyebrows. Babs Mason was showing an affected ambivalence that to him seemed like an attempt at protection; protection from her own guilt.

'Would you be prepared to take a lie detector test?' he asked her, and immediately saw a reaction in her eyes. The question had unsettled her.

'If you are going to charge me with my father-in-law's death, then I would agree. But not until you do, and only when I have my lawyer present, will I agree.' She had resumed her confident attitude.

Amos had no case, and he knew it, but he could scare her. 'I would also ask questions about the death of Senator Ann Robbins.'

Babs sat bolt upright. 'What are you talking about?'

Amos spread his hands. 'It's perfectly simple, ma'am; I have proof that Ann Robbins was murdered. And now I believe that Bill Mason was murdered. And you are the common link between the two deaths.'

'My God, Lieutenant, you certainly are clutching at straws.' Her voice had ratcheted up a notch. 'Ann Robbins was killed over, what ...' she struggled with this for a moment. 'Over four years ago.'

'Killed?'

Babs flustered for a moment or two. 'Well, she died. You said you believed she was murdered. That's why I said she was killed.'

'And that's probably why you would never agree to a lie detector test,' he told her, 'it tends to catch you out.'

Babs glared at him. He could see she was calming herself down, drawing deep breaths in through her nose.

'Lieutenant, I think you had better leave now. If you don't, I will call my lawyer and bring a charge of harassment against you and your department.'

Amos stood up. He had a thin smile on his face. 'You wouldn't do that, ma'am, because of the negative publicity it would bring. If this gets out into the open, the press will have a field day.' He could literally see the blood draining away from her face. 'So let me warn you; I will be digging deeper and deeper until I can bring a charge of murder against you. And believe me, I will.' He had been leaning forward, his hands on her desk. He straightened. 'I'll show myself out.' And with that he turned and walked out of her office.

Babs sat there mortified. She knew that the lieutenant was right; if this got out into the open it would deal a major blow to her husband's chances of getting elected. She shook her head in despair; as one problem surfaced and was dealt with, so another one reared its ugly head. Amos was a problem.

She picked up the phone. 'Jennifer, get my husband for me, please.'

Gus Mason was over in California about ready to address a meeting of the American Society of Newspaper Editors when he took the call from Babs. He had wanted Babs with him on the campaign trail, but she had decided it was too early for her. The truth was she didn't want to overshadow her husband too much in the early stages of his campaign for the presidency. He realized that her involvement would be limited beyond interviews with the fashion and lifestyle magazines, all trying to build her up into a fashion and beauty icon, while the TV chat shows would also be clamouring for air time with her. Far better, they decided together, for Babs to join her husband when his stock was growing and she could complement it.

He listened carefully as Babs explained what had transpired through Amos's visit. Gus could feel a sense of foreboding building inside. He turned to his press secretary who was idling away at a laptop beside him and put his hand over the phone.

'Jack, this is private. Could you give me a couple of minutes?'

His press secretary nodded and left the room immediately. Gus lifted his hand from the phone.

'Babs, I've got half these damn editors eating out of my hand,' he told her. 'At the moment they'll print only the helpful things about me. I've got a couple of them in my pocket, no sweat; old friends of Mort Tyler. They'll back me all the way. But if they get a sniff of that damn cop, they'll drop me like a ton of bricks.'

'What do you want us to do?' Babs asked.

Gus gave it a few moments' thought. There was only one answer. 'Get hold of Mort Tyler, tell him what's happened. He'll fix it. Tell him nothing physical. Get him to check the cop out, see if we can get anything on him. But tell him we've got to stop him.'

He said goodbye and put the phone down, a look of thunder spreading across his face. Then he called his press secretary back in and fixed a smile on his face. Time to talk to the men who could make or break him, but none of them could do more damage than that damn cop back in Newark. He had to be stopped.

Amos had put together a file on the Masons and taken it through to Dubrovski. A couple of hours later the captain had walked through the department to Amos's office and closed the door behind him. He tossed the file on to Amos's desk.

'Dangerous stuff, Amos.'

Amos pulled the file towards him and waited for the captain to sit down. 'Dangerous for whom, Paul?'

'It's pretty sketchy. I can see the links but ...' he hesitated, then shook his head. He had a habit of squeezing his lips tight together when he had a doubt about something. 'I'd like to see something a little more positive. Circumstantial evidence isn't going to help anyone.'

Amos agreed. 'Trouble is I know they're up to something.'

Dubrovski leaned forward and put his hand flat on the desktop. 'They are powerful people now, Amos, and they've got powerful backing.' He reached forward and tapped the file with the tip of his finger. 'They get uncomfortable with this and they'll hang you out to dry, you know that, don't you?'

Amos nodded quickly. 'I know.' He shrugged. 'I put some pressure on Mason's wife; see if I could get a reaction.'

'And did you?'

'Threatened me with her lawyer.'

Dubrovski relaxed and sat back. 'I have something for you,' he said, smiling.

Amos brightened. 'Oh, what's that?'

'The Demski family are taking an interest in Gus Mason.'

*

Amos pulled out of the parking lot and slipped into the traffic streaming past the 7th Precinct building. He had a lot on his mind, particularly the revelation from Dubrovski about the Demski family. He shifted down and accelerated into the middle lane, passing a slow truck. It was dark and judging by the amount of traffic on the road he knew he would be late in getting home.

Dubrovski had told Amos a little of his heritage. In a nutshell, the captain was a Jew. His parents hadn't been involved in the holocaust although they had lost relatives, but because his parents were third generation Americans, they only had a vague notion of what family ties they had in Europe.

But the slaughter had cemented the hearts of the Jewish nation in such a way that no other event, save the second coming of the Messiah could do. People like Dubrovski felt empathy with those who suffered at the hands of the Nazis, but little else. Although the young captain wasn't a member of any Jewish group in New Jersey, he still had associates willing to bring him up to speed with anything that they believed might be of interest. And the Demski family were always of an interest to Dubrovski.

He hadn't been able to enlarge on the small piece of information he had, but he told Amos that he understood that Isaac Demski had met with leaders of the mob and discussed Gus Mason and his bid for the presidency.

Amos waited for the lights at the intersection to change, digesting the supposition that any extreme right wing group in power would be inimical to Jewish interests. It didn't matter whether the Jews were right wing themselves or not, Amos knew it was simply a question of them against the Nazis. And history says there would only be one winner.

So what was Demski up to?

He swung right as the lights changed and put his foot down. He had promised to take his wife and daughter to the movies, and he was already running late. He had phoned his wife as he was about to leave the precinct but there was no reply. He decided she was probably at their neighbour's place and put the thought from his mind.

Amos always had a warm feeling come over him as he drove into the avenue leading up to his home. It was where he could let the tension of the day melt away as he settled into the company of the two people he loved most in the world; his wife and daughter.

The headlights of the car swept across the front lawn as he turned into the drive, picking out Holly's pink bicycle lying on the grass. He smiled to himself thinking about the number of times he had asked his little girl to always bring her bike indoors when she had finished playing outside.

He stopped in front of the garage door and killed the engine. The headlamp beams faded away as he opened the door and levered his bulky frame out of the car. He noticed that the side gate was open, but he thought no more of it.

He picked up Holly's bike and took it through to the back garden, closing the side gate on his way through. There were no lights on in the house which was unusual. Then he noticed that the back door was open.

Without any more thought, he dropped Holly's bicycle and ran into the house, calling out as he burst into the kitchen. There was no response to his calls; the house was completely silent.

He ran into the lounge, then tore upstairs and ran through all the bedrooms, calling out, each time his voice pitching up louder and stronger. He could feel sweat breaking out all over his body. He knew there was nobody in the house, and somehow he knew that his wife and daughter were not in with a neighbour. They had been promised a trip to the movies and would have been waiting indoors for him.

He ran back downstairs as the phone started ringing in the kitchen. He let out a yell and picked up the phone.

'Hallo honey, where are you?' His heart was pounding and his chest was heaving as he fought for breath.

'Is that Lieutenant Amos?' a voice asked.

'Yes, yes,' he snapped. 'Who's this?'

'Sir, this is the county hospital. Your wife has been admitted as a result of an RTA.' Amos knew this meant a road traffic accident. 'She's in emergency at this moment.'

'What? What are you talking about?' He was shaking his head.

'Sir, you are Lieutenant Amos, are you not?'

'Yes, dammit!'

'And your wife's name is Judith Amos?'

'Shit, yes! Oh my God, what's happened?'

'I've just explained, sir,' the voice droned on. 'Your wife has been seriously injured in a traffic accident. She is in emergency right now.'

'My daughter, is she there?'

'I'm sorry, sir. Your daughter?'

'My daughter, for God's sake. Is she there? She's only thirteen. She would have been with her mother.'

'I'm sorry sir, there was no one else involved in the accident. Your daughter wasn't in the car. Your wife was on her own.'

THIRTEEN

THE YOUNG WRITER *put her pen down and looked across the cell towards Babs Mason, an overwhelming feeling of revulsion towards her. But she could see defeat in the woman's body language. Babs had reached that point in her confession where it was evident that the plan was beginning to unravel.*

'It all went wrong from there, didn't it?'

Babs Mason allowed herself a wry smile and continued fiddling with the material in her skirt. Her features were etched in shadowy lines as the trauma of reliving the consequences of the audacious gamble began to backfire.

'It shouldn't have happened,' she admitted. 'But they knew that if they had simply shot Lieutenant Amos, the police would never have allowed any inquiry to fall off the rails. It would have been an abrogation if they had let the investigation become contaminated by the influence they held in the Precinct.' She shook her head slowly, studying the cell floor at her feet.

'I think this was really when I began to change my feelings towards everything my husband and his unholy gang stood for. Gus murdered his father, there was no doubt about that, and I think it made me realize that Gus had known for a long time who his real father was. This knowledge gave him power; it was like an aphrodisiac.'

She looked up at the young woman. 'There were two unstoppable forces now: my husband and Mort Tyler. Gus was on his way to the White House and nothing was going to stop him. Mort Tyler was getting too big for his boots, and was beginning to use force without the subtlety it needed. And when I heard about the accident, I began to change.'

'In what way?'

Babs smiled. 'You will see.'

Amos stood at his wife's bedside looking down at her swollen face. Apart from a heart monitor beside the bed, the only sound in the room he could hear was her coarse breathing. He held her hand, which felt cold, and massaged it gently in his own. A saline drip was connected to her arm on one side. On the other was another drip. Although he could see her face, she was practically unrecognizable. He didn't know if she was aware that he was there because she was in a coma.

Amos was trembling inside with a combination of anger and fear. He was angry because Mason's thugs, and that was the only way he would think of them now, had violated his family. He was afraid too, because he knew why they had done this and he knew what his duty was as a serving police officer. But to carry out his duty would be to put a death sentence on his wife and daughter.

He had been in the hospital for three hours now, waiting until the surgeons had finished operating on his wife. During that time he had only spoken to one police officer; Captain Paul Dubrovski. The captain had arrived at the hospital within twenty minutes of receiving a phone call from the hospital switchboard; one that Amos had asked them to put out. It took the captain less than a few minutes to assess the situation and put into operation a massive hunt for Amos's little girl.

Dubrovski was standing in the room now. He had just walked in, closing the door quietly behind him. Amos hadn't heard, absorbed as he was by his wife's condition. The captain walked across the room and stood on the opposite side of the bed. Amos glanced over and nodded.

'Got a minute, Amos?' he asked softly.

Amos was reluctant to leave his wife's side, but he knew he would have to speak to Dubrovski. He let go of his wife's hand and followed the captain out of the room. A police office was sitting on a chair in the corridor. He stood up as the two men appeared.

Dubrovski ignored him and steered Amos towards the end of the corridor.

'We've spoken to all your immediate neighbours. From what we can make of it, Holly was snatched from the house. Your wife must have fought with them because she came running from the house and went after them in her car.'

'Any ID?'

Dubrovski shook his head. 'No. Usual thing; no one really saw anything. Your wife's screams attracted the neighbours' attention. Someone saw a black BMW shoot off down the road. Your wife must have been a couple of minutes behind.' He put his hand on Amos's elbow and faced him, edging a little closer.

'The press will have a field day with this, Amos. I'll try to hold them off, but it's going to be difficult. There's nothing you can do, so why don't you look after your wife until we get your little girl back.'

'Her name's Holly.'

Dubrovski nodded a couple of times. 'Yeah, sorry, Amos. We'll find Holly for you.'

He patted Amos on the shoulder and watched him as he walked forlornly back to his wife's room knowing that the cards were stacked against them; he genuinely feared for Holly's life.

Jack Demski had been rebuffed by Babs Mason. His attempt at getting a meeting with her had been turned down with the uncompromising statement that she had no wish to associate herself with the family. Demski wasn't surprised, but he knew he would have to talk to her whether she was willing or not.

Babs finished the work her husband had asked her to do that day and took the elevator down to the underground car park. Jack Demski was sitting in a black Mercedes between two other high powered cars, waiting for Babs Mason to appear. As soon as Babs pulled clear of the car park exit, Demski's driver gunned the motor in to life and pulled out into the traffic ahead of her. The other two cars followed.

Babs had been assigned a bodyguard, but she had insisted he would always use another car. She had no intention of letting a stranger control her life. The bodyguard followed Babs out of the car park, unaware at that moment that there were two cars following behind.

Demski's driver kept to the nearside lane, driving at a relatively sedate pace until Babs moved up alongside them, unaware that she was the object of their attention. The three cars followed her out on to the beltway and kept a discreet distance behind her. Babs kept within the speed limit for a while, but soon began to exceed it. She wasn't worried about speeding fines because of her connections.

The first of the three cars pulled ahead of Babs while Demski's car pulled alongside. The third car moved up behind her which meant Babs was now separated from the bodyguard and part of a moving trap. At first she didn't connect the movement of the cars with herself, assuming they were making their own way up the beltway and would soon move off.

But then she realized that the three cars were slowly boxing her in. She hit the horn button and gestured wildly at Demski's car. There was no response. Babs sounded the horn again but could see there was to be no let-up in the provocative way in which the cars were hemming her in.

Checking her rear view mirror, Babs decided to slow up and force the car behind her to drop back, but what happened was so unexpected, she began to panic. The car did not slow up and Babs felt the two of them touch.

She lurched forward and almost hit the car in front. Demski's car kept station alongside her giving her no chance to move away. On her unprotected side was the Armco safety barrier, which meant there was no way out for her. She hit the horn button again, hoping that other motorists would see what was going on and maybe do something about it. But it was obvious that other drivers only had one thing on their minds and that was to mind their own business.

Up ahead Babs could see the junction exit and wondered if she could swerve off the road at that point, leaving the three idiots behind. But as the thought came into her mind, so did the realization that the others were coming with her. As she slowed they continued to slow with her and edge her towards the exit ramp. Babs had no option but to turn the wheel and continue along the exit road with her unwanted escorts alongside.

At the bottom of the ramp was a pull-off into a gas station. The three cars manoeuvred Babs into the forecourt and behind the main shop into the parking area. All four cars came to a halt. The driver of the third car, the one behind Babs, immediately leapt out of his vehicle and ran to the car being driven by the perplexed bodyguard. He tapped on the driver's window and pointed a gun at the man's face.

Babs waited, her hands trembling on the rim of the steering wheel. She couldn't see any of the occupants of the cars because of the blackened windows, so she waited. There was no choice for her; if she thought she could run from them, she had nowhere she could go and had no doubts that whoever was in those cars would soon catch her.

Eventually a figure climbed out of the car that had pulled up alongside her. He came round to the passenger window and waited for Babs to open it. As the window dropped, a man who she didn't recognize leaned in and spoke to her.

'Babs Mason?' She nodded but said nothing. 'This is a piece of friendly advice to you and your husband. Pull out of the campaign.'

Babs almost burst out laughing at the absurdity of the so-called friendly advice.

'I don't know who you are,' she snapped. 'Some bloody crank, no doubt, if you think my husband is going to pull out of the campaign.' She stopped. Who was this guy? she thought. 'Piss off before I call for the police.'

He smiled. It was quite disarming. 'We know the truth about your husband's birth right and your crazy little Nazi games. You've got one week. If your husband doesn't declare his intention to pull out, we'll go to the press.'

Babs sneered at him. 'You're out of your mind, whoever you are. And you're way out of your league. Now leave me alone.'

'One week. After that, if there's been no statement, we'll be back.'

Suddenly Babs realized who he was. 'You're Jack Demski.' She sounded surprised and relieved. 'You little shit; we'll have you for breakfast. Now out of my fucking way.'

She pushed the gear stick into 'Drive' and released the handbrake. Demski stood back from the car and waved the others away. He watched as she roared out of the car park and into the main stream of traffic. He felt satisfied for now. He hadn't expected anything other than what he had got, but now he had sown the seed of doubt in her mind and wanted to see some reaction from her and her hateful bunch of Nazis.

As the convoy of cars moved off, the bodyguard looked at the cell phone in his hand and shut off the call he was about to make to the cops. There was nothing left for him to do, so he slipped the cell phone into his pocket and followed Babs out of the gas station.

Amos was sleeping in the chair beside his wife's bed, dreaming about himself and Captain Dubrovski. They were sitting in the centre of a concentration camp, surrounded by Jews. A car came careening through the camp and crashed at their feet. His wife tumbled out and started screaming for Holly. He woke up and sat upright in the chair. He forgot the dream immediately and leaned forward, looking at his wife. She seemed to be sleeping peacefully. Amos had a bad taste in his mouth and needed a coffee, so he levered himself out of the chair and walked softly across the room to the door. The police officer was still sitting outside.

'Gonna get a coffee,' he said. 'You want one?'

The cop shook his head. 'I go off duty in thirty minutes. Thanks anyway.'

Amos sauntered off down the corridor thinking about Dubrovski and how serious he must have taken the threat to his wife by having a police officer posted outside the door. He had been told that his wife's accident was her own fault; she had driven through a junction at high speed and collided with another car. So why was the cop there? Was it to guard Judith or to keep an eye on Amos? He knew that sooner or later Dubrovski would be obliged to put a police officer with him permanently in case he decided to take the law into his own hands and go off on a wild search for his daughter. It would also be a safeguard against any of the kidnappers contacting Amos without the department knowing.

These thoughts continued running through Amos's mind as he helped himself to a coffee in the small kitchen at the end of the corridor. As he walked back to his wife's room, he began to think about Dubrovski and the Jews in his dream. He turned round before reaching the door and signalled to the officer he had forgotten to put sugar in his coffee.

He went back to the kitchen and put his cup down. He then went to find a pay phone. Although there was one in his wife's room with an outside line, he decided that he didn't want the cop outside the door to know he was making a call. It took Amos a while to find the number of the person he wanted, but only a couple of minutes to explain the situation. Then he went back to the room, put his coffee on a small table and resumed his vigil at his wife's bedside.

Thirty minutes later, Amos heard footsteps outside the room. He turned towards the door as it opened and the police officer who had been on duty popped his head in.

'Just going off duty, Lieutenant. Officer Steel is on. You want to speak to him?'

Amos shook his head. 'No thanks.'

The young man closed the door and left Amos to continue his vigil. Amos gave it about ten minutes and leaned forward, bringing his mouth up against his wife's ear. He whispered softly.

'Judith sweetheart, I don't know if you can hear me, but I've been doing a lot of thinking. I can sit here with you and wait until they find Holly, or I can go out there and find her myself. I know what you would want me to do, so I'm going to give it my best shot. I love you sweetheart. Always will.' He took hold of her hand and squeezed it gently. There was no reaction from his wife. Then he leaned closer and kissed her gently on the lips.

The cop outside looked up from the magazine he was reading as Amos stepped into the corridor.

'Just going to get a coffee. Be a couple of minutes.'

The officer nodded and went back to his magazine. About thirty minutes went by before he realized that Amos had not reappeared. He frowned and put his magazine down, then headed towards the kitchen. There was no one there, so he retraced his footsteps and looked in the room where Amos's wife lay. Amos wasn't there either. He noticed a cup on the small table beside the bed. He could see that it was still full of coffee. He swore and picked up the phone.

General Mort Tyler was not in the best of moods, having just received a call from Babs Mason about Demski's antics on the Beltway. She had sounded pretty upset, frightened almost. Tyler knew that the dangerous game they were playing was high risk, but he expected all his main players to accept that. The prize on offer was worth the gamble, and Babs Mason was a key player. Weakness was the last thing he would tolerate.

He considered the threat from Demski and decided that the man was pitching above his weight by threatening Gus Mason's chance of the presidency. Demski was a hood, a gangster, and understood intimidation and back alley murders. What he had never had to cope with was a full frontal assault by well-trained men. Although Gus Mason was now under 'light' security by the American secret service, there was no reason why they should be told of Demski's interest. If they picked up the head of the Jewish Mafia, he would shout his head off from the rooftops and the press would be all over it. Mason would be tarnished by any accusations Demski made, and all the denials in the world would not improve his chances at the election. No, Tyler knew he had to use his own men and get the problem solved in his own way. The press would then believe it was gang warfare. But Demski would be dead and that was all that mattered.

Captain Dubrovski got to the hospital as fast as he could, even though speed was not essential; Amos was not there. The young police officer could not be blamed for the lieutenant's absence. After all, he was only there to stop uninvited people going into the room. Dubrovski cursed his own lack of professionalism in not putting a police officer with Amos. It wouldn't have been the first time a cop had gone absent to deliver his own form of justice to a villain. In Amos's case it was pretty obvious he had got it into his head that he stood a better chance of finding his daughter than the police department. Bearing in mind the insidious control that Judge Lawrence had over the men who worked at the 7th Precinct, and up as far as Police Chief Holder, he could understand why Amos trusted no one. He arranged for a second guard to be posted at the hospital to compensate for Amos's disappearance and went back to his office hoping that the detective would get in touch with him. But he couldn't figure out why Amos had disappeared and where he thought he was going to go.

Gus Mason flew in from the state of California after enjoying a very successful campaign. There had been plenty of hand shaking, back slapping and promises of votes and funding during the visit. But behind the politician's veneer, Mason's heart was troubled. The latest developments involving his wife and the disappearance of Amos's little girl served no useful purpose other than to damage irretrievably his chances of making the White House. He had phoned ahead and asked for a meeting with Mort Tyler and Henry Lawrence. The limousine that picked him up from the airport took him straight to the Mort Tyler building and the office that the general used whenever he was in New York.

Mort Tyler and Judge Lawrence were in the room when Mason walked in. He tossed his briefcase on to a convenient chair and helped himself to a coffee as the two men stood up to greet him. He looked stressed out after the flight from the West Coast, and it showed in his demeanour towards the two men.

'You want to tell me what the fuck is going on here?' He kept his eye on the cup as he poured the coffee. 'I'm breaking my ass over on the West Coast while you're doing your level best to ruin my chances.' He slammed the glass jug down hard and looked at Tyler and Lawrence, anger blazing in his eyes. 'And who the fuck authorized the kidnap? What brain thought that one up?'

Mort Tyler approached him, a condescending smile on his face. 'Sit down, Gus. I know you're het up. You've had a long journey, so just calm down and let's talk about it.'

'And what about Babs? The Demski mob?' He sounded incredulous. 'They're nothing!'

Tyler put his hand on Mason's shoulder. 'That's all in hand. Babs won't be driving herself anywhere now; we're going to authorize a staff car and a permanent escort.'

Mason tossed his head back. 'She'll be bloody furious. One thing she values above all else is her independence.'

'There's no going back, Gus.' This came from Lawrence. 'The stakes are too high. No one is going to get in the way of your right to be president. We've got a lot of people in important positions who are there because we put them there. They will have more power than they ever dreamed of when we have control. And no jumped up little police detective or a gang of thugs is going to stop us. And if you want to know which brain authorized the little girl's kidnap, it was mine.'

Mason glared at him. 'What the fuck for? Why couldn't you just take Amos out?'

Lawrence shook his head. 'Taking Amos out would not have solved anything. We don't control the all the police departments in New Jersey. We have to show caution, Gus. We know Amos has his çaptain, Dubrovski on his side. Can't keep killing every damn detective who thinks he's on to us.'

Mason sat down and put his cup on the coffee table. 'So what happens now?'

'What happens now,' Mort Tyler told him, 'is that we deal with Demski.'

Mason looked away from the judge and fixed Tyler with a hard stare. 'And how do you plan to do that?'

'It's not your concern, Gus,' Tyler replied. 'All you have to do is keep pulling in the votes and acting like a president. We'll keep cleaning up behind you. We have more than enough men capable of taking on a few hoods.'

'Why is the Demski family involved in this?'

Tyler made a face. 'Demski told Babs that he knew the truth about your birth right; said you had to pull out of the election.' He raised his eyebrows and opened his hands in an empty gesture.

'But how would they know about that?'

Tyler shrugged. 'Demski was in Germany recently. He was with a guy called Haman. They went to see Franz Weber who was Hauptman Lörenz's driver towards the end of the war. He was in the Reich Chancellery at the end. They talked about Eva Braun and where she was taken to from the Chancellery. Weber's nurse reported the conversation to our Aryan League. The decision was taken by them to terminate Weber and his nurse.'

Mason raised his head a little in complete understanding of the warped justification laid on the act of murder; particularly that of the nurse who was only doing what she saw as her duty to the organization.

'Demski went to Switzerland, to the sanatorium. I think he realized we were on to him, but he managed to keep one step ahead of us.'

'But what made Demski go to Germany in the first place?' Mason asked.

'Gunter Haman. He was the German who contacted Isaac Demski. We discovered that he was in the chancellery as a boy soldier the day the Führer died.'

'How did you find that out?'

'Weber told the Aryan organization. Before they killed him,' Tyler added without emotion.

Mason switched his position and looked across at Lawrence. 'Your father was there. Did this German guy, Haman know about him?'

Lawrence nodded. 'We believe he did. So we kept an eye on Demski and Haman for a while. Demski went back to Germany. Our colleagues over there tried to take them out. They failed.' He said it simply, leaving out the spectacular details of the fire-bombing of Haman's place.

'So Demski's back here trying to finger us, is that it?' Mason asked. 'Can't we pay him off?'

Lawrence laughed. 'Don't be naïve, Gus; Demski is a Jew. He knows what we represent and will do his level best to stop us.'

'So that's why we've decided to take them out,' Tyler told him, 'the whole fucking bunch of them.'

'Don't you think that will draw attention to us?' Mason asked, seriously doubting the logic of such an action.

Tyler shook his head. 'We have enough influence with the press to make sure they see it as gang warfare. The public will believe what they read in the papers. And don't forget, Gus, you're hot stuff. The public won't have a bad word said against you. Anything else in the press and it will look like mudslinging.' He spread his hands. 'It's a cinch, believe me. Demski and his mob won't be a problem.'

Mason seemed to be satisfied at the general's explanation. His thoughts turned back to Amos's daughter. 'Where's the girl?'

'Best you don't know, Gus.' This was Lawrence who answered. 'She's safe and well looked after.'

'But what about Amos? He'll have the whole bloody police force breathing down our necks.'

Lawrence shook his head. 'Not so. He's disappeared. No one knows where he is.'

He then explained the situation regarding Amos's wife and the lieutenant's disappearance from the hospital.

Mason reflected on what he had been told and how the two men were managing the deteriorating situation. They didn't appear to be affected by it; they knew what they were doing. He conceded that they were right to keep him out of the loop because he needed to be fully committed to the campaign. And they were so close. Another week and the convention would be upon them, and he would almost certainly be selected as the party's candidate. It was that close he could almost taste it in his mouth. And he liked it.

'Right,' he said suddenly, looking at his watch. 'I've got the rest of the day off, so I'll spend that with Babs; we've got a busy day tomorrow.' He drained his cup and picked up the briefcase he had thrown on to the chair. 'Good day, gentlemen.'

The two men shook his hand and watched him leave. When he had gone, Tyler looked at Lawrence and heaved a big sigh.

'We're that close, Henry,' he said shaking his head and holding up his two hands. They were almost touching. 'That close.'

Babs Mason pulled up outside Bill Mason's place, spreading a cloud of dust as the wheels of her Jeep slowed to a halt. She hadn't been told of the change of plan that meant she would no longer be driving herself, but would have a chauffeur at all times. She hopped out and pulled the keys to the house from her handbag as she stepped on to the front porch. She paused for a moment, looking at the door and remembered the last time she had stood there. Bill Mason had opened the door. She could see him now, still handsome in the twilight of his years. Something stirred inside her and she felt a twinge of regret. Tears pricked the backs of her eyes and she blinked them away quickly.

She opened the door and stepped into the huge room that served as Mason's lounge. It was as if he had never left it. Nothing had been done to the place since the funeral; Gus had seen to that. He wanted no one to touch anything until he had been through his father's possessions.

She dropped her handbag on to a long sideboard and stopped. There was something odd, something she couldn't put her finger on. The house was quiet, but there was an eerie sense of a presence there. Babs didn't believe in ghosts and decided it was simply the fact that Bill had stamped his character on the place so indelibly, that there would always be something of him in the house.

She went through to the kitchen and lifted the kettle from the side. But as she picked it up, she put it down again. It was warm. She put her hand on the side of the kettle and was convinced there was some heat there. She looked around slowly and called out.

'Anybody here?'

There was no response and Babs told herself she was just being silly. The kettle was just beneath the kitchen window so it must have been the sunlight that had warmed it. She picked the kettle up and filled it with water, then put it on to boil. She decided she would need several coffees now because she was feeling a little edgy.

Babs had decided to take some time out of her daily schedule. She knew Gus would be arriving back from the West Coast and would expect to spend some time with her, even if it was only for the sake of appearances. When she reached Gus in California he told her he needed to get over to the ranch himself and pick up some paperwork. Babs knew that he would be terribly busy from the moment he touched down in New York, so she decided to be at the house when he arrived.

Once she had made her coffee, she began walking through the house, drinking the coffee and recalling fond memories of her time there with Gus's father. She began to open drawers and close them again, not really seeing anything in them. Her own reactions when she opened Mason's cupboards surprised her; she found herself becoming quite emotional. It was even worse when she realized that Bill had never thrown away any of the jackets or sweaters that she had bought him when they had been together during their first affair. She lifted the sleeves of the sweaters and could almost smell him. The tears came easily then and she had to leave the clothes alone and forget him.

As Babs was closing one of the wardrobes, she saw a small box on the top shelf. She pulled it out and opened it. Inside was a small hand gun; a Beretta. There was a box of cartridges with it. She immediately thought of Demski and decided she might be better off by having the gun on her should he come calling again. She took the gun and the cartridges through to where she had left her bag and slipped them in. Suddenly she felt a little more confident; having the gun in her bag gave her a lift.

She heard a noise coming from outside the house. She thought it might be Gus, so she went through to the front door and pulled it open. There was nobody there. She stood on the porch and looked around but could see nobody. She shrugged, deciding that she had imagined it.

Babs had no idea how long it would be before her husband arrived, so she decided to continue her trip down memory lane and walk around the ranch, recalling happier days. She knew that once Gus was president, there would be no freedom such as she was enjoying at that moment. She needed to make full use of it.

There was really only one place away from the house that could evoke fond memories of Bill Mason, and that was the barn where he kept his beloved Buick. She wandered across to the large shed and slid the door open. As it rolled back, Babs almost expected to see his car there. But it wasn't, of course. She walked into the barn and immediately saw a black Chevrolet Sedan.

As her mouth opened in a gasp, she heard a noise behind her. She was about to turn round when a hand came round to her face. Someone wrapped his arms round her and a soft cloth was pushed over her nose and mouth. Babs began to struggle and tried to scream out, but her vision clouded over and she felt herself being lowered to the ground. Then she blacked out.

When Babs came to, she was lying on the sofa. She lifted her head and looked around at the familiar surroundings. She sat up and put her hand to her head, trying to recall what had happened.

'Hey Babs, you're awake.'

Babs turned her head to where the voice came from as her husband walked into the room. He was carrying a cup of coffee.

'Looks like you've been having a quick nap.'

Babs sat up. 'What happened?'

'Eh?' He came over and kissed her, then sat down beside her. 'What do you mean?'

Babs looked puzzled. 'What am I doing here?'

Gus frowned. 'You're not making sense, Babs.'

She stood up and looked over at the clock above the fireplace. It was late evening. She spun round and ran to the front door. Gus put his cup down and went after her. As Babs got outside she saw Gus's car parked beside her Jeep and another car with Gus's bodyguards leaning up against it.

Gus came up beside her. 'You want to tell me what you're doing?'

Babs pivoted on her heel. 'Whose car is that in the barn?'

Gus screwed his face up. 'What car?'

She didn't answer but ran across to the barn. Gus followed her. The door yielded easily as she pulled it back and stepped inside. The barn was empty. Babs felt her whole body sag.

'There was a car here,' she told him.

'When?'

'This afternoon.' Her head snapped round. 'When did you get here?'

Gus looked at his watch. 'About fifteen minutes ago. Why?'

'And there was nobody here?'

He shook his head. 'Only you. You were fast asleep on the couch.'

Babs was stunned. Gus seemed quite relaxed about her manner. Perhaps she had been dreaming after all? But she was convinced that she had seen a car in the barn. She was now thinking about the sounds she heard in the house and the warm kettle. Had someone been there? And if so, what for? And why wasn't Gus concerned?

'I must have been dreaming,' she said eventually.

Gus took her arm. 'Come on; let's get back to the house.'

Babs allowed herself to be led back across the yard. The two men standing up against the escort car, standard issue Ray Ban sunglasses covering their eyes, were unaware of the little drama being played out, but watched with some interest.

Once inside the house, Gus briefed Babs on his meeting with Tyler and Lawrence. He kept out the sordid details but told her that she would no longer be allowed to drive herself but would have a car and chauffeur provided. It was for her own safety, he explained.

As he predicted, Babs was furious, but no amount of argument was going to persuade Gus she was to be allowed her own independence and freedom of movement. He also told her that it was time to get on the election bandwagon with him and be seen at his side more often. Despite her continuing objection, Gus beat her down with cogent argument until she relented and agreed to go along with his wishes.

He left her to her own devices for a while as he went through his father's papers, looking for the files he needed, although Babs didn't know what for. When he had finished, and they were about to leave, Babs went through to the back door of the house to make sure it was locked. Gus had said there was no need because no one had been there since the funeral, but Babs said she wanted to make sure anyway.

When she reached the rear door, she could see the key was still in the lock. She thought this strange because she knew Bill Mason never left his keys in the doors; he always put them in a drawer. Babs turned the key and locked the door, removed the key and popped it into a drawer.

Then she realized that the door must have been opened. That meant that someone had been in the house.

FOURTEEN

AMOS WAS SHOWN into Isaac Demski's villa after being frisked for a weapon. His police revolver was removed and left on a side table by one of the mob chief's huge minders. He was then taken through to a lounge where he was asked to wait.

Amos looked around the room at the trappings of wealth. He'd never seen such a display of quality and richness anywhere other than in films. Occasionally he would get to see similar gear during an investigation that took him in to the homes of some of the high flyers in his jurisdiction. But what he was looking at was an opulence provided mainly through the crime syndicate run by the Demski family.

It was late evening but he was just able to see the waters of the Hudson River, and the lights that dappled their blackness. He could see the silhouettes of large and small boats, their navigation lights showing dimly in the fading light. Soon these craft would be secure against their moorings and only the larger boats would be out there, running back and forth. He wished he could be there now with his wife and daughter, relaxing on somebody's yacht, without a care in the world. But instead he was caught in a nightmare from which he could see no escape.

A door opened and Jack Demski came into the room. Amos stood up and held out his hand. Jack shook it and asked Amos if he would like something to drink. Amos declined.

'So, Lieutenant,' Demski began, settling himself into a chair, 'strange call of yours. You sounded desperate, but I don't understand; how can we of all people be of help?'

Amos knew that Demski was alluding to the fact that they were on opposite sides of the fence, and would only get to speak to each other if the police were interested in the family's operations.

'My wife is lying in a hospital bed at this moment. She is in a coma and the doctors are not convinced she will recover.' Demski's expression of sympathy and curiosity only lasted a few seconds. Amos carried on. 'She was involved in a car accident going after the men who had just taken our little girl, Holly. My daughter is only thirteen years old.'

Demski back straightened. Amos's voice had no emotion in it, but the immediate statement of his daughter's kidnap had a distinct impact on him. Amos went on.

'I believe the people who did this are the men behind Gus Mason.'

Demski's interest sharpened. His expression changed as a deep furrow crossed his brow. 'Go on.'

'Under normal circumstances, I would expect to lead the hunt for my own daughter, but I cannot.'

'Why?'

Amos took a deep breath. 'I'd better start from the beginning, when Gus Mason was running for State. Did you ever hear of Senator Ann Robbins?'

Demski nodded. 'Yeah, she died, drowned in the lake. What, five or six years ago?'

And so Amos told him how he was convinced of Mason's involvement in her death and that of the chief medical examiner's change of heart. He told Demski everything he knew, or believed to be true, and how he also knew that the men who were behind Mason had some of his police officers on their payroll.

'So if I lead the hunt for my daughter's kidnappers,' Amos admitted. 'I know they will always be one step ahead of me. I would never find her.'

'So why have you come to me?'

Amos had given this a great deal of thought before he had phoned Demski from the hospital. 'I know your family are interested in Gus Mason. I also know you called a meeting this week to discuss him.'

Demski reeled back. 'How the fuck do you know that?'

Amos shrugged. 'How I know is not important. But what I believe is.'

'OK, I'll ask the question again: Why have you come to me?'

'I want you to find my daughter.'

It was almost midnight as four men climbed out the back of a nondescript van at Paulsboro refinery, just south of Philadelphia on the Delaware side of the Hudson River. They crossed the railway line and beat a path through the trees lining the banks of the river. All the men were wearing black fatigues and had balaclavas pulled over their faces. Each of them was carrying an AK47 rifle. One of them had an RPG slung over his shoulder. They clambered through the trees until they reached a clearing on the river bank. A small inflatable dinghy was tied up to a mooring post. It had an outboard motor on the rear board, lifted from the water. The last man into the boat lowered the outboard into the water and fired it up, using the pull cord. The engine roared into life and within seconds of climbing into the boat, the craft was powering its way down the river towards Bridgeport.

'Let me get this straight,' Demski said, his forehead creasing above his eyes. 'You want us to find your daughter?' Amos nodded. 'But you don't know where she is, and you can't lead the investigation because you believe it will be compromised.' Amos nodded again. Demski went on. 'And you believe that Gus Mason, or men connected with Gus Mason are responsible for taking your little girl?'

'Her name is Holly,' Amos told him.

'OK, Holly,' Demski responded a little irritably. 'So what's in it for us?'

'You get to find Holly,' was all Amos said.

Demski gave out a kind of half laugh and tossed his head back. 'Lieutenant, I'm sorry to hear about your little girl,' he held his hand up defensively, 'Holly. But what makes you think we could find her, and more importantly, what makes you think we want to get involved?'

Amos leaned forward in his chair. His expression had hardened and he even managed to look threatening, but he wasn't trying to intimidate Jack Demski; he was simply reacting to his own dilemma, and the fear of losing Holly for good.

'You want to get Mason off your backs for some reason.' He held his hands out in an open gesture. 'I don't know why, but you do. If you can find my Holly, and implicate Mason, then you'll get what you want and I will get my daughter back.'

The two men were quiet for a while, each one studying the other, weighing things up. Then Demski stood up.

'I'm going to speak with my father.' He glanced up at the ceiling. 'He's in his room at the moment, not too well, but he would need to make a decision on this.' He pointed a finger at Amos. 'But understand this, Lieutenant, if my father says no, you walk out of here and forget the whole business. Is that clear?'

Amos nodded. 'Very clear.'

The inflatable edged up to the bank beneath the private mooring that fronted Demski's place. The mooring was about a hundred yards from the house. There was a high wall that ran along the river bank and continued around the grounds of the house. Set into the wall was a security gate, unmanned, which gave access to and from the mooring. The four men climbed out of the dinghy and walked quietly up to the wall, pressing up close as one of them pushed a small wad of *plastique* explosive into the lock of the gate. A detonator was inserted into the *plastique* and attached to a small box. As the other three men stood clear, the fourth man pressed a button on the box. This was followed immediately by a small, but loud explosion. The gate flew open and the fourth man tossed the box into the river as the other three men ran through the opening and up towards the house.

'What was that?' Isaac Demski asked his son.

Jack was standing at the foot of his father's bed. He had spent about five minutes explaining the strange visit of Lieutenant Amos and the reason for it. But before he could give it a great deal of thought, the sound of the exploding *plastique* came thundering up against the house and rattled the windows.

Jack Demski spun round as the window shattered beneath a hail of bullets, each one peppering the wall alongside his father's bed. He dived for cover beneath the bed, pulling his father with him as he sought refuge beneath it.

The sound of returning gunfire could be heard, but it was practically lost as the four men literally hosed down the house with a hail of bullets. Then came the distinctive sound of the RPG being fired. The grenade screamed through the shattered, ground floor windows and exploded. It knocked out an internal wall and brought the ceiling crashing down on to the floor.

Demski pulled his father further underneath the bed, cursing loudly because he had no way of defending himself, and no way of letting his men know where he was. All he knew was that the men he had still in the house would be returning fire.

Another explosion rocked the house as a grenade exploded virtually beneath Jack's feet. He felt the floor tilt violently and suddenly give way. He struggled to hold on to his father as he began slipping away on the tilting floor, reaching out for anything he could grab hold of. Then it gave way and he felt himself falling. He heard his father call out but then nothing. He hit something hard which knocked the breath from his body, and then a terrific thump as his father fell on top of him. He passed out and the cacophony of ricocheting bullets and exploding grenades receded.

Ten minutes after the sudden attack, the four men were back in the inflatable and slipping away into the darkness of the Hudson River.

Dubrovski stood at the edge of the police tape surveying the scene of carnage. The police floodlights lit up the area like a film set, while the noise from the generators throbbed rhythmically in the background. The fire chief had declared the remains of the building safe, which meant the forensics teams could go about their business, and the paramedics could work among the dead and the injured as the coloured, flashing beacons from the police and emergency vehicles leant a surreal effect to the scene.

The alarm had been raised almost the moment the attack had reduced much of the building to rubble. Horrified neighbours had rushed out of their detached riverside homes in their nightclothes and witnessed a one-sided battle which they would talk about for years to come. It was too early for the police to gather coherent reports from the witnesses, but it was apparent that there would be very little for them to act on. Already the word was going round, put out by Mort Tyler's propaganda machine, that this was a gangland feud that had boiled over into all-out war.

Dubrovski had been hauled from his bed at about an hour after midnight, and was now standing inside the police cordon waiting for an opportunity to inspect the scene of the crime himself. It was obvious there had been more than one death, judging by the bodies lying covered on the ground. He was aware there were others inside the rubble but no numbers had been passed on to him.

A police sergeant approached carrying an evidence bag. He handed it to Dubrovski.

'This was found lying on the grass near the front of the house, Captain.'

Dubrovski took the bag from him. Inside the bag was a police revolver. Dubrovski studied it for a moment, feeling its weight, and then looked at the sergeant.

'Police weapon?'

The sergeant nodded. 'One of the forensics guys found it.'

'And did you trace it?'

'Yes sir; it belongs to Lieutenant Amos.'

Babs had not been able to sleep. The experience at Bill Mason's place had unsettled her, and despite her husband's assurances, she couldn't get it out of her head; someone had been at the ranch and had knocked her out. No way did she walk into Mason's house and fall asleep on the sofa; she had been put there.

She got up early and went through to the kitchen in the apartment they now rented in Newark. Gus was not with her, having left for a late flight to Oregon. He was back on the campaign trail canvassing among the Republicans who might be wavering. He had asked Babs to go with him, but she had declined because she wanted time to think and try to make sense of the situation. Gus was almost certainly going to be voted in as the next president of the United States. This would mean a complete stop to their lives as they would be put into a bubble from which there would be no escape. She was already under a form of guard since Jack Demski had threatened her. Once her husband was president, that guard would become official and unbreakable.

Babs had detected a change in her husband's demeanour too. No longer was there a self-effacing hope of success; it had been replaced by a singular, almost demonic assumption that he was now unstoppable. Gus's public persona was a metamorphosis from the man she first met; a Jekyll and Hyde change from the private person to the public person. Now Babs was unsure which man she had married, and she was now beginning to feel uneasy in his company.

She made a cup of coffee and switched the TV on to the local news. As she brought the cup to her lips, she stopped. There on the screen was a picture of Isaac Demski, described as the notorious crime boss. He had been found dead in the rubble of his home which had collapsed after a series of mysterious explosions. Babs put her cup down and reached for the phone. With a sickening feeling in the pit of her stomach, Babs knew that somehow, in some way, her husband had something to do with the awful scenes that she was now watching. She punched in her husband's number and waited for him to pick up.

Dubrovski stood at the foot of Amos's bed. The lieutenant was hooked up to a drip and the top of his head was covered in an elastic bandage.

'What the hell were you doing there, Amos?' he asked, his voice showing a kind of weariness.

Amos wasn't hurt, just a few bruises and a dislocated shoulder which had been put back. He had been hospitalized as a precaution and on the express wishes of Captain Dubrovski. He didn't want Amos disappearing again.

'I wanted Demski to find my Holly.' His eyes filled with tears.

Dubrovski put his hands on the rail at the foot of the bed and leaned forward. 'That's our job, Amos. We'll find your little girl.'

'Her name's Holly.'

Dubrovski nodded. 'OK, Holly. We'll find her.'

Amos shook his head. 'Why do you think I went to Demski? I can't trust the department, Captain; no way.'

'You can trust me.'

Amos looked at him sharply. 'You going to find Holly on your own? Because that's the only way you'll do it.'

Dubrovski shook his head. 'I've asked the NYPD to come in on this. I understand your concerns, but whenever an officer is personally involved, like you are, it's important to have an independent unit take care of it.'

Amos struggled up into a sitting position. The thin tube running from the saline drip went taut. Dubrovski stepped round the bed and loosened it.

'Captain, you don't know how deep Mason has his claws in this. He has powerful friends. Real powerful.'

Dubrovski shook his head. 'Nevertheless, I can't let you go off like a loose cannon. And God knows what you thought you'd get out of Demski, Amos. What did you offer him?'

Amos looked away in disgust. 'Nothing.'

'Others will say different,' Dubrovski suggested. 'And it's your career that will suffer.'

'Fuck my career, Captain,' Amos spat out. 'Holly's more important than my fucking career.'

Dubrovski put up a restraining hand. 'Calm down, Amos. Calm down. I know what you're saying, and I understand, completely. But think of your wife too. She's in this hospital, in a coma and you're in here all banged up because you wanted to climb into bed with Demski. That isn't going to do either you or your wife any good. So get a grip and think it out properly. Let me handle it. I'll keep you on side with the NYPD and we'll get Holly back for you.' He put his hand in his jacket pocket and pulled out Amos's police revolver. 'You left this at Demski's place. Bad move, Amos.' He put the gun back in his pocket. 'But that's as far as it goes. OK?'

Amos nodded and sank back on to the pillows. 'So what happened at Demski's?'

Dubrovski sat on the edge of the bed and told Amos what he knew and what he had been told. 'Isaac Demski is dead. His son, Jack is OK, but took a beating. About four of Demski's men were shot dead. It was a professional hit, Amos.' He made a clicking sound with his tongue as he shook his head. 'Too professional for a mob operation.'

Amos nodded thoughtfully. 'There's only one man who could organize something like that; Mort Tyler.' He looked up at Dubrovski. 'Demski told me something before everything went to rats. Gus Mason's backers are so far to the right they will be a major threat to the security of this country once Mason is president. Demski has something on Gus Mason, but he wouldn't tell me what it was. Mason knows of Demski's threat, and I believe this is how he or Mort Tyler has responded. And that's why they have taken Holly.'

Dubrovski considered it briefly. Then he stood up. 'So we'd better find your Holly quickly and somehow find a way of preventing Gus Mason becoming elected.' He shook his head despairingly. 'It would be fucking easier becoming an astronaut.' He then put on a firm expression and looked directly at Amos. 'I'm confident we can find Holly, Amos, but there's no way we can stop a juggernaut once it's rolling.' The reference to Mason's bid for the White House was not accidental; Dubrovski knew he wouldn't stand a cat in hell's chance of de-railing the Mason bandwagon. He took Amos's hand and shook it briefly. 'I'll keep you posted. Just get back to work as quickly as you can.'

He left and Amos wondered how straight the young captain was. All he could do now himself was get discharged from the hospital and make sure he had a close involvement in the search for Holly.

Mort Tyler took the call in his hotel room in Oregon. He told Babs that her husband was asleep and wasn't to be disturbed. It was still the early hours of the morning because of the time difference between Newark and the West Coast. Despite the hour, Tyler was already aware of the success, if that was the right word, of the attack on Isaac Demski's home. As a result of Babs's call, he now had the television on and was watching CNN, who were carrying the report. He was smiling as Babs railed at him for what she called the unnecessary violence.

'Babs, honey, you gotta remember that it was Demski who started this,' he drawled. 'He threatened you and we weren't gonna let him get away with that.'

'There must be other ways,' Babs insisted. 'Gus wouldn't have wanted this.'

'Don't you believe it, Babs; Gus was with us all the way on this. He's calling the shots now.'

Babs felt her mouth drop open, and for a moment she was speechless. She thought Gus would have opposed that kind of violence. But then she remembered how she was already beginning to see another side of her husband; one that she never believed existed.

'What about the press?' she asked. 'They are bound to uncover something that will connect us and Demski.'

'It's not a problem, Babs,' Tyler replied. 'The press will only print what they are told to print.'

He left the rest unsaid, but it didn't take Babs long to realize that Tyler meant he had most of the key editors and newspaper owners in his pocket. The gangland feud, as the attack on Demski's house was bound to be presented, was nothing more than a bauble compared to the news of Mason's electrifying drive to the White House.

'I want to speak to Gus,' she told him.

'No, I told you; Gus is asleep. He has a heavy schedule tomorrow and needs all the sleep he can get.'

Babs felt like an appendage to the campaign. It was as though she was to be sidelined if she became too much of a nuisance, despite the fact that Gus had told her he needed her by his side more often.

'He's my husband, Mort,' she argued. 'I have a right to speak to him.'

'Denied,' he answered perfunctorily. 'I'll get him to call you when he has a free moment. Goodbye Babs.'

'Mort!' But the phone was dead. Babs swore and slammed the phone back on to its cradle. Bastard, she thought angrily; Tyler was treating her like a third grade secretary. She felt anger building up inside her and wanted to strike out at something or somebody, preferably Mort Tyler. The campaign was taking precedence over everything, including her life, and she could see the distance between her and Gus widening. Sure, they would fetch her out when there was a convenient photo shoot, and some glamour was required, but close involvement seemed to be only on Mort Tyler's terms.

There was little Babs could do, so she decided to go back to Bill Mason's place and spend some time there, perhaps even figuring out what exactly had happened to her the day before. She showered and dressed, then buzzed down to the front desk and asked for her car to be brought round. Five minutes later she stepped out of the lift and walked over to the desk where one of Mort Tyler's men stood waiting.

'You my driver for today?' she asked airily.

He nodded briefly, most of it being lost in his massive frame. 'Yes, ma'am.'

'Good,' she said briskly, 'I'd like to go over to Bill Mason's place.' She looked at him, a bland expression on her face.

The heavyweight shook his head. 'I'm sorry, ma'am, it's off limits; Mort Tyler's instructions.'

Babs was stunned. The house was as good as their own property now that Bill Mason was dead. And here was some goon telling her that she couldn't go there?

'I insist,' she tried, rather weakly.

Again he shook his head. 'Won't do you any good, ma'am; Mason's place is off limits.'

Babs felt her breath pulsing in her chest as she tried to come to terms with what was effectively a restriction on her movements. And the goon who was standing in front of her telling her what she could or could not do was effectively a representative of what her husband Gus and his power brokers were bringing into American politics. She stamped her foot in disgust and swore at the man. Then she turned away and headed back towards the lift.

'Go fuck yourself!' she called back at him as the doors of the lift slid open. She stepped inside and punched the button for the penthouse apartment, wondering how on earth she was going to get out of the straitjacket Mort Tyler had put on her.

Jack Demski had moved into a suite in the Zuckerman hotel. He was in a pensive mood as he talked with Zeek Davidoff, his West Coast boss. The news of Isaac Demski's death had travelled swiftly among the organization bosses, and Zeek had flown to New York as soon as he was aware of the circumstances of Demski's death.

'Can't believe the old man's gone, Jack. He was too young.'

'He was murdered, Zeek,' Jack muttered through gritted teeth. 'Too young or not.'

Jack's arm was in a sling, and across his forehead was a long cut.

Beneath his clothes his body was covered in bruises. Two of his ribs had cracked when his father fell on top of him.

Zeek took a cigar from a small clip. He popped it in his mouth and showed his cigar lighter to Jack who nodded. Zeek lit the cigar. When he was settled, he asked Jack what he planned to do.

'I want to wait until after the funeral. No violence until we've paid our respects.'

Zeek grunted his approval. 'It's the right thing to do, Jack. Then we'll have a meeting. Do you know who did this?'

Jack shrugged and then winced. He put his good hand up to his shoulder and rubbed it gently. 'It has to be Mort Tyler. He was head of the National Guard before he retired.' He looked directly at Zeek. 'Lot of hot-heads there. Good pickings for any crackpot who wants to form his own army. Mort Tyler will have men ready to do his bidding, no question.'

'You sure it wasn't Granelli's mob?' This was a reference to the Italian Mafia who operated in parallel to Demski; both sides had clear lines over which neither group stepped.

Jack shook his head. 'No. This had militia stamped all over it; real professionals. They hit us quick and hard. There were seven or eight of us in the house, Zeek. Only me and Lieutenant Amos survived.'

Zeek pushed his shoulders back and raised his head. He took the cigar from his mouth. 'You had a cop there?'

Jack lifted his good hand. 'Yeah, he wanted me to find his little girl.' He saw the puzzled expression on Zeek's face and explained the bizarre request that Amos had put to him.

'Shit, you don't say. He thinks Mason has kidnapped her?'

Jack nodded. 'But it doesn't make sense. Mason is fighting a presidential campaign. Why would he jeopardize that?'

'Mort Tyler. Maybe he took the girl.'

Jack gave it some thought. Then he lifted his head. 'Zeek, it still don't make sense. This story about Mason being Hitler's son; that isn't going to faze him. Besides, Tyler's got that many newspaper owners in his pocket, they'll ridicule whoever comes out with it. And who's gonna prove it?' He shrugged as he put the rhetorical question to Zeek. 'Bill Mason's dead. His wife died a few years ago. And the old Sister in the sanatorium will be dismissed as a crackpot.'

'But the cop? He didn't know this, did he? So why have they taken his little girl?' Another cloud of cigar smoke followed the question from Zeek.

'He has something on Mason that could blow his whole campaign out of the water. That's why they took his daughter.'

'So where's the cop now?'

Demski shook his head. 'I don't know, but he won't be far away.'

'And what about his little girl? You going after her?'

Jack ran the fingers of his good hand through his hair. 'If we get a chance, yes. I'll put the feelers out, see what comes up. Trouble is, Zeek, if Tyler has her, there's no way we'll find her. No way.'

Zeek could see that Tyler's security would be watertight. There was little chance of one of his militia thugs opening up on where they had the little girl. It was best left to the police to handle the search.

'OK, Jack, I'll get back to 'Frisco. Let me know when you have a date for the funeral.' He got up from the chair. Demski stood up and they embraced.

'Shalom,' Zeek said to him.

Jack nodded. 'Shalom.'

The funeral was seven days later. It was in the same cemetery in which Bill Mason had been buried. The funeral cortège was enormous; half a mile of black limousines following the hearse carrying Isaac Demski's body. Following the procession was a line of police cars. Outriders flanked the limousines at regular intervals. All the traffic on the route to the cemetery had been stopped; all traffic lights on red until the cars had passed. Inside the perimeter, Lieutenant Amos stood motionless. Dubrovski stood beside him. The press were well represented as well as the Granelli family. At strategic points around the perimeter, armed security guards kept watch over the proceedings as Demski's coffin was brought to the side of the open grave. The ceremony, conducted by the chief rabbi of the Sharee Zion Synagogue was conducted in Hebrew and finally the coffin was lowered into the grave.

It was several minutes before Jack Demski climbed into the back of the waiting limousine, flanked by Zeek on one side and Levi Ben Haim, the union boss on the other. The car pulled away from the graveside and glided softly towards the large, open gates. The TV crews kept up their continuing coverage of the events as the paparazzi ran and flashed their cameras at the blacked out windows of the limousines.

Jack sat between the two men, motionless. Zeek glanced at him, understanding the pain and anger he must be feeling. Jack sensed the man's eyes on him and he turned his head.

'Zeek,' he said. 'It's time to unleash the dogs.'

FIFTEEN

BABS LIFTED THE phone on the third ring. It was the front desk of the apartment block.

'There's a Lieutenant Amos here wishes to speak to you.'

Babs let out a soft moan. 'Tell him I'm busy.'

'I already told him. Says he'll wait.'

Babs clicked her tongue and shook her head. 'OK, let him come up.' She put the phone down and glanced around the room for no other reason than it was an automatic gesture. Whenever guests called, Babs always made sure the place was presentable, but in this case, Lieutenant Amos was not a guest and she didn't give a damn what state the place was in. But she couldn't help the natural, quick look. It was almost as if she was looking for signs of incriminating evidence because there was a police officer on his way up.

The doorbell chimed musically and Babs opened the door wide. Amos was standing there, almost filling the door frame with his bulk. He looked different to the way he had looked the last time Babs had spoken to him. She thought she could see signs of bruising on his face. Amos walked through and waited for Babs to close the door and go through into the lounge.

Babs followed, her arms folded across her body, and sat in a leather chair against a small, writing bureau. She said nothing for a while, just kept her eyes on Amos. Finally she asked him what he wanted. There was a tension in her voice that she found difficult to control.

'My daughter, Holly, has been kidnapped.' As a statement, it was a simple fact. The force of it came from the fact that his daughter had been taken.

Babs felt herself recoil inside, and a sense of foreboding began to build rapidly, giving her more problems with her voice. She wanted to say something in answer to Amos's startling admission, but her voice seemed to choke on itself. She coughed and cleared her throat.

'I'm sorry, what did you say?'

'I think you heard first time, ma'am,' he replied almost impassively. 'But I'll say it again so you understand clearly. My daughter was kidnapped a couple of nights ago; taken from our home. My wife went after the thugs who did this but was in an accident. She's now in hospital in a coma.'

Babs felt small, tingling sensations at the tips of her fingers and down her legs. She felt weak and thought she was going to faint. She put a hand to her chest and could feel her heart thumping beneath her ribs.

'My God. Oh, I'm so sorry.' She stood up. 'Please excuse me,' she said. 'I want to get a drink of water.' She left the room and returned clutching a glass of spring water. Then she realized what she had done and forced herself to remember old fashioned courtesy.

'I'm sorry, Lieutenant Amos. Would you like a drink?'

He shook his head. 'No thank you, ma'am, but I would like to know where my daughter is.'

Babs was mortified. She realized that Amos believed she had something to do with the kidnapping, whereas the truth was she had no idea at all that Holly had been taken.

She shook her head slowly, disbelievingly. 'What on earth makes you think I know anything about your daughter's kidnapping?'

'The only reason Holly was taken was because you and your husband want me to pull my investigation.' His demeanour changed and he held out both hands in an appealing gesture. 'My little girl has gone and my wife may never recover. Is this what you want? Can you imagine what must be going through my little girl's mind? How terrified she will be? Can you imagine how I feel? Or is it because I am black that I don't matter? Don't you understand? Don't you know?'

Babs was close enough to see Amos's eyes filling with tears, and for the first time it was as though she was seeing through the colour of his skin and deep into his soul. It was the same colour as hers.

She dropped her head and looked into her lap, more to hide the growing feeling of shame than anything else. She recalled a little sister of hers, many years ago, dying from a child's illness. Babs was very young then, but could remember the deep loss she felt when her sister finally died. She could remember her mother's tears and the deep, deep sadness in her father's eyes; almost the same as what she had seen in Amos's.

She looked up. 'Lieutenant Amos,' she managed to say before her voice cracked and a sob lodged there. She coughed and cleared her throat. Fixing her eyes on the lieutenant's she said, 'I promise you I have no knowledge of the kidnapping. I wish I could make you understand that. I just can't believe you think I am involved in any way.' She got up and walked over to Amos, standing in front of him, showing that by her closeness she was demonstrating, or hoping to, that she was sincere.

'Please believe me, Lieutenant. If I hear anything, anything,' she repeated, 'I will let you know. I promise.'

Amos wanted to believe her, to trust her, but he knew and understood that her husband was about to become the most powerful man in the world, and she might value that above everything else; even his daughter's life.

He put his hand in his pocket and pulled out his wallet. He handed her his card. She took it from him, studied it briefly and folded her hands around it.

'You can reach me on those numbers any time, day or night. Thank you for seeing me.' He turned and walked to the apartment door, opened it and walked out without another word.

Babs watched him go; a dejected man. She heard the lift doors open and close, and the whirr of the winding motor as the lift descended with Amos in it. Then she realized she was still staring at the open door. She closed the door and saw she was still holding the card Amos had handed to her. She looked at the card and knew it was a cry for help.

She walked over to the desk for her purse. And as she tucked the card away she knew that if she heard anything at all that could lead the lieutenant to his daughter, she would tell him.

Come what may.

Holly woke up in darkness. She moved her head from side to side, searching through the blackness for something, anything that would tell her where she was. Her mouth was still bound by the duct tape that her captors had put there after her last meal. She had no idea how long she had been there, all she knew was that she was still scared.

She had no recollection of the kidnap because she had been knocked out with some kind of gag over her mouth. She recovered briefly in the big car in which her captors had her, but as soon as she made a sound, the gag was placed over her nose and mouth and she passed out again.

When she had regained consciousness completely, she found herself strapped to a bed with her mouth taped up. A hood had been placed over her head so she couldn't see anything. She began crying when she realized her predicament, but the gag restricted her breathing so much she thought she was going to suffocate. She panicked then and began kicking out, but the straps held her fast. As she was struggling she heard a door open and somebody came into the room. A hand was placed on her chest. She stopped struggling and waited. Then the hood came off and she could see someone leaning over her. He had a hood over his face.

'Stop struggling, Holly,' the voice said. 'We're going to give you something to eat and drink now, then you can go to the bathroom. Couple of days, honey, and it will be over. Just be a good girl and you'll be fine.'

She remembered they had given her some food and then taken her to a bathroom. She had no idea what kind of house she was in because they covered her face when they led her out. All she could remember of the bathroom was that it didn't smell as pleasant as her bathroom at home. Her mother always kept it clean and fresh. That memory had come flooding back and she wept solidly until she was taken back to her room.

All that had transpired some time ago. She had no idea how many days had passed; all she knew was that her routine had repeated itself with trips to the bathroom, meals and total boredom.

Holly's fear, so natural for a child in her position, had mellowed as time went by. She was still frightened, but now boredom was beginning to fill in the moments when she was able to think straight. Her captors had not been rough with her, and had treated her with reasonable kindness. This helped to give Holly the impression that she would soon be home with her parents, and all this will have been just a horrible nightmare.

She thought about her father a lot, him being a policeman and all, and the kind of questions he would ask her when he came for her, because she knew it wouldn't be long before he came. She remembered her father explaining to her mother what a kidnap victim should look for when being held. The kind of accent the kidnapper has. Any distinguishing features about the person's hands or face. Do they walk with a limp. Are they tall, short, fat, slim. Listen for sounds that filter through from the outside world. Any traffic noises. What kind of ring tones they have on their cell phones. Oh so many things. Too much for a little girl to think about, but Holly was determined to make her father proud, so she would make a mental note of all the clues she could muster.

But there was nothing Holly could think of that might help her father when he asked her about these things. Except one; there was a smell of horses.

It was a fine morning in Phoenix, Arizona when Hiram J. Wyatt stepped out of the municipal court house on the corner of Washington Street and Third Avenue. He had a good reason to be cheerful because he had just escaped prosecution for an alleged attack on a young, coloured girl. Wyatt was a lawyer by profession and had defended himself, knowing that the evidence procured by the prosecution was circumstantial and riddled with holes. Wyatt's other interest in life was a devotion to the Ku Klux Klan and the Republican Party, now on the verge of victory in the presidential election. He was also the Imperial Wizard of the Phoenix Chapter of the Klan. He was married and had three grown up children. He was also a personal friend of Judge Henry Lawrence. None of this was on his mind, though, when a nondescript car pulled up alongside him. He turned towards it as the rear passenger window was lowered. He didn't even notice the barrel of the gun or the shots that were fired at him. Hiram J. Wyatt fell to the ground as the car roared away down Third Avenue and left him bleeding to death on the pavement.

In the small town of State Line, in the Green and Wayne Counties, Mississippi, Bale Courtney walked into the State Line drug store for his weekly prescription of pills that would keep his blood pressure down. Courtney was the editor of the local newspaper, *State Line Voice*. His newspaper was a vociferous supporter of all things that Gus Mason's political party stood for. Some would have said that Courtney was an extremist, while he would argue that he was exercising his democratic right to express his views, providing they were not libellous, because of the freedoms that great Americans had fought and died for. He was also an admirer of George Lincoln Rockwell, the founder of the American national socialist movement, otherwise known as the Neo Nazis. Bale was married. He had a daughter and two grandchildren. He was thinking of them when he clambered into his pick-up truck and pulled away from the drug store. He was still thinking of them when the truck erupted in a massive explosion and ripped him apart.

The Democratic Party in Portland had set up a campaign office in Delsy Road opposite the Hillsboro School District, Harefield. There was plenty of movement around the area, what with the football stadium, baseball and soccer pitches drawing many youngsters in and around the area. It was a prize location for just one of the several offices that the Democrats had installed in the city.

The office was within site of the platform Gus Mason's party had set up in Harefield for a massive rally. Mason had even been condescending enough to offer a wave to the faces in the window as he drove past to meet the thousands waiting to hear from the man who was fast becoming a modern day messiah to millions of Americans.

It was about 4.30 in the morning when the call came in to the fire department, and the dispatcher sent the teams on their way to Delsy Road. But they were too late. When they arrived there was little left of the Democrat Party office but a burnt out shell, and all that remained was the need for a damping down operation before the investigation could begin into who or what caused the fire.

*

Edwin van Groenou, chief executive officer of Amalco, the American Aluminium Company, had good reason to feel pleased with himself having just tied up a massive deal with the representatives of EuroArm, the German owned arms manufacturer. The two companies were now involved in building hi-tech weaponry for the growing markets in Central Asia and the Far East. High on EuroArm's list of high demand items were their latest, short range missile, the super lightweight army personnel machine gun and the Cougar stealth tank. Groenou had received a lot of support from General Mort Tyler, a personal friend, during the negotiations with EuroArm. Several doors had been opened to help the delicate negotiations, including the very helpful promise of support should Gus Mason be elected President. Tyler had even produced Mason at a very private dinner with representatives of Amalco and EuroArm to endorse that promise.

Groenou had little else on his mind when he stepped into the lift of the luxury Olympus hotel on Fifth Street and took the lift to the nineteenth floor. He knew there would be a woman waiting for him in his room. This had been arranged by Mort Tyler; a free gift for Groenou's titillation and a thank you for the expectation of future cooperation once Gus Mason was president.

An hour after the time that the young woman had expected Groenou to show up, she was still alone. She phoned the only number she had been given and complained of being stood up. She never did see her client, and Groenou was never seen again.

The union man, Levi, faced Zeek across his desk at the Black Jack Casino in Reno, one of several gambling hotels in which Zeek was involved in Nevada.

'What the fuck did you hit the Democrats for?' he asked.

Zeek blew out a cloud of cigar smoke and waved it away with his hand. 'Give them something to think about.'

The two men were looking at ways of bringing the retribution that Jack Demski had ordered to an end. They both knew that a prolonged confrontation with Mort Tyler would achieve very little other than a lot of dead bodies on both sides. Jack Demski had gone into hiding, although that wasn't a word he would have used, because he knew he would be the prime target in a continuing battle. But it had been considered to be in the family's interest if Demski was out of the way. Consequently Zeek and Levi had been given the task of organizing strikes against key men in the Republican movement. That was why Levi had asked the obvious question: why the Democrats?

'I look at it this way,' Zeek went on. 'The guys we hit will not make national news.' He shrugged. 'Well, maybe briefly. But Mason will know he has lost some heavy support from those guys we wasted.'

'But the Democrats?'

Zeek put a hand up. 'Let me finish. They will think that some hotheads from Mason's party will have fire-bombed their offices. The Republicans will deny it, but then they'll think they may have some renegades in their party who think the Democrats hit the guys that we wasted. It will sow confusion.'

Levi grimaced and shifted his bulk in the chair. He reached for the drink Zeek had poured him and emptied the glass in one swallow.

'So how far we going to take this?'

Zeek shrugged. 'We wait for Jack. He told us to unleash the dogs, so that's what we're doing.'

'We got less than one week to the election,' Levi reminded him. 'Maybe we should take Mort Tyler out.'

Zeek shook his head. 'Wouldn't get near him while the feds and the secret service are watching every fucking move Mason makes. Tyler's an icon; everybody loves him.' He snorted as he said this. 'But Jack has suggested something spectacular.'

'What's that?'

Zeek shuffled his weight forward, leaning closer to the desk. 'Remember Gus Mason being asked about Camp David, and would he use it if he became president?'

Levi nodded. It was a news item that grabbed people's attention for a while. Gus Mason had been asked during a live, television broadcast about the presidential retreat at Camp David in Maryland, and whether he would use it as other presidents had done before him. Mason said that he would prefer to use the ranch his father owned out at Hutton. It was a massive spread, easily guarded and more like home than the impersonal, dull place that Camp David was reputed to be.

'Yeah, so what about it?' Levi asked.

'Like I said; it was something Jack came up with. When the world and its dog are concentrating on the election, we're gonna burn the fucking place down.'

Holly sat up as soon as she heard the door go. Her kidnappers were giving her more licence now; she was no longer tied to the bed, but had been told she must remain on the bed at all times. Failure to do this and she would be strapped down again.

The man who came into the room was hooded as usual. Holly studied him as carefully as she could; remembering the words her father had spoken to her mother. Look for clues, he had told her. Holly tried to figure out the man's height and weight, but she wasn't too good at that. She had figured something out about her room though, and that was the sun always came up on the far side. She had noticed the early morning light behind the black curtain that had been fastened securely to the window. It was opposite her bed which was up against a blank wall.

The kidnapper told her to stand up. This meant she was going to be taken to the bathroom before they brought her breakfast through. She stood and waited for the customary hood to be placed over her head. Then she felt the guy's hands on her and she allowed herself to be taken out of the room.

Holly now knew she was walking in a southerly direction. Whether this was going to help her father once he had rescued her, she had no idea. If the kidnappers took her away somewhere else, she might be able to tell him where she had been. She had grand schemes about writing a note and dropping it on the floor somewhere, hoping someone would pick it up and get help. But although her child's mind was considering clues that were in truth quite useless, one thing Holly did give a lot of thought to was that all pervading smell of horses. And it was as she was being guided to the bathroom that she realized she was being taken through some stables. She guessed this because of the fairly long walk she had before reaching a door through which she was taken before being led across a courtyard and into a building that contained the bathroom. So now she knew she was in some place that kept horses. Or used to because she couldn't hear any as she made that long walk. But at least she knew that she was being held on a ranch.

Gus Mason yawned and leaned back on the long sofa. His tie was loosened and his jacket had been tossed casually over the back of a chair. His empty glass resided on the coffee table by the sofa. Mort Tyler was just ushering the few remaining staff members out of the room as Judge Lawrence poured fresh drinks for the three of them. Mason lifted his glass and made a silent toast towards his two friends.

Tyler picked up his drink and acknowledged Mason. 'Two days, and that's it.'

'You figured out why some of our key men have been murdered?' Mason asked him.

Tyler just shrugged. He had given it a great deal of thought and had only loosely connected it with the attack on Isaac Demski. At the moment he couldn't see a firm link, and he had received no word from Demski, or any other organization for that matter, claiming responsibility for the attack. He decided to work on the old adage of revenge being a dish best served cold. Once Gus Mason was in power, he, Mort Tyler, would have almost unlimited control over the nation's security services and would put them to good use seeking out the perpetrators.

'We can cope without them,' he told Mason. 'Sad loss, but we have a lot of powerful backers in place, Gus. I'll deal with whoever was responsible when the time is right.'

Mason nodded. 'Good. Seemed a bit stupid to spring this on us so close to the election,' he observed. 'What do they expect us to do, call off the campaign?'

He laughed at the thought of people believing they could knock the Mason bandwagon off course.

'No changes to your schedule at the last minute then, Gus?' This was from Lawrence.

Mason grinned and shook his head softly. 'I need to be back in New Jersey. Babs will roast me if I don't show my face before the election.'

They all laughed. The absence of Mason's wife during his campaign had been the talk of the small press, but it had all been speculation and unnecessary editorial licence that most of the public chose to ignore anyway. The truth was that Tyler and Lawrence did not want Babs on the campaign trail with her husband because of the various key people they would be meeting along the way and Babs would be an unnecessary distraction for all of them. Babs had been quite happy about the arrangement. At least, that is what they all believed.

The truth was that Babs was not happy with the arrangement. Not now. She had been seeing her husband in a different light as he ventured further towards his political goal. His character had been changing, imperceptibly at first, and Babs had wondered if it had been her imagination. But she knew she had been guilty of the same offence, if that was what it was. Her feelings for Gus's father had been reignited by that fateful visit to the ranch, and had simply proved that her feelings had been lying dormant for some years, just waiting to be awakened.

It was the policeman's visit that had proved to be a catalyst in Babs's change of heart. She had the uneasy feeling that Gus had been behind the kidnap, or at least had sanctioned it. It had nagged away at her to such an extent that she needed to confront him. Trouble was, there was no way in which Babs could talk to her husband privately about Amos's daughter. Not now that Gus Mason was virtually public property.

She reached for the phone.

'Is the room bugged?' Mason asked.

They laughed. 'In few days' time, Gus, you won't have to worry yourself about details like that,' Tyler told him.

'So we can talk about the Bill of Rights, can we?'

Lawrence chuckled. 'Once we've got the Supreme Court eating out of our hands,' he said over the top of his glass, 'it will be like taking candy from a baby.'

'You'll be my first appointment, Henry,' Gus promised. 'I need you to work on the First Amendment.'

'It will be my pleasure, Gus,' Lawrence replied sincerely. 'A tribute to my father and everything he stood for.'

The three men stood up and snapped their heels together. Then they raised their arms in a Nazi salute. 'Zeig Heil!' they shouted and collapsed about laughing as the phone rang.

Gus picked up the phone. 'Mason.'

'Gus, it's me; Babs.'

Gus looked up at Tyler and Lawrence and mouthed the word 'Babs'. They both nodded and walked through to another room in the suite.

'Hi honey,' Mason trilled as the two men left. He looked at his watch. 'Shouldn't you be in bed?'

'I couldn't sleep,' she told him. 'Things on my mind.'

'Like what, the election night? Hey, should be great.' He sounded almost light headed; flippant. 'Don't worry about it, sweetheart, it's going to be great, I promise you.'

'It isn't that, Gus; it's something else.' She sounded mordant.

'Look Babs, this isn't a secure line,' he warned her. 'How about I give you a call in the morning?'

'No Gus, I want to talk now.'

He frowned. 'Well keep it tight, Babs. Understand?'

'I'm worried about a little girl, Gus. She's gone missing.'

Mason felt the muscles around his jaws tighten. 'Don't worry about that, Babs. Well talk about that when I get home. Goodnight sweetheart.' He put the phone down. Then he picked it up and dialled reception.

'No more calls please. None!'

Babs switched her phone off and tossed it on to the pillow beside her. She knew now that Gus was aware of the kidnap. There was no doubt in her mind. She sat there staring at the far wall wondering what she could do about it, knowing that there was precious little.

Something nagged away at her in the back of her brain. What was it? She shook her head in despair and laid back. Something was trying to get out and the awful thing was, she couldn't pluck it from those dark recesses of her mind. Maybe it would be clearer tomorrow, she thought. And with that, and the nagging realization that her husband was up to his neck in some treacherous game, she turned off the bedside light and tried to think of the election and the gala night they had been promised when Gus was confirmed as president elect.

And God help America, she thought.

SIXTEEN

BABS WAS NERVOUS. She had just watched her husband accept the congratulations from the defeated, Democratic presidential candidate by phone. It meant he was now locked in as President-elect of the United States of America. He was about to become the most powerful (and unapproachable) man in the world. Nobody would be allowed to get near to him if he didn't want them to. Already his phone and credit cards had been taken from him and sealed away. Gus was now a symbol, an imaginary crown on top of the nation. He was the people's property, no longer a private citizen. Only a select few would have his ear; those who would feather their own nests and enlarge their own, individual power and influence around the world. Those who would now further the cause of National Socialism under the guise of republicanism.

Babs had seen the movement growing over the years and seen the men who would come to finance the path to power and glory. Men who would control the military, men who would control the justice system through the power invested in their rise to the Supreme Court. Men like Henry Lawrence and Mort Tyler. There were also the faceless ones who embraced a political dream and philosophy, who had tasted power and wanted to gorge on it.

Babs had seen them come and go, but had never realized that it was a cancerous growth that was seeping into the nation's well-being. It had passed her by until it was too late to recognize the signs. Now the die had been cast; the fingers of power and political change would spread until a sleeping nation woke up to the fact that the democracy they had so cherished and died for would soon be in the hands of a despised and hated demagogue.

Yes, Babs was nervous. She wanted to stop everything. Call another election. Tell the world what an evil man her husband was beneath the media savvy front he showed to everyone. And as Gus stood on the platform and took the applause and the adulation of a crowd drunk on the sheer joy of seeing their man take the victory, Babs wanted to burst into tears; tears that would be confused with joy and emotion by the crowd, not recognized as tears of horror and bitterness.

Gus turned to her and scooped her up into his arms as the crescendo of noise became a wall of sound. Babs put on the fixed smile and showed the crowd, the supplicants, how much she was enjoying the absolute victory with her man, Gus Mason, the next president of America.

She wished it would all end, that there was some way of stopping all this. She wished it was a bad dream, that she would wake up and Gus would be a lawyer in the district attorney's office in Newark, just like it was in the old days.

Babs knew it had already begun, even as far back as that fateful day when Judge Lawrence agreed to support Gus's application for the State Senate. Ann Robbins had died because of her opposition to Gus. Did she already know? Was she aware of the danger that was threatened by the ideology that would surely follow? And did Gus kill her? Lieutenant Amos believed it was either her or her husband, but was kept on a short leash by his captain, another of Lawrence's acolytes. He also guessed that Bill Mason's death was no accident. But Babs knew the truth.

The noise and the cheering grew with each of Gus's movements on the platform. A hand wave, a look at Babs, a nod to the members of his staff who were on the platform with him. There was even a congratulatory pat on the shoulder to his running mate. The bunting fluttered wildly and the flags moved back and forth in an orchestrated movement of colour. The journalists who had been assigned to trail Gus's campaign now gave up their previously, unbiased reporting and clamoured like drunken graduates at the foot of the platform. Television cameras were vying with personal cameras to get the best shots of the new man; the new, world statesman.

Babs hated it. She wanted it all to end, but she knew she had no chance, none at all. Soon they would be doing the round of parties. First the official ball at the luxurious five star Marriott followed by smaller, more personal parties to show appreciation and heart-warming gratitude for services rendered. It was going to be a long night, and the more Babs thought about it, so the night seemed to stretch away into the interminable distance.

Lieutenant Amos was on duty outside the hotel. Dubrovski was close by. Amos wanted to be there, simply to watch Mason walk past. He had some kind of forlorn hope that he might catch a glimpse of the man who, he was convinced, had ordered the kidnap of his beloved Holly. Dubrovski had taken the unheard of measure of relieving Amos of his side arm because he was afraid of what Amos might be tempted to do. Amos had told him not to be a prick, but his captain wasn't taking any chances, so Amos went unarmed.

The crowds from the convention hall had spilled over into the roads making traffic control an absolute nightmare. There were the usual, joyous scenes as motorists toured the city, sounding their horns and generally making an unfettered nuisance of themselves. Most of it was harmless, but still meant the overworked police department had a great deal on its plate.

Amos couldn't help feeling resentment at his own colleagues, foolishly branding them all with the same iron as he looked around at them and wondered how many were on Mason's payroll. And how many were impeding their search for his daughter? It was probably true that none of those officers were involved in any aspect of the kidnap, and probably had no way of interfering with the investigation. The truth was, there was nothing to go on. No clues. No witnesses. No ransom demands, not that any were expected anyway, and nothing but total silence.

He had spent a great deal of time with his wife, who was still in a coma. He had talked to her and kept promising that he would find Holly. It was this continuous insistence that helped to keep Amos on an even keel. He was frustrated by his own helplessness, and by his department's failure to find any leads. Holly had simply disappeared off the face of the earth, metaphorically speaking, and there was nobody who could tell him where they were hiding her.

Amos saw the flashing blue lights of the police motorcycle outriders coming off the expressway. The sounds from the sirens echoed around the high buildings, announcing the arrival of America's next president. He watched as the escorts brought the motor cavalcade to a halt at the edge of the red carpet. Immediately two secret servicemen leapt out of the second car and opened the doors for Gus Mason and Babs.

Amos was standing on the edge of the red carpet, about five yards from the car. Dubrovski was beside him, trying hard not to touch the gun nestled beneath his jacket. He knew there were police marksmen on the roof of nearby buildings, and he had personally briefed two of them to watch Amos. Any unexpected movement and they were to bring him down. He tried to look casual and at ease, living easily with the sense of the occasion, but in truth he was under tension, and it showed on his face.

Mason stepped out of the car and on to the red carpet. He turned and held his hand out for Babs, who emerged to a battery of flashing cameras. The noise from the well-wishers close by reached a crescendo, and Babs turned to acknowledge as many as she could with the smile fixed permanently on her face. Gus kept her hand in his. He could feel the tension in her body and put it down to all the excitement and nervous anticipation. He led the way with the smiles and the waves and the finger pointing as he recognized someone in the masses of people squeezed into such a small area.

Then Babs spotted Amos and her smile dropped. Amos looked at her. He was quite solemn. He gave a small, almost indiscernible shrug and turned his hands outwards in a gesture of emptiness. Babs knew exactly what he was saying and felt his sadness pierce her heart. For a brief moment she thought she was going to break down and cry, but she kept her presence and remembered her duty. The smile returned and she looked away from him. Amos watched her walk by, not two yards from him, and didn't take his eyes off her as she followed her husband into the grand foyer of the luxury hotel.

As the television cameras continued to roll and the flash of many cameras scattered shotgun blasts of light that bounced off the glittering celebrities, Amos wondered why and how such people as Gus Mason could fool people into believing he was some kind of modern day messiah. The real powers behind this man, the faceless ones, would be kept away until the day Mason took the oath of office. And then, perhaps he would get his beloved Holly back.

Inside the grand ballroom, Babs kept up the glamour pose and did her best to show that she was almost beside herself with happiness. But the truth was, she was growing more bitter as the evening wore on. She was becoming tired of the glad-handing, keeping a fixed smile on her face until she felt like the Joker from *Batman*. And she kept remembering the awful look on Amos's face, and the distress in his body language.

Babs kept her true emotions beneath the surface, continually watching the clock until it was almost midnight. Then she told Gus she was going to her room. There was an elongated goodnight from Mason and her well-wishers, until eventually she was free to ride the elevator, with a security man, up to the penthouse suite.

She closed the door behind her, leaning up against it to enjoy a moment of solitude. It was peaceful there. No sound came up from the grand ballroom. She looked around at the huge suite with its brand new furnishings, magnificent drapes that shrouded all the windows, closed for security reasons. Babs wanted to fling them open and breathe in some of the cool, night air.

She kicked off her designer shoes and left them where they came to rest. Then she pushed away from the door and walked across to the drinks cabinet and helped herself to a straight shot of bourbon. It was Bill Mason's favourite tipple. Babs had grown quite accustomed to it. The amber liquid burned her throat as she tossed it back. She poured another and went through to the bedroom.

The second drink followed the first and she slid the empty glass on to the dressing table. She studied herself in the mirror, looking at her trim figure, wondering what Bill would have done had he been there at that moment. The dress came off quickly, thrown to the floor like a discarded rag. She couldn't get Bill Mason out of her mind now. It annoyed her because she should have been giving everything to her husband, the wonderful messianic Gus Mason. She almost spat the words out as she looked away from the mirror and pulled open a drawer, selecting a silk slip that she intended to put on after taking a shower.

That was when she saw the gun. It had slipped out of an evening bag she had brought with her that morning. Babs couldn't understand why she had kept it with her. It was the small, silver Beretta that Bill Mason had given her such a long time ago. She had never wanted to carry the gun, but when she had last visited Bill's ranch, she had come across it by accident, almost. It opened up so many memories.

She pulled the gun from the drawer and looked at it. It had been studded with small, industrial diamonds; a lady's gun. Babs had never fired it. Now she held it in her hand and felt the weight of the loaded magazine. The safety catch was on. She put the gun back in the drawer and covered it with a pair of panties. Bill would have loved that, she thought.

Her brassiere and panties were thrown to one side as she stepped into the shower, allowing the stinging needles of water to punish her body; a body that women would die for and men would kill for. She didn't want this, Gus's victory; she wanted to go back through the years and think only of Bill. She slid down the wall until she was leaning back against it, her knees drawn up around her ears.

She began to cry, her tears vanishing in the stream of water that poured over her. She so much wanted this not to be. She knew now that her husband was only interested in power; extreme power. She knew he had murdered for it, and had kidnapped Amos's little girl for it. Babs could not forgive him for the deaths of others, although she had learned to accept the inevitable truth. But to allow his thugs to kidnap a frightened little girl was beyond reason. It meant he would stop at nothing.

And Babs now understood the reason why his father had been so vehement in his objection to Gus's Nazi leanings, and why Gus had killed him. Bill Mason was a threat to the growing rise to power of the Nazi zealots. He knew that America was in danger of succumbing to the Phoenix; the birth of the new Reich. Anybody who stood in their way would be killed; it was as simple as that.

Babs turned the water off, stepped out of the shower and reached for a towel. She was drying herself down when she heard her husband come into the suite. His voice was light and cheerful as he said goodnight to the security men who were stationed outside in the corridor. He closed the door and locked it.

'Where are you, Babs?'

'I'm in the bathroom. Be out in a minute.' She tried to sound cheerful, on a high even, but her voice and her feelings almost betrayed her.

When Babs came through into the bedroom, Gus was standing at the foot of the bed, a drink in his hand. He didn't have his jacket on, and his tie had been pulled loose. He had closed the door.

'Wonderful night, Babs,' he said through a smile that Babs had got sick of looking at. He walked across the luxurious carpet towards her, his eyes gleaming and an expression on his face that was unmistakable. One side of Gus Mason's character that was never revealed to the outside world was his propensity for rough sex. It happened on few occasions, and usually when he was drunk or had something to celebrate. Babs had tolerated his darker side, learning to endure it, but now she wanted no part of it, no part of him.

She felt her skin tighten, and tried not to show her instant rejection of the idea of having him crawl all over her.

'Gus, honey, I'm all freaked out. Later, eh babe?'

Gus's expression changed. The fixed smile faded into nothing and then was replaced with a frown.

'What's got into you, Babs?' He moved towards her, the drink still in his hand. 'You were always up for it.'

'I think it's the pressure of the whole day, Gus,' she lied with an apologetic shrug. 'Too much.'

He put the glass to his lips and sipped the drink slowly. There was now a menace to his body language. He took the glass away and stood with his legs apart, like a quarterback on heat.

'I'm the president, honey. Or hadn't you noticed?'

'You're not the president yet, Gus,' she reminded him.

'All but,' he countered. 'People jump to my tune now.' He put the glass down on a small table. 'And that means you.'

'Is that why you had that little girl kidnapped?' She snapped at him. 'Because people jump to your tune?'

He stepped forward and grabbed hold of her arm just above the elbow. She could feel the pressure of his fingers biting into her muscle. The gratuitous violence he had suppressed for so long was returning, released by his elevation to the highest rank in the land and given almost unlimited power.

'Gus, you're hurting me.' She tried to prise his fingers away, but he was far too strong for her. 'Is this what your men will do to that little girl?'

'Never mind about her. She's as good as done for anyway.'

The look on Babs's face turned to ice. 'You bastard, what have you done to her?' She continued struggling, getting angrier by the minute.

'All's fair in love and war, honey,' he laughed. 'Nothing must be allowed to stop us. No black, fucking nigger cop, nor his offspring.' He grabbed Babs's face with his free hand. She could feel his fingertips squeezing the blood from her skin. 'No way are we going to be intimidated by blacks, nor by Jews nor by any Spick who thinks he's entitled to a free ride in this great country.'

Babs began struggling wildly and pulled away from him. 'You're crazy, Gus,' she snarled at him, flecks of spittle flying from her lips. 'You don't think the American public are going to let you get away with this, do you?'

'They already have,' he declared. 'That's why I'm here.'

He grabbed her again and flung her on the bed. As she fell her legs opened, revealing everything. This seemed to inflame Mason and he leapt on her, pulling the belt around his waist free. He wrapped it around his fist, leaving a small length, and whipped her across her ribcage.

Babs screamed and turned away from him. He pulled her back and lashed out again. Babs could see he was beside himself, out of control. She swung a clenched fist up at him, catching him on the side of the head. He took the blow and put his hand up to where she had caught him. Then he smiled at her.

'You're going to pay for that one, honey.'

Babs went wild. She knew he would beat her where it wouldn't show and hated him even more because of it. She kicked out and rolled away from him, slipping from the bed and falling to the floor. As she pulled herself to her feet, she grabbed hold of a drawer handle and pulled the drawer out. It fell on top of her, spilling its contents on the floor. The gun fell beside her. Babs picked it up and scrambled to her feet. She pointed the gun at Mason.

He froze. 'What the fuck do you think you're going to do with that?' he asked her sarcastically, as though he had no fear. But the reality was that Mason was caught by surprise. It was enough to stop him briefly, but not that long. He took a lunge at Babs who threw herself back.

'Don't come near me,' she said through gritted teeth. 'You do and I'll shoot you, so help me.'

Gus still had the belt in his hand. He allowed it to unroll so that it was hanging by his side. He lifted it and took hold of the end of the belt, pulling it tight.

'You're going to get it, bitch,' he said slowly, and launched himself at her.

Babs flicked the safety catch off and shot him. The sound of the gun filled the room as Mason took the bullet in the chest. He staggered backwards and collapsed on to the bed. A red flower of blood blossomed on his white dress shirt and dribbled on to the pristine sheets. Mason put his hand to his chest and then looked up at Babs. His face was distorted with pain. He lifted his hand and looked at the blood running from his fingers. As he struggled for breath, blood bubbled from his mouth. He gave Babs one last, distorted look and died.

All hell broke loose then. The two guards outside heard the shot and burst through the door, splintering the wood as it gave way beneath the weight of the two men. They had their weapons drawn and swung them left and right, the way they had been trained, looking for what they believed would be armed terrorists or something equally as dangerous. They couldn't see anybody in the room and immediately ran to the bedroom door. The door flew opened as they tumbled into the room.

What they didn't expect to see was Babs Mason, half naked, holding a gun and pointing it at them.

'Don't either of you move,' she screamed at them.

The two men were now in a quandary; do they shoot or do they wait to be shot? Their training should have kicked in, but they had never been taught how to tackle the First Lady-elect who was holding a gun and threatening to use it.

'I want one minute on the phone and then I'll put my gun down. Deal?'

They didn't answer.

'Deal?' she shouted.

They looked at each other. 'Deal,' one of them said.

Babs nodded towards the bed. 'My bag. Take the phone out.'

One of the men did as he was asked and took Babs's cell phone out. He held it out towards her.

Babs shook her head. 'No, leave it there and back away. Across the room. Now!'

When they had retreated to the other side of the room, Babs lifted the phone and punched in a number, keeping her eye on the two men. She spoke briefly and tossed the phone on to the bed. Then she tossed the gun after it.

'OK guys, now you can arrest me.'

SEVENTEEN

AMOS WAS SITTING beside his wife's bed in the private room. He was talking to her, holding her hand and praying from time to time. He'd been there almost three hours since leaving the hotel where Mason had begun his victory tour. His wife's complexion was pale, her pulse regular but faint. Her hand felt cold to his, and he had to fight to stop the tears from welling up and rolling down his face.

He tried to think of Holly, but while he looked at his wife, the memory of his daughter could not impose itself upon his deep, deep despair. This made Amos feel culpable, almost negligent in not being able to find his little girl and bring her home. He knew his wife needed him and he kept whispering gently, leaning forward, bringing his cheek to touch her face lightly and tenderly.

He felt something vibrate. It startled him and he looked up, wondering which machine was signalling an alarm, but there was no other sound in the room save that of his wife's pulsing heart monitor, and the almost imperceptible hum of the air conditioning. The vibration came again and he suddenly realized it was his cell phone. Amos had turned the sound off and set the phone to vibrate on an incoming call.

He sat up straight and pulled the phone from his pocket. He looked at the screen and frowned because he didn't recognize the number. He put the phone to his ear as he pressed the 'accept call' button. What he heard almost riveted him to his chair in an unexplainable reaction to the words that followed.

'Amos, this is Babs Mason. Your daughter is being held at Bill Mason's ranch. Go and get her.'

The phone went off and all he could hear was the buzz of a closed line. He took the phone away from his face and stared at it for a brief moment, as though it was some alien device. Then, quite suddenly he cried out, 'Oh Jesus, yes!'

He rammed the phone back into his pocket, kissed his wife on the cheek and said to her, 'Honey, I'm going to get Holly.'

The approach to Mason's house on his ranch was a gravelled drive leading up from a huge gate, which was closed. There was nothing ostentatious about the place, something Bill Mason had cultivated down the years, never wishing to present a front that shouted wealth to the local Hutton residents. In daylight, the house had the look of old money about it; an inheritance handed down through the generations. It was three o'clock in the morning and the house was in darkness now, looking empty and lifeless. Beyond it the barns and stables were just vague shapes, barely lit by a weak moonlight in the November sky.

None of this was of any concern to the two men who sat in a stolen Chevvy pick-up truck parked about a hundred yards away, concealed off the road beneath a covering of trees. They were dressed in black and had plain ski masks pulled down over their faces. One of them checked the time on his wrist watch and nodded to his companion. They opened their doors and climbed out of the truck, taking with them a small bag each.

Coming out of the trees, they sprinted across the road and clambered over the closed gate, taking care to keep to the trimmed lawn on one side of the gravel path. When they reached the house, they stopped immediately outside the front door and listened carefully. Satisfied that there was nobody inside listening to late night TV or to the radio, one of them jemmied the sash window and eased it up gently. Within seconds they were inside.

A quick sweep of the house told them it was empty, as they suspected it would be. They then walked from room to room; taking flares from the bags they were carrying and setting them off at random. As the house began to burn, they forced the rear door and ran out into the open yard. They both stopped and turned towards each other. They nodded and grinned beneath their masks, then looked across the open yard towards their next objective; the stables.

Lieutenant Amos was almost iridescent with anger as his captain, Dubrovski, failed to grasp the fact that he now knew where Holly was being held. Dubrovski had garbled something down the phone about the shit hitting the fan and all available officers were heading for the hotel where Gus Mason was staying. He mentioned a shooting, but he was so wound up and hyper about the 'situation' that he wasn't making sense. Not to Amos anyway.

Amos knew he couldn't go over to Hutton without back up, and a phone call to the precinct at that time would yield nothing. All he could do was ask the dispatcher to put out a call to all mobiles and ask for assistance at Mason's Ranch in Hutton. Whatever response Amos got, he was not going to leave his daughter one second longer than necessary. He decided to go alone.

The house was now beginning to burn well, filling the shadowy corners of the ranch with a flickering, yellow light. The shadows began to stretch out ahead of them as the two men raced across the yard. They stopped beside one small outbuilding and hurled a flare through an open window, then ran on towards the stables.

Amos hit the road in the Crown Vic police car he had been using, culled from the police pool. He wanted its power and reliability. With anger still burning in his veins he took the expressway south, put his foot down and switched on the car's sirens and flashing lights. Then he pulled his cell phone from his jacket pocket.

The stable doors opened with little effort. But as the first of the hooded men was about to step inside, the rattle of machine-gun fire peppered the doors and showered him with massive splinters. He swore and leapt back into the yard. He could feel the trickle of blood seeping down his cheek. His partner, thinking quickly, ripped a flare and tossed it through the small gap between the doors. As the flame blossomed he could see the shape of a four-by-four vehicle. He had no time to ask himself irrelevant questions, but understood that they had come up against someone who they didn't expect to find in the stable. He grabbed the other man by the shoulder and pulled him away as another burst of gunfire hit the doors.

Then there was a sudden explosion as the flare that had been tossed inside hit something inflammable and set the entrance to the stable burning furiously.

Jack Demski lifted the phone from his bedside table, still half asleep despite the shrill ringing. He held it to his ear, closed his eyes and lay back on his pillow.

'Demski.'

'Demski, this is Lieutenant Amos. Listen, I'm going after my daughter. I need help.'

Demski pressed the phone to his ear. He thought he could hear a police siren and the sound of a roaring engine.

'Where are you, Amos?'

'I'm on the expressway, heading south. I know where my daughter is and I need help. I can't explain. Can you get there?'

Demski thought the policeman sounded crazy, not thinking straight. 'Why isn't your department helping you?'

'I ain't got time to explain. Can you help me?'

Demski took a deep breath. He could have done without this. 'I'll try. Where are you going?'

'Mason's ranch at Hutton. That's where they're holding her.'

Demski had relaxed just a little, but when Amos told him where Holly was being held, he sat bolt upright and swore. 'Oh, shit!' He climbed out of bed and turned on the main lights. 'Listen, Amos, now it's my turn not to explain, but two of my guys are there right now. You get there as fast as you can.'

He turned the phone off and immediately dialled another number.

Holly woke to the sound of gunfire and an explosion. She sat up on her bed and screwed her face up. It was dark in the room but she was now familiar enough with the layout to get out of bed and walk across to the door. She tried the handle but the door was locked. She shrugged and went back to the bed. She sat on it and wondered what was happening. More gunfire erupted, but this time it was coming from outside of the stable building. She could clearly hear the impact of bullets as they thudded against the tough, wooden framework.

Then she smelt something. It was smoke. She cast around but couldn't see anything. She thought of the door and went back to it. The smell was stronger now and she realized that somehow the smoke was seeping through the gap at the bottom of the door. She ran to the bed and pulled the blankets away, then dragged them across to the door and tried her best to ram them into the small gap at the bottom. After a few minutes the smell of smoke began to dissipate. It gave her a little time, but it didn't help to calm the terror that was building up inside her. She began pounding on the door, battering it with her little fists, screaming for someone to come.

Amos roared up to the gravel driveway of Mason's ranch and smashed through the wooden gates with the Crown Vic. The car juddered as the timber gave way and slewed across the gravel. Amos ducked as the windscreen shattered but kept his foot down, steering by feel rather than by sight. After fifty yards he slammed on the brake and leapt from the car, shards of glass falling from him. He left the doors open, the engine running and the flashing lights blazing as he sprinted up to the burning house. Already tears of fear were streaming down his face as he pictured his beloved Holly trapped inside the building. For a moment, he didn't know what to do. He was helpless. No way could he force his way into the inferno and get to his daughter. He was about to lift his cell phone from his pocket and called the emergency services when a hooded figure appeared. He was holding a gun and pointing at Amos.

'Put the gun down, Lieutenant!'

'It's not a gun, it's a phone.' Amos held it up for the apparition to see.

'Put it down anyway.'

Amos bent his knees and dropped the phone on to the gravel. The hooded figure walked up to him, still keeping the gun out at arm's length.

'Lieutenant, Jack Demski called us, told us about your daughter. We think she's in the stable round back. We're gonna try and help get her out. We got a problem though.'

'What's that?'

The hooded figure lifted his head and nodded towards the rear of the house. 'Couple of guys in there we reckon. Can't get near them.'

'Who are you?' Amos asked. 'How come you got here so damn quick?'

'Never you mind. We're Demski's boys,' he replied, 'so we're the good guys. OK?'

Amos didn't want to ask any more questions. He didn't give a damn who they were or how they knew who he was or that his daughter was there; he just wanted to get her out.

He picked up his phone and slipped it into his jacket pocket. 'Let's go then,' he said, and followed the hooded figure towards the burning stable.

Now Holly was beginning to shake in fear. Although she was a child, she understood the dangers of being trapped inside a burning building. She could smell the smoke again, but this time it was much stronger. She jumped off the bed and pulled the mattress away, dragging it across the floor. She hoped it would prevent more smoke coming through, but she couldn't flatten it enough to block the smoke off.

She turned as a flicker of orange light danced across the bedroom wall. It was brief, but as she stood there, it appeared again. That's when she realized the light was coming through the black shrouds that had been pinned up against the small window. She glanced down at the metal frame bed she had been sleeping on and a thought came to her.

She grabbed the bed and turned it on its side. It was quite a struggle for her because of her size, but she eventually managed to get the bed standing on its end against the wall beneath the window. Then forcing her feet into the cross mesh of the springs, Holly pulled herself up until her face was level with the bottom edge of the window. She reached up with one free hand and began tugging at the curtain.

When Amos reached the other side of the house, he almost stopped as the scene opened up before him. The long building was on fire in its centre, spread over about thirty feet. He could see the silhouette of a man crouching some distance from the flames. He was facing them and appeared to be aiming a gun. Amos couldn't figure out if he was firing because the sound of the fire and the burning timbers filled the night air and roared above everything else.

Even as he reached the second man, Amos had pulled his cell phone from his pocket and was dialling the emergency services.

'My daughter's in there,' he shouted as he jammed the phone back into his pocket.

The guy who was crouching turned and stood up. 'What d'ya say?' he shouted.

'My daughter,' Amos pointed frantically. 'She's in there.'

The heat was now reaching out to them and Amos was forced to shield his face from the flames. The other two had a small advantage in that they were both wearing ski masks. Both of them glanced at each other and then looked at Amos.

'Sorry, man; there's no chance.'

Just then the centre of the building erupted and a massive column of flames and burning timbers punched up into the night sky. Amos felt his body freeze in a terrifying grip of indescribable fear.

'My daughter!' he screamed. 'Oh my God, my Holly.'

Holly gradually levered herself on to the small lip of the window frame and pushed her hand against the window. It was hinged at the top and swung outwards. She had to lift the window opener from the small, metal spigot that was fixed to the centre of the bottom edge. She felt the top edge of the bed beneath her feet beginning to slide away, so she hauled herself up the last few inches and was now lying almost prone along the length of the windowsill. Then the middle of the stables exploded.

The pressure wave from the explosion ripped through the building. It hit the door that Holly had jammed with the bedding and the mattress, blowing it off its hinges. It smashed into the bed beneath her with a force that jarred her enough to make her wobble on the thin edge of the window frame. Then the force of the pressure wave hit her and knocked her through the window. But as she fell, Holly's dress caught on the metal spigot. The tiny spike tore through the thin material and held her fast. Now she was dangling like a rag doll on the end of a rope as the dress began to slip up her body and gather around her neck. Holly started to struggle, but with each movement, the dress rode a little higher until she could feel it tightening like a noose. She screamed as the awful dilemma hit her and uncontrollable fear took over. Holly was hanging by the neck, and all she could see in front of her was the darkness as her screams vanished into the empty night.

Amos heard it. A faint, high pitched sound. He looked from side to side, his mouth wide open. Where did it come from? He heard it again and took off, running as fast as his unfit body would let him. He reached the far end of the stable and turned the corner. And there, hanging like a rag doll was his daughter.

'Holly! Holly!'

The little girl struggled, gripping the dress with her tiny hands to gain some relief from its deathly grip. She tried to look down towards the sound of her name being called, but she couldn't bend her head enough. She struggled but the dresse rode up and was now virtually closing her windpipe. Her screams were choked off until she could no longer breathe.

Amos immediately took in the dreadful struggle his daughter was under. He tried to reach her feet by standing on tip toe, but was still woefully short. He jumped, but slid back. He knew that if he managed to reach her he would only add to her body weight and she would surely die.

He ran back round to the front of the stables and called to the two men, waving his arms frantically.

'My little girl,' he kept shouting, and pointed beyond the end of the building. The two men responded and ran towards Amos as he went back to where his daughter was fighting for her life.

When the two men reached him, Amos shouted at them and pointed. 'Lift me up!'

As he leaned up against the side of the stables, the two men grabbed Amos's legs and lifted him bodily. This brought him face to face with Holly. He put his arms around her and lifted her gently, taking the pressure off the strangulating dress. Then he released it from the spigot. Holly started drawing in deep draughts of air as

Amos held her tightly. Slowly the two men lowered Amos and his daughter to the ground.

The next few minutes were a blur to Amos. He ran away from the burning building carrying Holly in his arms and stopped about a hundred yards away. He then sank to his knees and held on to his little girl and simply didn't want to let her go.

He was still kneeling in that way, holding on to Holly, when the emergency services arrived. He heard a voice and looked up. It turned out to be one of the fire fighters who had been despatched after Amos's 911 call.

'Are you OK, sir?'

Amos looked up and nodded. He didn't say anything.

'Sir, we've got a paramedic with us. I think you'd better let them take a look, eh?'

Amos stood up. His knees were stiff and sore, but he didn't care; he was happy. He followed the fire fighter across to an ambulance where a paramedic attended to Holly.

'How did you get your little girl out of the building?' the medic asked.

Amos pointed somewhere out into the night. 'There are two guys here. They helped me,' he told him.

The paramedic looked up from attending Holly's superficial wounds. 'What two men?'

'Two guys out there,' Amos told him. 'They were here when I got here.'

The medic shook his head. 'Well, they ain't here now,' he said, applying a plaster to another small wound on Holly's leg. 'Just you and your brave little girl here.' He looked at Holly as he said it, and was rewarded with a self-conscious shrug and a big smile.

Amos didn't care where the two men were. He would probably never find out anyway. He didn't want to. All he wanted to do now was get Holly to her mother and begin another rescue.

It was to be another twenty-four hours or so before Amos could take his daughter to see her mother. He had to give statements while Holly was attended to by a child psychologist to help her get over the trauma of the kidnap and the fire. Amos refused to leave Holly's side, so he gave his statement to a police officer in a side room close to where Holly was being treated.

Over at the hotel it was bedlam. Captain Dubrovski had conceded defeat to the FBI and the secret service, allowing them to assume control of the investigation into Mason's shooting. None of the television units had packed up, so there was plenty of coverage for them to gorge on. Damage limitation was being dished out in spades by the spokesman for the security service. The hotel had been cordoned off and no one was going in or out.

Except Babs Mason; she had been escorted through a rear entrance and been driven away in a police car. Dubrovski understood that she had named Tyler and Lawrence as culpable in the kidnap of Holly Amos, which had been enough for the captain to place both men under arrest.

There was no way anybody was able to keep even a smidgeon of the developments out of the news, and within minutes of the shooting, the wires were singing all the way to the other side of the world and back again. It was all media frenzy, with weirdoes coming out of the woodwork and claiming they had seen all along that Mason was a Nazi but nobody would listen to their spurious claims.

But none of the genuine reporters, or the proclaimers were aware that Gus Mason had been conceived in Hitler's Reich Chancellery, and had always nursed an ambition to continue the philosophical bloodline into another thousand year Reich.

Amos stood holding Holly's hand. They were in the room where his wife lay in a coma. Amos felt a mixture of relief and fear. Relief that he had done as he had promised, and brought their daughter home safely; and fear that his wife would never recover.

They approached the bed. Amos leaned towards his wife and whispered softly in her ear. 'Hallo sweetheart, I've got a little present for you.'

He pulled Holly gently towards the bed and took his wife's hand. He then placed Holly's there and closed his hand around them. Holly kissed her mother on the cheek and then gave her a big hug.

'I love you Mom.'

Amos watched, and waited. Suddenly the heart monitor changed its note and his wife turned her face towards him. There was a hint of a smile as her eyes fluttered open. Then she closed them and sighed gently.

Amos saw his tears drop on to the pillow and he shook his head, thanking God for giving his wife back to them. He pulled Holly gently away from her mother.

'She's OK now, honey. Now she knows you're here, your Mom is going to get better. A whole lot better.'

EPILOGUE

THE YOUNG WRITER *stopped writing and switched the small recorder off. She put her notepad and pens into her bag, then picked up the digital recorder and slipped that in too.*

'Quite a story,' she admitted, snapping her bag shut.

'And all true,' Babs replied. 'Every last, damn word.'

The young writer stood up. 'I feel privileged to have been asked to do this.'

Babs gave a weak smile. 'I think you deserve it, Holly. After all, you're part of the story. It will make a bestseller; get you started in life.'

'It seems so long ago now,' Holly said wistfully.

Babs agreed. 'Must be what, almost ten years or so?'

Holly came over to her and gave Babs a little hug and kiss. 'My mom and dad will be thrilled. Thank you so much.'

Babs shook her head. 'No, Holly, thank you.' She breathed in a deep sigh that seemed to settle on her shoulders in a profound way. 'Now, if you don't mind, I am tired.'

Holly smiled. 'Of course.' She tapped the side of her bag. 'I'll get on to this right away. I'll bring you a copy when it's published.'

A sadness fell over Babs's face. 'Thank you,' was all she said. 'Now go, enjoy the rest of your life.'

Babs watched Amos's daughter walk out of the cell. She looked fabulous and was blessed in that she had never had a reaction over the terror she had been through. And Babs was thankful that she herself had been able to do something right for once.

She stood up and pulled her skirt off. There were thin gaps in the material where she had been pulling the threads out. She gathered up the threads from where she had been hiding them and held them out across her body. They were now long enough to twist into a thin, but strong cord. She finished making the cord and tied the ends off. Then she ripped her skirt apart, using the weak areas from where she had removed the thread. A few minutes later she had successfully made a noose, which she placed over her head. Then she pulled out a chair and stepped up on to it. The light above her was now within reach. She passed the cord through the small protective grill round the lamp and knotted it carefully, making sure it would not open. Then she offered up a prayer and kicked the chair away.

Babs had come a long, but torturous way in life. She had loved and lost, and made bad choices. Her last thought was that she hoped she had made amends. She would never know, but perhaps the world would.